TITS-OUT TEENAGE TE|

Steven Wells left school in Bradford in 1978, became "skinhead poet" **Seething Wells** and founded the social-surrealist **Ranting Poetry** movement. Then he went to work for the **New Musical Express** as rock-journalism's first transvestite hack **- Susan Williams**.

He's written for **On The Hour** and **The Day Today**

And made documentaries and pop videos.

And tons of other stuff.

He lives in London with an Apple Mac.

Also published by **ATTACK!** books

Satan! Satan! Satan! by Tony White
Raiders Of The Low Forehead by Stanley Manly

Steven Wells
TITS-OUT TEENAGE TERROR TOTTY

ATTACK! is an imprint of Creation Books.

First published in 1999 by ATTACK! Books
83 Clerkenwell Road, London EC1 5AR
Copyright: Steven Wells 1999
Design by Rom
Original artwork by Paul McAffery
Printed and bound in Great Britain by
Woolnough Book Binding Ltd
Irthlingborough, North Hants

THANKS!

For love, encouragement, plot, inspiration and

TOP SEX!

To David Quantick, Tony White, Irvine Welsh, Stewart Home, Joe Strummer, Digital Hard Core, The Prodge and Tommy Udo. And GOD!

What a

NUTTAH!

HERE

it comes now! Stumbling through the undergrowth, the brittle skulls of small rodents cracking like gunshots under the savagely spiked heels of its steel toe-capped Dolce and Gabana fuck-me stilettoes.

Those oh-so familiar doe-like eyes fix madly on the middle distance, ignoring the brambles and branches that lash at that brutally scarred but oh-so-beautiful face. On its back, surgically attached and purely decorative, are two massive wings of compassion. On its lurching torso is a matt-black strapless Versace gown. In its gnarled fists it carries a razor toothed chainsaw. And in its heart - **HATRED!**

She's **BACK!** Stop **CRYING!** Princess of the Pod People! Queen of Hearts! Empress of Empathy! Duchess of Despondency! Monarch of Melancholy! Sovereign of Sobbing! Czarina of *WANGST!*

England's Rose is risen from the dead and this time - **IT'S PERSONAL!**

Sewn back together by an especially formed team of the world's top neurosurgeons and made **more** beautiful, **more** perfect, **more** saintlike, **more** compassionate, **more** doe-like and better equipped to deal **instant death** than ever before!

Her reconstituted flesh covers a titanium skeleton. State of the art micro-circuited laser weaponry hums under her peach-like skin.

She lurches to a stop and scans the horizon.

A lone paparazzo - the penile telescopic tools of his evil trade slung around his scrawny neck - lies concealed by camouflage just a hundred yards to the front, blissfully unaware of the savage death that awaits him.

"**QUEENMOTHERFUCKA**" screams Spencerstein as she scoops a fistful of upper-class quality cocaine out of her Chanel handbag and rams it wastefully up her oh-so-perfect nostrils before ripping the massive chainsaw into rabidly barking life. The startled paparazzo looks up suddenly and shitshocks savagely as he whirls round with whiplash intensity to witness the senses-shattering sight of Diana's zomboid horrorcorpse tottering towards him at impossible speed, slashing the air insanely with the fume-spewing chainsaw and screaming like a banshee on crack.

CRUMP! CRUMP! CRUMP! CRUMP!

Spencerstein charges, spitting with fury, bog eyed with hatred and

KABOOOOOOM!

gets blown to bloody bits as she accidentally steps on a landmine.

Ooh! That's **got** to fucking hurt!

"**SHE'S DEAD - AGAIN!**" scream an ecstatic British press.

"**HUZZAH!**" roar an orgasmic British public as they whip out millions of still tear-soaked and snot-stiffened union jack hankies and prepare for another week of utterly debasing, undignified, snivelling, grovelling and utterly nauseating forelock-tugging mass hysteria as, once again, she's scooped into a coffin and obscenely paraded through the streets of London in an orgy of braindead emotional masturbation.

Earl Spencer's speech the second time round is even more controversial. "**KILL THE BITCH!**" he screeches, pointing a pudgy finger at the quaking Queen and sure enough the grieving mob storm the Abbey and chase Liz, Phil and Charlie Boy out into the street where they are eventually cornered, strung up by their ankles from lampposts and beaten to death with floral tributes.

But in the confusion the coffin lid is knocked off and Diana's corpse is ripped to formaldehydespurting bits by the frothgobbed mob. It takes the deployment of the entire British Army to restore order, collect up the bits of tattered flesh and finally put Diana back together again.

But so incredibly successful is this second mass blubfest that the decision is taken to once again bring the corpse back to life, dress it up in a Little Baby Bunting style fox cossie and have it hunted down with many a "yonks!" and a jolly "tallyho!" by sabre-wielding paparazzi on the backs of massive chopped hogs accompanied by packs of slobbering killer dogs.

The British nation, its hysterical blood'n'blubbing appetite merely whetted, hysterically insists that the ritual is repeated again and again. This week she's crucified on Salisbury Plain, the next hung from a crane on a bungi rope and dipped repeatedly into a pit of blind crackbabies armed with machetes and razor sharp stainless steel false teeth. And each time she dies the entire nation unites in heartwarming compassion and emerges strangely purified.

The sun never stops shining, Tony Blair never stops smiling, the crime rate drops right off the scale and Ole Granny Britannia can once again toddle off to the local corner shop with her dog Ole Togger to buy three pence ha'penny of humbugs and a copy of The Daily Star without having to fear the malevolent attentions of smack addled 9 year old muggers on illegally motorised skateboards.

Armed secret police squads are empowered to burst into the homes of citizens suspected of not being sad enough. Concentration camps are built for the cynical, the sneering and the uncompassionate. Great golden statues to the Goddess Diana are raised in every town centre where deeply spiritual ceremonies involving much weeping, wailing and gnashing of teeth are made compulsory twice a week on pain of stoning and Elton John's 'Candle In The Wind' stays at number 1 for ever with the Sex Pistols especially re-written 'Di-Anarchy In The UK' lodged permanently at number 2 with all other music, art and non-Diana related broadcasting permanently banned just on the off-chance that it might contain something which might possibly give offence to any one of the millions of shitbrained spunkgibbon corpse-worshippers who nightly roam the streets armed with rolled up copies of the Diana Princess of Wales Tribute Edition of Hello! magazine with which they are willing to beat to a fucking pulp anybody caught not wearing black and mournfully screeching like a fiend from hell.

New Britain! New Labour! New Hysteria! A Nuclear Love Bomb Holocaust turns Britain's cities into Emotional Nagasakis permanently swept by the firestorms of compulsory compassion as 55 million stiff upperlips tremble as one and the gutters run red with the foaming blood of dyed-blonde Di-lookalike former hard-men transvestites who slash their wrists in mass suicide pacts in tribute to the fairytale princess whose life was oh-so tragically wrecked by the jug-eared parasite androids of The House Of Windsor.

I have seen the future! It is the image of a steel toe-capped Dolce and Gabana fuck-me stiletto stamping on a grinningly grateful peasant face - **FOR EVER!**...insanely flashbacked Jello Cobain as

SNONK!

three highly toxic grammes of ground-up crackbaby pelvic bones insanely frankensteined up two greasy fivers to savagely smash into the 8 million screamingly sensitive nerve endings at the scab encrusted rear-ends of his red raw nostrils.

"FUCKING *OMMMMMMMMMMMMM!"* screamed the full lotus-positioned bald Buddhist bastard beatifically as he simultaneously farted through his nose, shat through his mouth, vomited spunk out of both his ears and spat ten-pints of hot steaming liquid toe-jam through the painfully distended gob of his nightmarishly spasming cock (whilst his massive bald head spec-tacularly rotated 360 degrees at 347 RPM inna Linda Blair stylee - natch!).

"BOOM SHANKA!" screeched the highly successful publisher of cutting edge trash fiction insanely as he thrashed like an epileptic baby seal getting brutally booted hither and thither across the anabolic steroid ampoule littered concrete floor of a heavily strobed blind nazi skinhead gabba disco DJ'ed by a syphilis deranged Detective Chief Constable off his fucking box on illegally confiscated peyote, PCP, smack, coke, pot and ten hastily gulped ten-gallon sized earthenware flagons of mutant hookworm larvae infested and Hepatitis B infected rancid crab-apple brandy laced with lashings of CIA-experimental strength LSD whilst injecting himself in the left eyeball with a syringe full of DDT and laughing like a wanking chimp on crack.

"**HALLELUJAH!**" gibbered Cobain maniacally before savagely relaxing as if every cancer-ridden bone in his brutally abused body had been suddenly liquified by a spectacularly gruesome strain of species-barrier leaping mutant myxomatosis, causing him to suddenly and savagely smash straight down face-first into the syringe-strewn surface of his stainless steel desk with a sickening crunch as his nose interfaced violently with a cut-glass decanter containing 47 grammes of top-quality crystal meth - sending blood, snot, drugs and chunks of glass studded nasal cartilage splattering all over the pictures of naked teenage Brazilian street children that Cobain kept pinned to the spunkstained walls of his seedy office for when he needed to suddenly wank.

"**NIRVANA!**" he squealed brutally as his fat plastered naked body underwent a series of terrifyingly traumatic involuntary spasms whilst the crushed wreckage of his impact shattered olfactory organ instinctively hoovered up all the crushed-glass contaminated crystal meth in its immediate vicinity with fevered gusto.

"**EUREKA!**" he roared as he leapt to his sock'n'sandal-combo clad feet, ran across the office and booted open the door to the secret cellar where he kept a score of semi-lobotomised ex-rock music hacks chained to word processors and attached to drips which fed their festering semi-corpses a stream of watery gruel and just enough dangerous drugs to keep their bodies numbed and their crippled minds constantly teetering on the brink of total psychosis.

"**WORK, YOU BASTARDS, WORK!**" thundered Cobain as he strode between the ranks of glassy eyed author-serfs cracking a huge rhino-hide bullwhip and spitting with fury as the skeletal fingers of his mindless minions tip-tapped away at 200 words per minute as they did for 24 hours of every day of every week of every year churning out an endless stream of pulp fiction classics with titles like **HUGETITTED SPUNKSUCKING NAZIS-NAKE SLUTNUNS IN CYBERSPACE!, FISTFUCK TO FREE-DOM!** , **JOYRIDING INTELLECTUAL CRACKBABY BLOOD-FIENDS!, GASHCRAZED MEDICAL STUDENT CANNIBAL PARTY PAEDOPHILE CRACK-MASSACRE!, SUBMISSIVE BOOTBOY SMACK ADDICT SEXTOY!, I KILL FOR LAGER!, SKINHEAD TAKES IT UP THE SHITTER!, MENTAL SELF-MUTI-LATION FRENZIED KUNG FU GLUESNIFFER SPUNK RIOT!, I SHAT THE HOT-CUM OF A BILLION NEW LABOUR SPIN-DOC-TOR SCUM IN A CRACK-WRAP LITTERED AND BADLY-LIT BACKSTREET BOMBAY BUMBOY BROTHEL FOR BASTARD YONKS!, MY LIFE AS THE DRUG-DERANGED AND SAVAGELY UNDERPAID MAD MONKEY WAGE SLAVE OF CUTTING EDGE ENFANT TERRIBLE BAD BOY NOVELIST MARTIN AMIS FOR PEANUTS AND LOVED EVERY FUCKING MINUTE OF EVERY CUNTING DAY!** and **SHITSURFING FISHNETSTOCKINGED INTELLIGENTJUNGLECRAZED MUTANTFERRETSEXSLAVE CANNIBALSPUNKADDICT SINGLEMOTHERDRUGALIEN CRACKSMUGGLING COPKILLER ANDROID RIOT-GRRL WHORENUNS FROM RE-HAB CLINIC COLD TURKEY HELL VERSUS THE COCKSUCKER MERCENARY SKULL-FUCKEDPSYCHODRUGKOP SPACEFASCIST RANGERS FANS FROM SPEEDGABBA KEBABPUKESMEAREDMINICAB-HELLPLANET 9 ON SMACK! 2 - THE SCREENPLAY** which sold in their millions and made Cobain's Pining Shaft publishing house the most successful small business in the EEC.

"The secret of my success?" asked Cobain archly as he stared at his own disgusting reflection in a snazzy little onyx-backed drugmirror balanced precariously on top of the scab plastered head of one his furiously typing employees upon which he was chopping out a massive line of dead cheap smack laced with clinically pure cocaine and desiccated baby pygmy chimp adrenal-glands with the bloodrusted razorblade that he kept as a souvenir of his 3rd wife's 18th and most successful attempt at suicide.

"Why I'd have to say it's the probably the way I utilise the very latest developments in communications technology to keep my team of eager writers bang up to speed with the very latest trends and fashions!" boasted Cobain as he airily waved a podgy needle-pocked paw at the stinking ranks of pulpspewing semi-android hacks whose hideously swollen heads all sported heavy steel headphones which blasted cutting edge extreme pop sounds straight into their shaking skulls whilst banks of video machines spewed looptapes packed with horrific images of slaughter, torture, kid's cartoons and triple-X rated hardcore-europorn straight into each slackjawed slave's visual cortex through a complicated spaghetti of multi-coloured wiring.

"And it all comes out...*SNONNNNNNNNNNNK! uh! uh! uh! uh! uh!*.....**HERE!!!!**" screeched the porcine parasite excitedly as he romped like a psychotic sumo to the back of the dank rat-ridden subterranean room where he kept the state-of-the-art laser printer from whence savagely spewed yet another utterly psychotic sure-fire smash-hit but shudderingly subliterate teen-sploitation novel mindlessly churned out in a few hours by the utterly drugboggled brain of an anonymous kidnapped rock hack whose finer sensibilities had been mercilessly crushed by a relent-less and totally desensitising non-stop barrage of gratuitously violent, overtly sexual and utterly tasteless cultural effluent and then smashed into atoms by the computer generated super-orgasms that thrashed his emaciated body as a reward each time he concocted a savage sentence, sordid sex scene or sickeningly violent pig-getting-his-ear-sliced-of-in-Res Dogs style scenario that leapt clean over the boundaries of civilised good taste and fell screaming into the abyss of barbarity, perversion and dangerously demented decadence beyond.

(But the last laugh was with the writers - for little did the pillpopping porcine parasite piss-artist, pimp publisher, part-time pot pusher and hard core kiddy porn peddler realise that these were actually the best working conditions that any of the rock hacks had ever known.)

"Come to me, my baby!" chortled Cobain brutally as he eagerly snatched up the first page of

TITS-OUT TEENAGE

TERROR TOTTY

and started to read...

CHAPTER ONE

FOX!

'Trust is good. Control is better.'

Joseph Stalin

MEANWHILE, *dahn sarf*...

JUSTICE, JUSTINE: Witch, pagan, nutter, bodybuilder, tattoo artist, serially monogamous to a series of pretty teenage boys. Breathtaker, spermseeker, ballbreaker, widowmaker, Helen Bonham Carter eyebrowed, cruise missile breasted, long-limbed, steroid munching borderline psychopath. Judo, aikido, kung-fu, gung-fu, karate, kickboxing and general all-round, no-holds barred fuck-U-up street fighter blessed with a hair-trigger temper and a prehensile cunt.

Her hobbies include writing original and contemporary free-form Anglo Saxon poetry, satanism and breeding a new strain of mutant super ferrets which she feeds kidnapped lap dogs and hypnotises with candle-lit readings from the obscure and allegedly non-existent humorous writings of Friedrich Nietzsche.

THE PLACE: The soft, effeminate and distinctly unimpressive Hampshire countryside. Upper middle class WWI British Army officers, screechily breathing their last through mustard gas lacerated lungs in some far corner of some muddy, blood-drenched and entrail strewn distant foreign field, dreamed of such landscapes. Of the satisfying thwack of leather upon willow, of warm, pissy, southern beer and of nuns cycling through sunlit mist towards the gently peeling bells of Evensong, of peachcheeked 3rd formers spreading arse under crisp white sheets, of the shatterveined faces of bent-backed family retainers sacrificing their minds, bodies and lives for the perpetuation of the terrorgrip dictatorship of sordid Norman sperm, of daddy and teachers and the big, clean limbed and aloof lads of the upper sixth slashing at distended buttocks with canes, slippers and freshly oiled cricket bats. Of ENGLAND! OI! OI! OI! Of a country worth dying for.

THE TIME: Now.

Justine rested her enormous yet staggeringly firm breasts on the mossy bank and peered eagerly through the still crystal sharp German binoculars that her Grandfather - the legendary anarchist drinker and mural artist, Crazy Frank Justice VC - had liberated from the trembling hands of a shitscared Waffen SS officer after Frank had single handedly wiped out the cringing Nazi's entire column of horse drawn kitchen wagons using a shitload of cap-tured *panzerfaust* and his justly infamous impression of a firmly buttocked palomino mare in heat to lure the Nazi horses onto the perfect ambush position (Crazy Frank had been Wilfred Owen's samesex lover in the stinking trenches of the previous war - an act of class treachery which the Justice clan overlooked only because it entitled and enabled future generations of Justice offspring to annoy their English Lit. GCSE teachers with the information that it was an ancestor of theirs who had popped the great poet's rectal cherry).

Framed in the two perfect circles of nazi glass was a scene so foul that it sickened Justine Justice to the pit of her perfectly muscled proletarian stomach. A fox hunt. The parasite class at play. A class directly descended from the swivel-eyed barbarian cattle-thieves, serial killers and child-rapers of the Dark Ages, now forced to play out their genetically pre-programmed blood-lust fantasies by dressing up like twats and, with the aid of forelock tugging classtraitor bumpkins and packs of slobbering killerdogs, go charging around the countryside in an attempt to corner and rip to bloody shreds a poor innocent foxy. **Oi! Oi! Oi!**

The hunt was just about to be "ambushed" by hunt saboteurs - stinking middle-class young townies whose inane sentimentality and hatred of their own species had led them down the self-righteous path of Animal Rightsism. The hunt sabs were all vegans. Deficient in protein, devoid of both the sensory pleasures of flesh consumption and of the essential amino acids needed by the human body for it to function at anything like optimum capacity, the hunt sabs were no match for the sunkissed, brawny armed, hairy chested, nail-studded baseball bat waving, knuckleduster clenching, Mace wielding and manically carnivorous members of the Hunt Supporters Association (moronic, brown nosed, flag-waving, immigrant hating, roast beef and two overboiled-to-a-mush veg munching, Jeffrey Archer reading, rectal cancer bleeding dickheaded lickspittles every one) who tonned out of screechily parked Range Rovers, whooping and hollering like the kids from 'Lord Of The Flies' (an anti-human piece of life-denying fascist literature, the basic message of which - that we **NEED** a rigidly censorious and powerfully armed state ready and prepared to smash any flowerings of individuality or deviance from a "normality" exclusively defined by a ruling class as an ideological weapon designed to justify and thus protect their own vast and unearned power and wealth which the Hunt Supporters - being knucklegrazing Tory voting brain-doners to a man and woman - forced their children to read as part of an unconscious, entirely instinctive and yet massively effective regime designed to create yet further generations of thick boned and Pavlovianaly loyal rural serf scum ready to die for their chinless, haemophiliac Norman masters) and laid into the wasp waisted, pasty faced, home grown organic "ganga" blasted, soapdodging, dog-on-a-stringing, carrot-munching, mungbeancurryslurping, foxhugging, sexually promiscuous, French film watching, filthy, reeking hedgemonkey vegetarian scum with gusto and battered the living fucking shit out of the shrieking, weeping and pitifully quick-to-bleed homosapiens-phobic hippy bastards who fought like incredibly soft girls and were **MASHED! Oi! Oi! Oi!** By Mr and Mrs Bully British Beef and their sturdy bulldog, Roger! **Oi! Oi! Oi!** It was a Coleman's Olde Englishe Mustard advert shot by Sam Peckinpah on Vietnam-era CIA experimental combat-acid (like in the film Jacob's Ladder) and designed to elicit the response "It makes me **WANK!**" from a sneak preview test audience composed entirely of land mine manufacturers, thus causing them to unleash mottled, heavily veined and purple headed pythons from pin striped trousered flies and frig them vigorously until they spat spunk and spattered the balding and skin-cancered heads of the similarly wanking capitalist scumbags in the row in front. **OI! OI! OI!**

Justine Justice sharpened the focus on her nazi-manufactured binoculars and cackled.

When the last squealing, nutroastmunching hunt sabber had been booted, kneed, punched, clubbed and battered into a boo-hooing bag of still stinking crusty crap by the jolly English yeomen and yeowomen (red faced, green wellied and black hearted she-nazi Conservative And Unionist Party jumble sale organisers, Radio 4 listeners and howling fuckmad sexsluts to a woman), the hunt proper came roaring around the corner with a yoiks, a tally ho and many a cock or clit stiffened by the scene of carnage that greeted their sweetsherryblurred eyes.

"Huuuu*AAAAAAAAAARGH!* " roared the subhuman scabs of the Hunt Supporters Association, waving their bloody cudgels and feverishly doffing their caps as the scarlet jacketed scum of the earth swept by on their steaming steeds.

"Time to **DIE!**" murmured the watching Justine Justice as she leant her entire muscular weight onto the plunger.

"KA-BOOOOOOOOOOOOOOOOOOOOOOOOOM!"

went the genuine 15th century stone humpbacked bridge as the 490 kilograms of semtex packed underneath exploded in a fireball that emptied bowels and shattered windows in 5 counties.

"**Plit!**", "**Pa-lop!**" and "**Smat!**" went the soggy and rough edged body parts of the hunters, the hunt horses, the hunt hounds, the hunt supporters and the hunt sabs as they pitter-pattered down all around like some strange and yet strangely stimulating, grisly, quarter cooked rain of death into the trees, bushes and gently rolling meadows of Jolly Ole England for miles around.

"K e r -RUMMMMMMMM! K E R -**RUUUU-UUMMMMMMMM!!!!!!**"

roared the engine of Justine's self-built 3,000 CC Harley-based motorcycle throatily as Justine prepared to make her getaway, laughing her fucking cock off (metaphorically speaking) at the Pol-Pot pure of mashed flesh with which she had defaced a southern English countryside so associated in her mind with the soulcrippling and spiritwithering fantasies of an English nationalism that was so limpdickishly effete, so cuntfearingly corrupt and so arselickishly servile that she would have nerve gassed and nuked it into a smoking slag heap and then covered it over with a concrete concocted from the powdered blood and bones of its vowel mangling southern denizens if only she had the time and resources.

She roared with laughter, tears streaming down her muscular cheeks, her long red hair whipping out behind her in the breeze, as she thrashed her monstrous bike down the flesh spattered English lanes. Then she saw the fox.

Foxy sat in middle of road. Foxy exhausted. Men and dogs and horses no longer chase Foxy. Foxy safe! Foxy go kill chicken or duck. Take home to Mrs Foxy and baby Foxies.

"SPLAT!"

went Foxy, his pathetically small brains spurting out of his cute little pointed ears, as Justine Justice ran her deliberately aimed monster motorbike front wheel over the chicken and duck slaughtering little ginger-furred psychopathic animal bastard!

Having already laughed one metaphorical cock off, Justine Justice aimed her sturdy juggernaut of a massive, lead-spurting, unsilenced motorbike towards the North, Bradford and home and laughed off several more metaphorical peni as she did so.

CHAPTER TWO

DOG!

'Drugs Make Your Eyes Bleed'

American T-shirt slogan, The ABC of Terror series, 1980's.

That night, up north, in the picturesque city of Bradford.......

The sickeningly gusset-drenching hot-bod of the 24 year old sexual athlete, bisexual porn star, subliterary genius and clit'n'-cock stiffeningly droolsome epitome of male beauty known to the world as Mad Mick The Needle lay tucked up snugly under a sperm-stiffened Teletubbies duvet cover snoring savagely through steel-plate reinforced nostrils made sexily cavernous by the lad's totally irresponsible anabolic steroid abuse plus his utterly disgusting habit of snorting toilet-bleach adulterated bathtub sulphate through rolled-up greasy fivers at regular four hourly intervals in order to maintain the fragile state of nervously twitching punk rock psychosis so fashionable among the urban terrorist cognoscenti amongst whom Mick was undisputed uber-hund thanks chiefly to his massive following amongst Northern Britain's vast hordes of puppylovestruck terrorist groupie teeny-boppers who wasted hours of their preciously short teen years drooling over the vaginal juice'n'vaseline smeared poster of our Mick buck naked and ready to fuck which Smash Hits had once printed by mistake and which had since become the major masturbatory aid of choice for an entire generation of frustratingly socially inept but incredibly randy suburban schoolgirls who, as we speak, frig clit vigorously in their baby-doll nightied millions whilst fantasising savagely about being brutally taken from behind by the very same horse-sized length of rock hard cock meat which currently sticks out obscenely from Mad Mick's Postman Pat jim-jam bottoms to form a deliciously rude bulge in the used tissue strewn and sperm-stiffened Teletubbies duvet cover under which the most sexually desirable male who has ever lived lies blissfully aslumber whilst a liberated NHS hospital drip pumps 200 potentially lethal milligrams of Lithium a minute into the chemical sewer that is Mad Mick's bloodstream and a pair of dead flash headphones thrash the lad's impressively overmuscled eardrums with a 200 decibel loop tape of hissing white noise wrecked extreme Speed Garage stroke Gabba versions of 'Abba's Greatest Hits Vol 1' whilst Mad Mick slumbers on little knowing that he is indirectly responsible for the hideous poltergeist storms which nightly sweep the neatly privet-hedged avenues of suburban Yorkshire as the Mick-centred orgasms of millions of sticky fingered individual teenage terror-fetishists release screaming tendrils of pungent psykick energy into the atmosphere where they inevitably coagulate into hideously visaged demons who channel the wanked-out lasses' deranged but perfectly healthy sexual hysteria into acts of senseless vandalism which result in garden gnomes being decapitated agogo and many a suburban bus-shelter being mysteriously sprayed with the slogan **MICK IS FIT!** and suchlike.

And, as he twitches and fiddles and writhes, Mad Mick The Needle *dreams* (in full, gaudy, eyeball-melting 1940's style technicolor and eardrum puncturing state-of-the-art Sensuround sound) that he is dressed sexily in gleaming white power-assisted combat armour and off his incredibly pretty face on experimental combatstrength battlecocaine whilst leading the assault of a hand-picked team of top terrorists on a hideously gothicgargoylestudded Scottish castle which conceals the secret HQ of an evil mung-beancurrymunching, lentil-loving, ducksqueezing, treehugging, crustoid hedgemonkey, New Age ning-nang-nongmerchant Animal "Rights" outfit that is being, annihilated, obliterated and generally mashed into a pink-tinted, steaming and still screaming human flesh pâté for having dared to have ruined Mad Mick's moment of glory in the Kicking Off Swans' Heads competition.

In this dream he punches a loose-boweled, trembling, squealing, naked vegan up the cock and pulls his entrails out through his urethra with a state-of-the-art power-assisted combat glove before whirling the screaming veg repeatedly around his helmeted head like some weird slimy-stringed puppet, scything down the scum's filth-caked friends like stinking, carrotmunching dogs trousershittingly hiding themselves in the tall grass from a satanic combine harvester driven by a dog-hatred obsessed factory farmer ripped to the sunkissed ruddy tits on cider and snorted insecticide. Mad Mick smiles, sexily. One muscular hand snakes down under the duvet to toy with his massive erection. Now he's pulling the top veggy's head off with a sickening *RIIIIIIP!* and staring savagely into the scarlet flecked and John Denver specced face of his messily decapitated foe. Mick laughs, hysterically. But then,***SUDDENLY!!!!*** , the head starts to change spookily ala post Jurassic Park (the 19th best movie ever made despite the stomachfucking, sheetsniffing babyboomer family values "message" nailed clumsily onto the end) top notch horror movie spesh FX. The flesh peels off and falls to the floor with a sickening slap. The gleaming skull that Mad Mick holds in his power-gloved hand now laughs **BACK!** Like the skeletoid warriors in Jason & The Argonauts - only ***not as jerkily!*** It is no longer the face of a disgusting, patchouli-reeking animal rights crustoid scumnutter vegnazi. **NO!** It has changed. It has changed into...the face of...

DEATH!!!!

MEANWHILE....*dahn sarf*

Sucking savagely on the slim surrogate tit of a Silk Cut adulterated with killer crystal meth stolen from the backstage rider of ripe young fleshlings Torso! (Britain's first openly and rampantly homosexual tennybopperfodder toyboypopcombo), rock impresario, Loaded subscriber, record label owner (and former Crasstifarian anarchoveg punk rocker) Charlie Barker sneered at the cringing figure of the six and a half foot tall skinny hippy tosspot who slouched pathetically on the office couch and pouted like a petulant dog with no bones.

"Fing is, Dicky boy" smiled Charlie Barker savagely as he twirled a black cassette tape between the heavy gold-sovereign ringed fingers of his pudgy left hand, "vat ve tested art yer new demo onna focus group ov espeshlee picked panters ie long-'aired teen'h'age chicks wif a fing abart skinny-looking miserable 'ippy barstards plas a sma'erin' ov sick lickle indie boys what gets off on music what makes 'em feel even more fackin' sad an' miserable, the sick cants, an' they **ALL** said it was **TOTAL FACKIN' SHIT!** You *CANT!!* "

"Yeah. Well. Huh." shrugged Ashley Richards, incredibly sensitive lead singer and main songwriter for ironically monickered miserabilist indie combo, The Zest.

"I dunno! You ain't cammin' ap wif ver goods no more! You still takin' the smack?"

"Yeah. Course." grunted the hippy.

"An' are you like still rilly fackin' bammed art?"

"S'pose..."

Barker leant forward suddenly and rammed a fat digit straight into the skinny hippy's face.

"You gorra fackin' bird, you cant! Untcha!? **UNTCHA!?**"

Richards cringed, cowering from the music mogul's thrusting finger, his lower lip wobbling frenziedly whilst hot piss trickled down the inside of the stinkingly filthy leather trousers that floppingly encased his incredibly long, skinny and needlepocked legs.

"**I FACKIN' KNEW IT!**" roared Barker, slamming a Mighty Joe Young style fist into the desk, "I fackin' **KNEW IT!!!!!** What did I tell you, you fackin' **SHIT 'ED!?** Eh!? Eh!? **EH!?** You fick fackin' smack'ed **CANT!!!!!!!** The *only* fackin' reason your last album ov piss-miserable self-pityin' whinin' **SHITE** sold so many fackin' copies was 'cos you was inspired by your fackin' bird leavin' you for your best fackin' mate 'cos she said you was a miserable fackin' 'ippy cant, **savvy?** You gorra keep miserable, **capiche!?** You fick fackin' miserable lickle 'ippy **CANT!?!?**"

Barker was now standing, leaning right over the desk and

prodding the trembling musician hard between the eyes with each syllable.

"**DO -YOU-UNNER-FACK-IN'-STAN'? HELL-OH! ERF-CAL-LIN' PLA-NET-FACK-IN'-'IP-PY! IS-THERE-ANY-ONE-AT-FACK-IN'-'OME?** Oh my giddy aurnt! You're pissin' on me carpet! You fackin' *DIRTY* lickle **CANT!**"

Barker slumped back into his seat, cradled his enormous greasy head in his podgy hands and sighed. Your average punter probably thought that running a record company was piss easy - find the talent, stick 'em inna recording studio, feed 'em smack and whack the shit out - bish bash bosh- SORTED! Ha! If only they fackin' knew!

"'Ere!" snarled Barker, reaching into his desk to extract a bag of smack which he flung at the pissing hippy. "Shat ap, jack ap an' then fack off, I've got fackin' work to do, you useless **CANT!**"

Still shaking his head and tutting, Barker emphatically whacked the ON button on his elephant-cock shaped blood-red dictaphone and roared: "Tamara! Track dahn that mad Karen Skull bitch an' tell 'er I'm apping the offer to 50 mill for a five album deal on the proviso that she gets 'er kit off on in the first vid and duets with Myra Hindley onna cover versh of the Nancy Sinatra classic 'These Boots Are Made For Fackin' Walkin'. Oh yeah, an' sacks my fackin' cock, the dirty fackin' little cah, **ARF!**"

"Tell her yourself" spat back disgusted posh rock secretary Tamara Palma Farmer, "she's *hgggggggggggghhhhh! GAH!* "

BAM! The heavy onyx doors of Barker's disgustingly opulent office flew off their solid gold hinges and sent scores of expensively framed platinum records crashing like so many guillotine blades into the shag pile carpet where they stuck quivering hideously as the lithesome and black PVC clad hot bod of the world's sexiest female terrorist strode briskly on lime green killer stilettoes towards the fear-paralysed Barker, clutching a bloody tooth-edged machete in one hand and the glassily staring head of a posh bird in the other.

"**PUGH!**" coughed Barker explosively as Karen Skull brutally backhanded him across his fat, greasy and coke wrinkled fizog with the spurting head of his recently slaughtered posh bird employee, knocking the drugfag down his throat so he choked violently like a dog who'd just been fed a lump of juicy mince with a huge dollop of Colemans English Mustard hidden inside by some sick bastard who hated dogs and liked to wank on them as they coughed their tortured canine guts up.

"Hear this, **scum!**" purred Karen, seductively, as the fat rapist of workingclassyouthculture flapped and panic-attacked like an epileptic crackbaby being kicked down the stairs of a Glaswegian tenement building inside a metal dustbin by Tamasipanaddled Rangers fans for a laugh.

"Tamara I have terminated because she was called Tamara and was thus, by definition, **crap!**" spat Karen, slinging the machete over her incredibly sexy shoulder (so that it thudded harmlessly into the bony forehead of the massively musclebound Res Dogs suited armed bodyguard who had just emerged from behind a secret panel clutching an Uzi and smiling), whipping a gleaming stainless steel scalpel out of her Batman-style utility belt and performing a lightening-fast tracheotomy on the purple faced pig even as she spoke.

"Aw, fuck it! " she roared as she accidentally slashed through Barker's jugular, causing a savage jet of warm, watery and chemically adulterated blood to erupt straight in her scowling face, ruining her carefully applied make up and brutally kicking her permanent PMT into homicidal overdrive which inevitably sent her on a 4 hour killing spree during which she brutally butchered every single employee of Apocalypse Records above janitor level which, whilst permanently removing 498 utterly crap individuals from her Anti-Crap Jihad Hitlist, ultimately did nothing to slow the progress of the Thundering Crap Juggernaut that Karen instinctively and intellectually knew was effortlessly crushing the human spirit into the dust of despair and total boredom despite all her efforts to slow its progress by savagely slaughtering as many crap types as she could before the sad but inevitable day when she got trapped by the SAS and then shot in the back after she'd surrendered. And that *really* pissed her off.

Police reports would later reveal that the only person left alive in the entire building was a skinny hippy who lay sprawled on the couch in Barker's office in a pile of his own shit and a pool of his own piss, dribbling out of both sides his stupidly grinning gob at the same time whilst an empty syringe dangled from his incredibly thin left arm.

MEANWHILE....

Mick awoke spurting sweat and screaming like a highly strung and hysteria-prone operatic soprano who'd just had her chubby hands whacked into a couple of oversized liquidisers by a white coated and psychopathic mad scientist as part of some sick and ultimately pointless but fun experiment.

SUDDENLY...

the 48 inch state-of-the-art flat screen Sony Trinitron TV suspended directly above Mad Mick's huge bed by the soldered entrails of a vulturised Apache attack-helicopter burped into life and spat visual and aural crap ie the opening credits for the hip, happening, wacky, zany, irreverential, groundbreaking early morning youth TV dominantideology agitprop-popprogramme **MAD HIPPIES ON DRUGS!** We see through Mick's sleep encrusted but utterly beautiful eyes the slo-mo footage of grim-faced, arms-linked, doggishly-devoted-to-decency, rock-hard cockcop Britrozzers (note the gritty, gut'n'groinstirring strains of 'Land Of Hope And Glory') and note that this heartwarming footage of embattled bobbies is interslashed with shots of black youths (huge spliffs dangling from slack lips), picket lines, Arthur Scargill, violent hippy demonstrators taking drugs and diarrhoearing savagely onto bonfires built from kidnapped white working class babies, bibles and jolly unionjack bunting etc. We hear through Mick's incredibly pretty but still extremely masculine ears the aggressive junglist-reggae music competing with, overwhelming and ultimately kicking the crap out of the patriotic tune in a cowardly 10-onto-one, beer-crates-in-the-pub-car-park-after-dark, crack-fuelled sneakysmack-attack caught on securi-cam and exhibited on prime time Crimewatch UK as further proof (if proof be needed) that crime is a genetic disorder that will only be finally and irrevocably surgically sliced from the otherwise healthy body politic by the judicious and moderate application of fascism.

Take a breath and....*slow* zoom in on the ruddy puffing face of an arms-linked peeler who in an ideal world would be telling the time to rosycheekedkiddywinkies before cuffing them gently on the side of the head with a heavy leather glove stuffed with ball bearings to send them home screaming with blood pumping from both smashed ears for scrumping apples from the village orchard and being cheeky because being smashed on the side off the head never did anybody any harm and stops children growing up into childmolesters and pissing in the racial gene pool by engaging in underage and video-nasty fuelled sexual shenanigans with strangely dressed and badly postured drug dealers in return for clingfilm wrapped blocks of mindblowing ganga. For what stands between YOUR family and the gibbering hell of simpering samesex politically-correct limpwristed lesboid commiepoofter hardcore pornoterror, hmmmmmmmmmm? Did the Spitfire pilots crawling on the beaches of Dunkirk with Japanese shells exploding all around them die in their tens of thousands so that an entire lost generation of sickly, animal-pornography addicted, juvenile delinquent ne'er-de-wells could be cosseted and coddled in cosy comprehensive kindergartens by the predatory homosexual stormtroopers of let-it-all-hang-out *maaaaaaaaaan* slackness and depravity? NO! Where are your children? Having non-sexist fairy tales read to them by do-gooder social workers in meat-free hessian kaftans under which they frig swollen genitalia vigorously. Think on.

In this week's episode a bunch of multiracial hippies with black beards and hippy wigs and tie-dye T shirts are holding a busty blonde mini-skirted woman hostage in a New Age traveller caravan. The beautiful blonde woman holds a beautiful blonde baby to her ample yet incredibly firm bosom.

SUPERINTENDENT WITH A MEGAPHONE
Come out, you travellers, we've got the place surrounded!
(Off megaphone)
Sergeant, get that crowd of civilians back out of harm's way.

HIPPY 1
Come and get us, pig! Just come one step closer and we shoot the woman...

HIPPY 2
Yeah! And eat the baby inna Babylon an' ting!

BOTH HIPPIES
Heh heh heh heh heh heh!

SERGEANT
Come along you lot, there's nothing to see...

CROWD
Rhubarb, rhubarb.....

SUPERINTENDENT WITH MEGAPHONE
I have to warn you that you are in contravention of the Criminal Justice Act 1995 and that if you do not surrender immediately....

HIPPIE 2
Surrender THIS, fascist!
(Fires machine gun out the window)

The crowd of onlookers - a line of respectable and innocent civilians including a war veteran with lots of medals but only one leg, a young mother with a baby in each arm, a young girl in a wheelchair, some brownies, a little girl on a pony, a granny, a little blind boy and his guide puppy dog and a cute two-year old girl clutching a teddy bear - are raked with machine gun fire in slo-mo ala Sam Peckinpah.

CROWD
AAAAAAAAAAAAAAAAAAAAAAAAAAAAAAARGH!

HIPPIES
Heh heh heh heh heh heh heh heh heh heh!

YOUNG PC
Th-th-th-they've killed them in cold blood! Those bloody rotten murdering travelling rotten drugged up bloody scrounging facepainting unwashed filthy hippy bastards!

SUPERINTENDENT
Get a grip, Constable! We're professionals! Sergeant, bring up the water cannon!

An armoured car with a water cannon is driven up.

SERGEANT
(Clutching a huge box of soap)
Soap ready, sir!

SUPERINTENDENT
Load the soap!

SERGEANT
(Tossing the empty box over his shoulder)
Soap loaded!

SUPERINTENDENT
Fire!

CUT TO INT. CARAVAN
The hippies and the woman scream as the water crashes through the smashed window. The hippies run out screaming like girls and roll in the mud to get the soap off them. The buxom blonde woman follows them out, unzips the "baby" and pulls out a massive 45 Colt Python.

BUXOM BLONDE WOMAN
Freeze, scum!

She fires the gun **(BLAM! BLAM! BLAM!)** and boots their stinking hippy corpses. The rest of the police open fire. Sam Peckinpah style slo-mo shot of the hippies writhing and jerking as the slugs hit home...

Having leapt out of bed and ripped off his pyjamas to reveal the body of a statue of a Greek God but with much larger genitalia and loads more muscles, Mad Mick savagely pumped weights for two hours and then consumed a hearty breakfast consisting of cold strawberry flavoured Pop Tarts, Coco Pops in sugar free soya milk, five whole pots of streaming hot Ashbys Of London Organically Grown Coffee, half a dozen raw organic free range eggs from corn, worm and chicken shit fed chickens, Joe Weider's Olympian Performance Advanced Formula Muscle Builder Protein Rich Powdered Drink Mix With Added Free Form

Amino Acids, Vitamin, Minerals And Added Dibencozide (mixed in the Kenwood blender with a half pint of single malt whisky, a banana and a punnet of fresh strawberries -mmmmmmm! De-LISH!), 500 milligrams of Pro Performance Laboratories Pure Creatine Mono-Hydrate, a big fat juicy organic beef steak with grilled prawns and steamed vegetables, assorted gigantic and strangely coloured pills, great gulping gobfuls of the anabolic steroid Anatrofin, 15 Tetrapacks of chilled 1996 Saint Chinian rose (Jean de Roueyne) and 200 Silk Cuts dipped in liquid beta-blocker before engaging in a 30 minute aerobic and cardiovascular work-out by using as a punchbag the swinging body of the young priest who Mick had seduced and fucked the screaming arse off the night before but who had then, unfortunately, whilst stupidly stricken with overwhelming guilt, silently hung himself with a crude rope made from strands of his own tattered and spunkspattered black cassock.

Mick's carpet-bombed bowels then trembled and quaked like a shit-caked and soon to be ripped to bloody shreds and eaten whilst still barely alive but fully conscious and well able to feel pain cute little bunny rabbit hypnotised by the evil beady red eyes of a slaveringly hungry, needle-fanged mutant super ferret on an all-out, no holds barred, take no prisoners, berzerkoid ATTACK! ATTACK! ATTACK! Destroy-All-Rabbits-And-Fuck-Their-Corpses "tip" whilst listening to top-volume post-unification rockhard-core German techno on a mutant super ferret sized Walkman and psyched up to the max on horror videos and moralitydestroying illegal drugs.

Mick wrenched open the bathroom door and whined with frustration.

"MUTHAPHUKKKKKKKA!!!!!!" he screamed and shat standing. Yet another long-dead bog-eyed froth-mouthed poodle-wigged lurex-lacquered teen-scream wet-dream drag-queen plankspanker sat slumped on the dry-vomit encrusted plastic bog seat with tendrils of faecal hamburger dangling from his needle-pocked ass, swinging like fetid swamp vines between knees made vile knobs by tumours, ruptured veins and semi-sentient acne contracted from filth-encrusted Levi 501s previously owned by a witch-cursed leprous wretch in Bangkok who had sold his last pair of jeans for the price of a slice of Wonderloaf to the visiting rock star whose belief in the insane teachings of Aleister 'Creepy'

Crowley had led him to make many such bizarre wardrobe choices. This was the third time that week that Mick's early to mid morning dump had been delayed by the necessary but messy removal and burial of a dead rock musician. Proof, he thought, that these truly were the last days.

As he tossed the bin-bagged and quickly stiffening cadaver into the crowded open grave he'd originally hacked out of the back garden to accommodate the corpses of visiting Mormons, Jehovah's Witnesses and cats that pissed on his roses, Mick listened to the portable radio in the shape of a panda he'd been bought as a 14th birthday present by his aunt, the infamous anarcho-sex therapist Alice Nutter (who'd later been shot in the back after she'd surrendered by armed police after ramraiding the Conservative Party Conference but not before she'd taken out 74 delegates with a chain gun and grenades, seriously injured another 187 and put Tory elder statesman Horatio Messeltine on a life-support machine for the rest of his evil life). The plastic panda spoke with Buddhaesque calm of strange goings on at the Idle Conservative Club, of massed packs of frock-coated and top-hatted zombies roaming the streets and the declaration of martial law throughout the Greater West Yorkshire Conurbation before segueing seamlessly into the 'Buggery' remix of the Revolting Cock's golden oldie industrial disco classic 'Beers, Steers and Queers' which had only last week been officially adopted as the Mexican national anthem by the new revolutionary government to celebrate the completion of the re-annexation of Texas which had ended with the ritual pissing on and demolition of The Alamo and the sexual desecration of Davy Crocket's corpse by lobotomised giant chihuahuas on live TV.

As he shovelled dirt and whistled, Mick mulled over the events of the previous night when he and the rest of his Girlington Police Boys Club Viet Cong Style Karate, Kickboxing and Kung Fu Class had visited the Vaults bar in downtown Bradford in search of fascists to kick to death and had found themselves instead in the midst of the screaming, thrashing, uncontrollably spurting frenzy that *IS* a Helen Keller's Iron Lung gig.

CHAPTER 2b

TEDZ!

'Kung fu! Do what you do to me! I haven't been the same since my teenage lobotomy!'

'Kung Fu' by Ash

Mad Mick and his straw-hatted, black pyjama'ed muckers clung to the walls, scanning the pogoing crowd for signs of corporatism, trying hard not to tap their slippered toes and failing - for it had to be admitted that The Lung kicked arse so hard that they left indelible steel-toecapped boot prints on the inside of the skull for ever.

Helen Keller's Iron Lung were the world's first genuine satanic rock band and used, instead of electricity, psykick energy tapped from the crushed remains of the kidnapped corpses of Keith Richards, Jimi Hendrix, Elvis Presley, Robert Johnson, Ozzy Osbourne, Peter Waterman, Ed S*M*A*S*H, Kurt Cobain, Ginger out of The Wildhearts, James out of EMF, Billy, Fatboy Slim, Robbie Williams, Joyce Grenfell and Sid the Vish which the Lung's lead singer, Stalin, kept inside an antique McDonalds World Cup '94 mini-football slung from his neck on string woven from dried fetal gizzards scavenged from the dustbins of an abortion clinic in Bristol. He sought only one more corpse, that of Australian soap star turned pop singer turned movie star Kylie Minogue who, now that she had forsaken her mortality and become Robokylie, no longer had any real need for her mortal remains but none the less had hidden her cadaver from Stalin out of sheer spite.

Fuelled by the trapped and tormented spirits of so much tortured talent, The Lung were the ultimate rock band - in your face, down your trousers and up your arse like a shit eating rabbit on speed. As they roared through their legendary version of the reformed Sex Pistol's take on Lawnmower Deth's version of Stretch And Vern's gabba remix of 2 Unlimited's techno interpretation of Extreme Noise Terror's hand-bag style rip-off of The Verve's adaptation of Everything But The Girls plagiarism of Steps re-visiting of Jive Bunny's murdering of Eddie Cochran's Greatest Hits, the air seethed as if infested with a microscopic mist of mutated, flesh stripping streptococci.

Most of the audience, lacking the Girlington Police Boys Club Viet Cong Style Karate, Kung Fu and Kickboxing Class's control of their chi, were already coughing up blood, shaking like strobed epileptics and grinning like porpoises with vibrators stuck halfway up their slippery asses.

The music, of course, wasn't to everybody's taste. A posse of deluxe retroTeds, lard dripping form their teetering two-feet tall quiffs to form pools of congealed gunk on the padded shoulders of their lime green dayglo drapes, gave vent to their disgust at the band's alleged buggery of Eddie Cochran's corpse by hurling half-empty Newky Brown beer bottles which, although intended to cripple or intimidate, was a little like feeding a 'roid-raging bull chimp with amphetamines and then poking it with a cattle prod and calling it a puff in front of its bird without first donning all over chain mail and carrying a pump action shotgun with a snazzy underbarrel white phosphorous grenade launcher ie **VERY DANGEROUS**.

Guitarist Animal rocked back on the top of the speaker stack upon which he was perilously perched and launched himself into a 20 ft kamikaze death dive. *CRUNCH!* One steeltoecapped boot crushed the skull of the Ted known as Stuttering Steve who screamed *"F-F-F-F-UCK! "*, flapped and fell. The crowd roared. *KRAK!* Animal's other steelie spanged off the stubbled jaw of Tedzilla - the world's hardest Ted - and sent his yellowing dentures whistling across the room to smash with a sickening thud into the pimpled forehead of Detective Sergeant Alan Clarke of the West Yorkshire Metropolitan Police Drug Squad who had disguised himself as a busspotter in search of human adrenaline ampoules.

The pig roared, projectileshockvomited and collapsed. **DEAD!**
SNIKTHUNK! The bayonet protruding from the front of the still
descending Animal's black painted Gibson Deathmaster Japanese
copy penetrated the left eyeball of Little Ted, the diminutive leader
of the West Bowling Rock'n'Roll Appreciation Society and killed
the tiny Ted twat instantly.

    Even before Animal's goreslimy feet hit the spit, blood,
brain, snot, sweat, lager, semen, shit and sawdust encrusted floor,
he had punched the strap-button on his chest that freed his guitar
and enabled him to go into a roll which ended in a crouch from
which he pivoted on his left foot whilst driving the toe of his right
so far and so hard into the groin of the Ted known as Rockin' Stan
that it severed his penis and recessed his testicles into his
stomach causing a massive and messy haemorrhage and
instantly fatal traumatic shock. Animal (who had trained for 5 years
in a secret Tibetan Satanic monastery and thus knew that the
sound of one hand clapping was exactly the same as that made
by a fleet of nuke laded B52 jet bombers crashing into a field of
gibbering born-again Christian steel drummers on drugs), skidded
across the floor, his right foot trapped in the still twitching torso of
the torn apart Ted like some giant, dayglo carpet slipper.
Wrenching his killer foot free, Animal whirled, picked up his still
screaming guitar, and whirled again, the deadly edge of the mock-
Gibson's sharpened flexi-steel strap describing an arc which
ruptured the jugulars of another 2 Teds and slashed open the
femoral artery of a third. Only now did Animal pause for breath.
And the air he breathed stank. Of **DEATH!**

    The bodies of the six slaughtered Terror-Teds jerked and
spasmed beneath the lashing feet of the mercilessly disrespectful
crowd except for one which still staggered, blood gratuitously
vomiting from a gaping neck wound. Summoning his chi, Animal
kicked the still standing Ted under the jaw with both feet. *BOK!*
The Ted's head came clean off, dragging a not insubstantial
section of nerve-dangling spinal column with it. The body leapt
high into the air in a spastic parody of demented and drugridden
disco dancing, the blood geysering from the ragged remains of its
neck. The head whirled across the room, the trailing vertebrae
whisking like the tail of some enormous mutant super-sperm,
slashing through flesh and clothing, to land with a **THUNK!** in the
huge, hairypalmed hands of Iron Lung singer, Stalin, who, whilst

crashing backwards under the impact, raised the Tedskull's still warm lips to his own and inserted his tongue causing the band's homophobic cockernee roadie, Dagenham Pete, to involuntarily projectile shockvomit with disgust at the side of the stage.

The crowd roared. The 27 white polyester skinny rib T-shirted, bud-breasted E'n'speed addicted 14-year old teenyboppers who lined the front of the stage screamed in unison, releasing a yellow river of steaming urine as they involuntarily voided their cider engorged bladders. Three of them collapsed, writhing in orgasmic frenzy on the piss-slippery carpet of entrails where they were trampled into unconsciousness by their now delirious peers, all of whom were now teetering on the brink of a pelvis shattering hysterical mass orgasm of such intensity that (when it exploded 3.7 seconds later) it triggered a poltergeist storm which exploded every piece of glass within a 2 mile radius and raised the dead in nearby Undercliffe cemetery.

Unaware of the imminent gorefest, the band played on. The drugs, the violence, the fury - all feeding into a psykick feed-back loop of the sort that momentarily opens up dimensional port-holes and allows life-hating demons to stick their crab-like claws through the thin fabric of the reality/screaming-fucking-nightmare interface like some shellshocked, mad slasher ex-Para with sharp-ened garden shear blades for fingers trying desperately to gouge out the hawk-like eyes of a blue rinsed fascist lace curtain twitcher with roast chicken skin and a bulging colostomy bag.

The resulting rupture of the very fabric of the universe had seriously negative knock-on FX for a secret meeting of freemasons conducting child-sex fuelled satanic rituals at the local Conservative Club when the multi-phallused entity known to our prehistoric Cro-Magnon cousins as Ole Spunker flickered into corporeal existence in the very midst of their perverted shenanigans and shagged them all to living death with 13 of its six hundred and sixty six prehensile, multi limbed and steel fanged peni whilst tap dancing with its cloven hooves and whistling the bass riff from Rage Against The Machine's punkrock fuck-off classic 'Bombtrack'.

CHAPTER 2C

JEEEEEZUS!

'We were very surprised to see them walking, we had never seen that before...They went down in their hundreds. You didn't have to aim, we just fired into them.'

Anonymous German machine gunner, 1916

Ripped to the rigidly grinning satanic tits on the totally legal Yank bodybuilding workout drink Ultimate Orange (which makes you want to shit, piss, puke, fuck, fight and run screaming to your mummy all at the same time) that they'd "scored" after their gig in Bradford, the psychotically shaking Helen Keller's Iron Lung posse were bombing down the M1 at 170 miles an hour in their souped-up transit van which, of course, was fuelled by the trapped and screaming souls of the innocent Christian dead.

Like Dr Who's Tardis, the Lungmobile was substantially bigger on the inside than it appeared to be from the outside and contained, amongst other things, a huge unholy-waterbed, a martial arts dojo and a massive fuck-off unholywater filled jacuzzi in which several members of the band were busily frolicking and fornicating with a dozen nubile groupies of both sexes while

Dagenham Pete, the band's homophobic cockernee roadie, sat in a corner reading his copy of Loaded and disgustedly grunting about having to work with "fackin' paffs!".

"Aye up, lads! We've got us a Christer!" yelled the band's manger, Aleister Crowley, suddenly as the van's satanically powered radar unit started to viciously ping whilst he expertly steered around the furiously burning wreckage of a top rock band's tour bus which, thanks to a distortion in the space-time continuum, doesn't actually blow up 'till later in the book.

"**WHERE!**" demanded singer Stalin, violently, as he leapt from the jacuzzi mid orgasm and accidentally sprayed Dagenham Pete's straight in the face with a geyser of hot cum.

"**LEAVE IT ART!**" screamed the furious fat cockernee hysterically, bursting into tears and pissing his outsized Levi 501's in disgusted homophobic frustration.

"Dead ahead! Range 8 miles and closing!" barked Crowley who wasn't, as you might have presumed, named after the famous dead satanist and Fester from The Adams Family lookalike Aleister 'Creepy' Crowley (aka The Most Evil Man In The World) but **WAS** in fact the famous dead satanist and Fester from The Adams Family lookalike Aleister 'Creepy' Crowley (aka The Most Evil Man In the World)'s ghost. Or so he said. And, as he'd kicked the fuck out of the last 598 people who'd laughed at him and called him a fucking liar, I think you'd better believe him, OK?

"Get me a lock!" screamed the still naked Stalin hysterically as he feverishly strapped himself into the padded seat of the van's built-in rocket-powered harpoon gun.

"You're locked on!" bellowed Crowley, excitedly. "Target in range in 12 point 4 seconds ex.......**ZACTLY!**"

"Weapon armed! Switching to radio mike!" screeched Stalin as the roof of the transit van slid aside and screaming hydraulic jacks pumped the twitchingly adrenalised and bollock-naked satanic harpoonist out into the cold night air.

"Passing target!" babbled Crowley frenziedly. "Target is in driver's seat of red Ford Sierra! Do you have target, Devil 1?"

"This is Devil 1 calling Big Al. That's a roger!" snarled Stalin.

"Reducing speed, good hunting Devil 1!"

"Fucking right!" laughed Stalin as he flexed his trigger finger and gobbed out a huge wind-direction-testing greeny.

"Dance, dance, wherever you may be! For I am the Lord of the dance said He!" sang beatifically smiling and tastefully pullovered born-again-Christian folk singer Jonathan Fisher as he tapped the steering wheel of his sensibly driven red Ford Sierra and sobbed with heavenly joy as his body rippled with tingling waves of orgasmic ecstacy while the song playing at a sensible volume on the car's deck tape filled him once again with the Love Of Our Lord God who had sent to Earth His only son Jesus Christ who was crucified so that we might have Eternal Life!

"Hallelujah!" he roared, tears pouring down his cheeks as the certain knowledge that he, Jonathan Fisher, was certain to spend eternity with God because he had accepted Him as his personal saviour and been washed in The Blood Of The Lamb while everybody else (ie Jews, Hindus, Moslems, Buddhists, Mormons, Catholics, Atheists and Agnostics) would burn in extreme agony in a sea of fire for ever for stupidly not believing that every single word of the Holy Bible was the Word Of God and thus the literal truth! The mugs!

*"And I'll lead you all, wherever you maybe! And I'll lead you all in the dance sai**HUUUUUUUUUUUUUUUUUUUUUUUUUUUU-URK!**"*

"GORRIM!" woofed Stalin excitedly as the harpoon smashed through the red Ford Sierra's insectcorpsesplattered windscreen and whacked the bespectacled godbotherer smack in the middle of his weedy chest - atomising the top of the steering wheel, slashing the safety belt and nailing the fucker to the car seat with extreme prejudice as it did so.

"Oh sweet Jesus! This must be The Rapture!" thought Jonathan Fisher blissfully as he felt himself suddenly fly through the petrol fume polluted air (referring to the bizarre belief amongst born-again-Christian types that God will pluck them all (including the dead ones) up safely to heaven shortly before The Last Days when the Anti-Christ will rule the earth and everybody will have to wear 666 bar codes on their heads and God and his team will then take The Dev and his mob on at Armageddon and kick the fuck out of them as allegedly prophesied in The Bible).

"HALLELUJI-***EEEEEAAAAAAAAAAAAAAAAAARGH! OH FUCKING BASTARD CUNTING HELL!***" screamed Jonathan Fisher as his ears were savagely ripped off by the jagged edges off the shattered windscreen.

"**DANCE, LITTLE FISHY!**" screamed Stalin, insanely, as he slowly winched-in the writhing Christian, artfully smearing the insanely screaming tambourinebanger over the tarmac as the now driverless Ford Sierra swerved into the central reservation, mounted the crash barrier and flipped over to land on its roof on top of a BMW driven by a coked-up record company video commissioner going in the other direction who veered violently into the path of a mini-bus full of delegates returning from a Conservative Party constituency workers' rally in Eastbourne which piled into the Sierra-topped BMW and steered it straight under wheels of an articulated lorry which was rushing vast quantities of the new U2 album northwards causing it to roll completely over and send a coach packed with pissed up neo-nazis returning from a fascist rally in Bruge skidding wildly out of control and right up the arse of a Sun reader driven lorry carrying chemical fertiliser and shunting it directly into the path of another Sun reader driven lorry carrying chemical fertiliser causing both trucks to spill their loads onto the motorway where they mingled explosively and were ignited by a cigar butt tossed out of the window of a Rolls Royce driven by a pissed up property speculator, thus causing a massive explosion which set off a Dresden style thermal chain reaction fire storm which detonated the fuel tanks of every vehicle on the North- bound carriageway for 40 miles in both directions (all of which just happened to contain complete and utter bastards including a well known yoof-TV and pop radio morning show presenter, a Channel 4 programme commissioner, a minibusload of public school rugby players, a coachload of paedophiles, a people-carrier full of New Labour spin doctors, 19 transit vans containing shitty little under-achieving jingly-jangly "indie" bands, The Loaded Roadshow convoy, and 846 other assorted vehicles which all carried hilarious stickers claiming that members of the assorted drivers' chosen professions all did "it" in a position relevant to the aforementioned profession) for the Lord moves in mysterious ways His wonders to perform.

"Stop playing with your food, Devil1!" bellowed Crowley as the van's satanic radar unit detected police and other emergency vehicles (which would doubtless notice a satanic gargoyle studded transit van dragging a screaming Christian along behind it) already heading towards the worst (and, in a way, best) traffic accident the world had ever seen.

"Oh, all right!" mumbled Stalin petulantly as he whacked the auto-reel button on the side of the harpoon gun and hastily pulled on a rubber devil mask in case the Christer was still alive.

Which, fortunately, he was! Hastily scrubbing up and donning his blood red theatre gear, guitarist Animal (who, luckily, was a fully trained surgeon) dragged the blubbering wreckage of the Christian folk-singer's almost skinless yet still breathing body over to the van's mini-operating theatre where, after punching the fucker unconscious (because Dagenham Pete had snorted all the anesthetic) he battled valiantly to keep the Christian from croaking so that the bastard could be lightly roasted on a giant spit and then slowly eaten alive in the medieval banqueting hall of the lovingly restored Elizabethan mansion house of the decadent young aristocratic fan of the band who had invited them to a party that very night.

It was a top party - packed with smackedup supermodels, lithesome strippers, top-draw whores, roaringly drunk and brutally fruity-voiced mad posho British actors who'd last made anything even vaguely approaching a decent film way back in the '60s, snorty posh birds panting for a portion of proletarian knob, thick-as-pig-shit-but-utterly-fit 12milliondollars-a-movie yank himbos who had all the acting ability of a desiccated dog turd but mysteriously possessed the ability to make the majority of heterosexual women in the world spurt just by being in the same room, an Indian guru who everybody thought was utterly profound (because he smiled all the time whilst talking complete shite but who was actually just a savagely brain-damaged buffoon with charisma and a python-sized cock) and Bobo - the famous pygmy chimp with a American sign language vocabulary of over 600 words who proved very popular with the coachload of deaf and superbly thighed American cheerleaders who turned up looking for directions to Cheltenham where they were meant to be attending an international cheer-leader conference (sponsored by Channel 4 as part of its ongoing and utterly futile campaign to help the utterly shite sport of American Football take root in this country which is a total waste of time seeing as how we've already got what the Yanks call "soccer" which is not only a vastly superior sport but is also, as was recognised by Prof. Eric Hobsbawn in his book The Age Of Extremes, an artform inferior to none) but decided to stay at the party and shag the film stars instead. And, like all the best parties, it wasn't just loads of boring grown-ups sat around chatting or (even worse) loads of people just wiggling about to disco music, but involved lots of great games like Postman's Knock and Blindman's Bluff and Musical Chairs and Hide'n'Seek and that one where you pick the name of a famous person out of a hat and have to stick it on your forehead without looking and then guess who it is by asking other people questions to which they can only answer "yes" or "no". And, of course, tons of drugs and shagging.

At dawn the entire (by now completely stoked-up) party trooped outdoors, leapt on a fleet of waiting souped-up golf carts and raced off to the ancient druid grove at the bottom of the decadent aristocrat's 3,000 acre garden where they sacrificed a Etonian 3rd former to Odin as the sun came up and then bombed back up to the house where the long-suffering Filipino staff had whipped up a delicious breakfast of kedgeree and kippers and kidneys and tons other stuff that you only ever see in films about posh people before the entire lot of them - except Helen Keller's Iron Lung who had a gig in Aberdeen that night and wanted an early start so they'd buggered off straight after the sacrifice taking the deaf cheerleaders and Bobo the talking chimp with them - were massacred by the long suffering Filipino staff (who had been infiltrated by an MI6 agent provocateur who was actually a "sleeper" under the control of the infamous terrorist Karen Skull) who burst in wearing red bandannas, lobbing fragmentation grenades and firing Chinese made AK 47's from the hip whilst quoting vast chunks of Chairman Mao's Little Red Book in the original Mandarin from memory before blowing the house to rubble with the 50 tons of chemical fertiliser they'd secretly stashed in the mansion's copious cellars, revealing, when the smoke had cleared, that the house had been built directly over the entrance to a vast subterranean maze of natural tunnels in one of which were discovered the oilskin bound and still perfectly preserved copies of 23 hitherto unknown Shakespeare plays which revealed that the bard was in fact an atheistic primitive communist and fanatical anti-royalist (which was presumably why the plays were hidden in the first place). But we digress.

CHAPTER 2D

GOTH!

'There were three ravens sat in a tree/they were as black as black might be/The one of them said to his mate/Where shall we our breakfast take?'

(Trad)

Meanwhile, back in Bradford....

Pop video director Hilary Hilton, like all men called Hilary (or Toby or Julian or Sebastian), sucked. London based mock-vampiric Nouveau-Goth "New Grave" band, *Lesalt* , sucked. Shooting a video in a Victorian cemetery sucked. The track sucked. The drugs sucked. The weather sucked. Undercliffe cemetery played host to a suckfest of lethal proportions.

Zombies, however rule. Thus it was that when the dead awoke, smashed their way through granite, marble and sandstone with fists made diamond-hard by spooky zombie magick and tore the band, director and crew apart like parcels of dog food wrapped in tissue paper, the needle on the Coolometer whizzed from Suck to Rule and stayed there. Throbbing.

"This is really fucking cool!" yelled *Lesalt* drummer Simon Le Death who slept in a coffin and went everywhere with a white albino rat called Hitler perched on his emaciated left shoulder as the animated corpse of the only male child of a celebrated 19th

Century Bradford mill owner bit his left shoulder off and spat it clean across the graveyard into adjacent Peel Park from whence a startled Hitler ran off into the bushes, squeaking. The rest of the band said nowt. Struck dumb with terror they merely squitted and died. Like **DOGS!**

The shambling mass of zomboid Victorians, their fleshlust tweaked by the recent snack, headed towards the city centre moaning as they went about the litter and the architecture and the general decline in standards since they were alive. An observer might have remarked that, actually, zombies only *really* ruled whilst they were engaged in their fave activity of shuffling after, cornering and consuming the living but that the rest of the time, due to the fact that, like all old people, they stank and held extremely conservative views, they sucked big time.

*Meanwhile...*in the leafy London suburb of Lewishan, Hong Kong born gun-opera movie director, John Wong, ran red-hot action-babe, Sonia Small through her paces in scene 57 of the long awaited factually-based martial-arts bio-epic The Anti-Crap Jihad of Karen Skull. Dressed in a tight black mini skirt, steel-toecapped monkey boots and a "Terror Worldwide" T-shirt (from the ABC Of Terror series), the young Sonia Small (in the role of Karen Skull) suddenly realises that every single car parked in the leafy Lewisham street down which she is walking has a Garfield doll attached the rear streetside widow by transparent plastic suckers. Enraged, she proceeds to destroy every single one of the 27 rear windows with a typhonic blitz of roundhouse kung-fu kicks. This done, the hysterically screaming Small/Skull then drenches the entire contents of her economy sized box of Tampax Tampons with highly flammable nail-polish remover, hacks crude holes into the car's petrol caps with her nail file, forces the hastily improvised fuses into the jagged holes, lights the tampons with her shocking pink Bic lighter and

BA-BA-BA-

BOOM!

converts the leafy Lewisham street into the Basra Road.

Mr Wong smiles.

CHAPTER 3

FOLK!

'The English language is neither a hot-house orchid nor a precision tool but a gibbering mutant.'

David 'Crater Face' Bates

After bathing in Dettol, Mad Mick The Needle threw on a blue satin kimono, slumped on the lime-green dayglo calf-skin sofa and sulked like a motherandfatherfucker. Today was obviously going to be shit. He zapped the TV on and raced through the 897 channels in search of some mindless pap, some chewing gum for his third eye with which he could settle his chi and possibly get a wank out of. BBCSKYB 298 was showing Stewart Homes's classic 'If 2'. It was the best scene. The one where David 'Craterface' Bates, the school swot loosely based on Cuthbert Cringeworthy from Leo Baxendale's epic comic strip The Bash Street Kids, finally snaps under the New National Curriculum's philistinism, crass Eurocentricism and crap cultural conservatism.

"The English language is neither a hot house flower nor a precision instrument, rather it is a gibbering mutant!" roars Bates as he applies his Bic lighter to the neck of a home made Napalm molotov and tosses it at the startled teacher. The teacher's cheapo-brand armoured exoskeleton immediately bursts into fume-spewing flames as the screaming pig topples into a row of desks, his cries of agony drowned out by the animalistic hooting and hollering of the naked schoolboys who pelt the flaming fascist with spitballs fired through empty biro tubes and dare each other to dart in and penetrate flabby academic ass with compi dipped in VD infected dogwank. The scene obviously owes much to that bit in Masque Of The Red Death where the aristo in the monkey suit is strung up and burnt to death by a revenge crazed and class hatred enthused dwarf but is none the less artistically valid, thought Mick, otherwise I wouldn't be nursing this massive, purple headed erection that looms from the silken folds of my nice blue kimono like some hideous snail-munching lizard. Look how it writhes and twitches.

Mick now faced the most existential of all existential dilemmas - to wank or not to wank? To settle for a few minutes of sensual pleasure or to preserve his tantrick energies for the day ahead? Normally Mick thought that sensory deferment sucked but today, with its aura of impending total crapness, he might need every ounce of **umph! ugh!** and **aaaaaaaaaaaargh!** he could muster. He'd shave instead.

Like most of his generation, Mad Mick loathed facial hair with a passion. A man might as well tattoo **DOGSCOCKSUCKER** on his forehead as grow a beard.

Mad Mick The Needle stared in horror at the volcanic pimples that seethed beneath his facial epidermis like dolphins trying to break the skin of an ocean of cold custard before they died, still grinning but in mortal agony, from brain damaging oxygen deprivation.

"Curse Body Shop Sensitive Skin Shaving Foam from the Mostly For Men range" roared Mad Mick as he smashed the shaving mirror with one blow from his Mighty Joe Young style fist.

"Curse Anita Rodick and her intellectually insulting attempted marriage of milch-cow biologically determinist feminism with market forces!"

Mad Mick strode from the house, naked and erect, savagely rabbit punching and drop-kicking a path of shattered bone and ruptured internal organs through the hordes of zombies and screaming innocent bystanders who clogged the streets. By the time he'd reached the city centre he discovered that the army were in full control of the situation and so was forced to kill and strip a copper to bluff his way past the roadblocks.

Snatching up a Pekinese tied to a lamppost and chewing his way through the leather lead, Mad Mick entered The Body Shop, grabbed a plastic bottle of Lychee And Strawberry Shower Gel And AntiDandruff Shampoo For Regular Use and thrust it in the bemused and bespectacled face of a young man in a cute forest green mock Fred Perry.

"Can you assure me that this product has most definitely NOT been tested on animals?" barked Mick.

"Yes" smiled the shop assistant.

"Right!" said Mick, ripping off the bottle top with his teeth and squeezing a jet of greenypink liquid straight into the red and rheumy eyes of the screaming peke which he then threw with great force straight into the gingerfreckled and still smugly grinning face of the speccy lickspittle who collapsed as if poleaxed as the distressed dog latched onto his face like an Alien facehugger with a hard on and speedgnawed its way into plastic surgery history.

If the shop assistant screamed then that scream was lost under the nerveshredding shriek of metaljacketed, titanium-tipped 9mm dum-dums that spat from the muzzle of the snazzy little sub-machine gun that Mad Mick had liberated from badly manicured and shockrigidly frigid digits of the offed pig. The slugs smacked like steel wasps into Body Shop product and punter alike.

"Everything alright, Sarge?" chirruped a cheeky cheerful cockernee corporal from the devastated Body Shop doorway.

"Hippies" grunted Mick, pointing with the stunted tip of his still smoking pig-issue Krupps Kommando at the writhing mass of gibbering consumerflesh that bucked and twisted on the floor in front of him.

"**Sorted!**" snarled the 15 year old squaddie.

By noon the zombies had all been located, decapitated, staked, incinerated and reincarcerated in holy water drenched soil. This ruled. Mad Mick The Needle, however, was being stalked by a Vatican Death Squad for the third time that week. This sucked.

These particular assassins were vastly superior to the Killer Katholik Kommandos Mick had previously destroyed with the aid of a series of cunningly planned ambushes involving the use of fervour-triggered demonic hellmines which he'd bought from a PO box address in the back pages of the Crowleymania Postermag.

This new lot were different. These geezers were the creme de la creme de la creme of militant fundamentalist Catholicism.

Crusaders against Heresy!

Hardcore Holymotherfuckers For Christ Rampant**! HARD** men.

These guys were so celibate that they hovered fully erect, their massive sexual energy rechannelled into miraculous anti-gravity. They formed the Pope's personal bodyguard which was cool because they were his biggest fans and would willingly slap to death anybody who said he was crap or talked bollocks. They swallowed amphetamines and steroids like popcorn and every evening they ripped each others' broad and muscular backs to shreds with monomolecular steel wire whips before the long, sleepless hours where they'd lie, screaming in torment, strapped to their iron beds by steel bands whilst a specially created team formed from the most cockteasingly horny nuns in Christendom, frolicked and fornicated in front of them, occasionally leaning in close to gently blow on huge, trembling, steaming and rigidly red hot cockheads because sleeping and ejaculation were for puffs and Protestants which were the same thing anyway, right?

They were hard. Rock hard. And permanently pissed off. And now a top team of these psychopathic Papist superpigs were seconds away from tearing an utterly innocent Mad Mick The Needle into screaming, shitting, squealing pieces of organic rag. Shit, man, this was bad. To say that the situation sucked the stinking cock of an enormous dog with terminal cock cancer would be a massive understatement. One had to ask the question - how much more suckier could this situation be? And the answer was - none. None more suckier.

Meanwhile, heading north....

The blindfold that Crowley wore as he drove the screamingsoulfueled Lungmobile (at lunatic speed through savagely twisting southern English country lanes made greasy-slick with mist and cuckoo-spit) still stank of the sweat that Bruce Lee had wiped from his oh-so-perfectly formed armpits mere seconds before he popped his kung-fu-clogs and thus became a 20th Century Legend.

A reversed loop-tape of Chris Spedding's Ton-Up Boy tribute single 'Motorbikin'' screeched from the satanically-enhanced transit van's stadium-sized stereo speakers and was relayed to the world outside from the gobs of enormous robo-gargoyles that perched atop the vans massive gothic fog-lamps but gave insufficient warning to the pipe-sucking shepherd, two bog-eyedly rigid collie dogs and the flock of sheep that suddenly appeared in front of the van as it screamed round a blind corner on two wheels and smacked them screaming skywards to be grabbed by the eager fists of the vehicle's semi-sentient tantrick force-field which stripped their flesh, syphoned their souls and spat their bones into the fields on either side.

"Wor I don' underfackin'stan'" whined Helen Keller's Iron Lung's homophobic cockernee roadie Dagenham Pete as he slouched with his size 19 18-holer steel-toecapped cherry-red DM-shod feet stuck up on the transit van's endangered species skull-encrusted dashboard and casually flicked through a spunk-stiff-ened copy of Paul Raymond's Model Directory, "is 'ow no uvver facker seems fackin' bovvered by the fack that when I started workin' for this fackin' band two fackin' months ago they were yer average bogstandard fackin' run-of-the-fackin' mill indie-schmindie combo and now they're a bunch of fackin' 'ard-core fackin' satanic psychopaths and all this fackin' "magick" shit is fackin' going on!"

"Can you have a look in the glove compartment and see if there's any of those boiled sweets left?" replied Crowley between yawns as the transit van piled headlong through a 20 strong convoy of posho teenage pony-trekkers.

"An' anavver fing!" exclaimed Dagenham Pete, his simian brow furrowing in confusion, "'ow come I talk in this fackin' ridiculous cockernee accent all the fackin' time when I'm from fackin' Newport? Eh?! And 'ow come every facker calls me fackin' Dagenham Pete all the fackin' time when me fackin' name's fackin' Julie? And 'ow fackin' come fackin' Tristan's called Stalin and how fackin' come....."

Dagenham Pete paused, caught sight of his reflection in the rear view mirror and started to scream.

"HE'S HAVING ONE OF HIS FUNNY TURNS!" roared Crowley into the van's intercom, bringing guitarist Animal rushing forward with a huge icing-sugar bag sized syringe full of rhino-tranquilizer which he rammed savagely into the thrashing cock-ernee's tree-trunk sized neck.

Dagenham Pete froze and then turned to looked at

Crowley. The scowl with which the bigoted 24 stone cockernee behemoth usually viewed the world was gone, replaced with wide eyed and frightened surprise.

"Alan?", he said in a softly girlish Welsh accented voice. 'Where are we, Alan? Where are the children?"

"DON'T CALL ME ALAN!" screamed Crowley, taking his right hand off the steering wheel, forming it into a fist and rabbit-punching the fat cockernee bastard hard in the face an incredible 26 times in the space of 5 seconds inna speeded-up Bruce Lee stylee.

"Shit!" muttered Animal anxiously as he hastily prepared another potentially lethal hypo-load of zoological knockout drops. "He's almost totally regressed! Hit him again before he remembers everything!"

"WHATCHEWFACKINITME4CHEWFACKINCANT?!" roared Dagenham Pete, spraying the windscreen with a fine mist of blood, blobs of crushed nasal cartilage and bits of broken tooth.

"Phew!" sighed Animal. "Emergency over! He's back!"

"CHEW1SAM?! CANT! EH?! CHEWFACKIN1FACKIN-SAMOFVIS?! CHEWFACKINSLAG!" roared Dagenham Pete whilst adopting the ridiculous traditional fighting posture of the outraged cockernee male.

"Shirley Manson!" barked Animal. The hideously fat homophobic cockernee roadie immediately collapsed like a boneless dog and started snoring.

"What's **UH!** going **UH!** On **UH!**?" asked Stalin, who had wandered up from the back of the van still vigorously humping the impressively thighed and ra-ra-skirted deaf yank cheerleader who was wrapped around his naked waist and was giving vent to the incredible orgasms that racked her superbly fit bod as only a drugged-up deaf yank cheerleader being expertly shagged by a bull-elephant cocked satanic rock singer can.

"Old Dagenham was having one of his fits" explained Animal, taking the snoring cockernee's pulse, "but he's alright now."

"Thank **UH!** fuck **UH!** for **UH!** that **UH!**" exclaimed the still pneumatically pumping satanic vocal chore handler as the deaf yank cheerleader lass thrashing insanely on the end of his inhumanely large beef bayonet suddenly hit and maintained a top C so pure that it shattered the stained glass lenses of his ultra-cool non-prescription Lennon spex.

"Cos **UH!** little **UH!** does **UH!** he **UH!** she **UH!** know **UH!** that **UH!** he **UH!** stroke **UH!** she **UH!** is **UH!** in **UH!** fact **UH!** the **UH!** hu **UH!** man **UH!** gate **UH!** way **UH!** bet **UH!** ween **UH!** the **UH!** curr **UH!** ently **UH!** exist **UH!** ing **UH!** hyp **UH!** er-re **UH!** al **UH!** ity **UH!** in **UH!** which **UH!** we **UH!** are **UH!** a **UH!** dead **UH!** cool **UH!** sat **UH!** anic **UH!** rock **UH!** com **UH!** bo **UH!** who **UH!** make **UH!** Mar **UH!** ilyn **UH!** Man **UH!** son **UH!**, prime **UH!** early-**UH!** Sab **UH!** bath **UH!** and **UH!** Deic **UH!** ide **UH!** comb **UH!** ined **UH!** look **UH!** like **UH!** Every **UH!** thing **UH!** But **UH!** The **UH!** Girl **UH!** on **UH!** val **UH!** ium **UH!** and **UH!** the **UH!** incred **UH!** ibly **UH!** knee **UH!** chew **UH!** ingly **UH!** dull **UH!** real-**UH!** real **UH!** ity **UH!** in **UH!** which **UH!** we **UH!** are **UH!** a **UH!** path **UH!** et **UH!** ically **UH!** shite **UH!** little **UH!** sub **UH!** urban **UH!** jin **UH!** gly **UH!** jan **UH!** gly **UH!** indie-**UH!** schmin **UH!** die **UH!** band **UH!** who **UH!** sound **UH!** like **UH!** Her **UH!** man's **UH!** Herm **UH!** its **UH!** cros **UH!** sed **UH!** with **UH!** The **UH!** Smi **UH!** ths **UH!**"

"Ugh! Don't remind me!" spat satanic zen-master Animal.

"DOCKLMPHFF!

AGAAAAAAAR! SHTMMPFHHHHH-

HHHHHHH!"

spluttered Satan by way of reply as he suddenly started savagely spurting sizzlingly hot sperm into the deaf yank cheerleader's greedily guzzling gash.

"UH! UH! UH! AROOGA!

AROOOOOOOOOOOOOOO-

FUCKINGAH!"

screamed the impaled deaf yank cheerleader chick savagely, using every single-square centimetre of her incredibly well aerobicised lungs as she sensed every single one of the still stridently stallioning Stalin's semi-sentient satanic sperm splosh savagely into her shag-shocked womb and came like the Big Bang on crack.

"Fee Fi Fo Fum! I smell the blood of some crustie scum!" chanted Crowley suddenly as he pulled up his blind-fold to reveal gapingly empty eyesockets.

"Quick!" yapped Animal, "put your eyes in and have a look at the satanic radar!"

"Hmmmmm! Two hitchhikers. Male. ETA about 40 seconds." murmured the hastily re-eyeballed Crowley.

"Then slow down for fucksake!" barked Stalin, who was gently caressing the ecstatically sobbing deaf yank cheerleader still trembling on his slowly wilting cock.

"Nose plugs in, lads!" ordered Crowley. "I'm picking up strong traces of marijuana, patchouli, stale urine, sweat and - here's the clincher - mung bean curry flatulence! It's crusties alright! A couple of real hard-core stinkers by the look of things!"

"There they are!" roared Animal, hastily fumbling with his noseplugs as two caucasian-dreadlocked scruffy bastards with acoustic guitars slung over their filthy shoulders suddenly appeared on the horizon.

The hideously gothic transit van skidded to a halt.

"Where you going, er, man?" asked Crowley, winding down the blasphemously stained glass window.

"We're goin' to a folk festival in a hamlet called Little Beezleycombe, man!" drawled one of the hippies in a hideously fake folk-singer style pseudo-rural cum Thames Estuary accent that made Crowley's inhumanly pale skin crawl with revulsion.

"Far out, man!" exclaimed Crowley, fighting down the almost irresistible urge to leap from the van and beat the stinking hippies to a pulp with a tyre lever.

"Cos that's where we's heading, man. We a folk band, man! Hey-nonny-fucking-ho, man! Can you dig it?" said Crowley as the transit van's side-door silently slid open to reveal an impossibly dark interior which, the crusties would have noticed had they not be so totally zonked on a potentially lethal combination of home grown skunk and the unbearable stench of their own unwashed flesh, stank strongly of sulphur and was illuminated only by the gleam given off by several score pairs of slowly blinking yellow eyes.

"Farkin' dark in this here van, man!" exclaimed crustoid

folkie Stephen Pemberton aka Juggling Jim as he laid his acoustic guitar down in the gloom and groped for something to sit on.

"Yeah, ain't you got any farkin' lights back here, man?" whined Dalrymple Hetherington-Beakley-Cloughforth (pronounced "Clufth") aka Patchouli Pete as Crowley smashed the pedal to the metal and the van once again lurched forward savagely with a loud, throaty and extremely unmachinelike growl.

"Oh, I'm sorry!" purred a voice from the blackness. "Y'see we're all blind and we sometimes forget...."

The reassuringly friendly if ridiculously saturnine face of Animal suddenly appeared in the yellow sulphurous glow of a flickering firebrand.

"If you'll just give me a minute..." he smiled as the flame danced slowly in the gloom and left a trail of spluttering, spitting and obscenely gothic candelabra in its sinister wake.

"**Far farkin' out, man!**" gasped Juggling Jim as his skunk slaughtered senses were savagely assaulted by the Hammer Horror/Mondo Goth/punk rock on crack, smack, nazi crank and benzedrine drenched nasal inhaler innards interior of the speeding transit van.

"**Crikey Hell!** I mean, er farkin cosmic, man!" lapsed ex-public schoolboy Patchouli Pete slackly.

The crusties stared around them in awe. They found themselves slouched on huge velvet covered bean bags of incredible softness whilst surrounded by a similarly slouching mob of leather jacketed muso types with evil goatees and Keith from The Prodge-style spiked hair, a shit load of obviously very recently shagged semi-naked cheerleaders and a chimp dressed in an Elvis in Vegas style rhinestone karate outfit - all of whom were wearing Ray Charles style wrapround Ray Bans and grinning at them reassuringly.

"Er, don't look up, man!" drawled Patchouli Pete, urgently tugging on the sleeve of Juggling Jim's festering cheesecloth kaftan.

"**FARKIN' HELL!**" gasped the folkie as he suddenly found himself staring up at an exact-but-500-times-larger reproduction of the ceiling of the Sistine Chapel except done entirely in fluorescent dayglo colours as they would be seen by a cat off its tiny little skull on magic mushrooms (and with God, Adam and all the angels having much bigger knobs, natch) through gently scudding fluffy white clouds.

"This vans got it's own fackin' ecofarkinsystem, man! That ceiling must be farkin' *miles* away!" gasped Juggling Jim.

"Wha's farkin' goin' on, man?" demanded Patchouli Pete, suspiciously.

"Well you know about Atlantis and the hollow earth?" smiled Animal, reassuringly.

The two crusties nodded knowingly.

"And you know about corn circles and crystals and pyra-mid power and how Stonehenge was built by aliens and how Dolphins are really intelligent and that pixies and faeries really exist only we can't see them because we've been brainwashed by the hideous imposition of "civilisation" which has crushed the human race's ESP with its evil "science" which is why rocket ships are always shaped like penises and eject their debris into the Sun which is our cosmic mother and all that?"

"Yeah, obviously, man!" grunted Patchouli Pete petulantly, offended that a fellow folkie could even assume that a crustie as hard-core as he could possibly be ignorant of **"The Truth"** that **"They"** didn't want us to remember.

"Well we're, uh, Atlantean aliens from inside the hollow earth who have, um, been summoned forth by the crystals buried under the corncircles made by the visiting Venusians who built Stonehenge and the Pyramids and uh..." improvised Animal hastily.

"And we've been summoned forth to the surface to serve Mother Gia by the Grand Druidic Quadbunal consisting of the Queen Of The Fairies, The Lord Of Misrule, the King Of Khaos and the, er, Duke Of The Dolphins.." chipped in drummer Daemonic Dave, helpfully.

"Yeah, cos, like, this is the dawning of the Age of Aquarius!" shouted one of the lip-reading deaf yank cheerleaders, getting into the swing of things.

"Yeah! A New Age where the forces of materialism will finally wither on the vine of the sick and perverted "science" which gave them birth!" yelled Animal.

"Yea, verily! For mine eyes have seen the glory of the coming of the Lord! He is trampling out the vineyards where the grapes of wrath are stored!" roared the lipreading yank cheer-leader excitedly as her impressively thighed and sexily ra-ra-skirted cheerleader chums all spontaneously started loudly humming the tune to 'The Battle Hymn Of The Republic'.

"And, er, so that's why the van is sort of, um, bigger on the inside than it looks from the outside. And stuff." finished Animal, feebly.

There was a tense pause. The two crusties looked at each other with raised eyebrows.

"So is that why you're all blind then, because you're from the centre of the earth where there's no light?" asked Juggling Jim, hesitantly.

"Like the mindless followers of The Mole Man out of The Fantastic 4?" added Patchouli Pete.

"Uh, yeah!" said Stalin, convincingly.

"Phew! Thank fark for that!" laughed Juggling Jim, "I thought I was having a bad acid flashback, man!"

"FLASHBACKS! *FLASHBACKS!!* **"** roared a loud homophobic cockernee voice from the front of the van, **"FLASH-BACKS ARE FOR PAFFS WHO CAN'T HANDLE THEIR FACKIN' DRUGS! POOOO! COR! FACK ME! WOS THAT FACKIN' ORRIBLE FACKIN PEN AND FACKIN' INK! HAS SAM CANT FACKIN' SHAT BACK THERE OR WHAT!?"**

"Who's the fascist, man?" asked Juggling Jim, suddenly suspicious.

"And why is the driver coshing him with a tyre lever, man?" added Patchouli Pete.

"That's, er, a Golem!" improvised Stalin hastily.

"You obviously don't mean the mythical monster from the Rabbinical version of the Frankenstein myth," mused Patchouli Pete, once again unconsciously lapsing out of Crustiespeak. "So am I safe in assuming that it's actually a physical embodiment of all the materialistic vileness like racism, sexism, homophobia, disabilism, ageism, hygienism, speciesism and carnivorism that you, as representatives of Mother Gia on a secret mission the Grand Druidic Quadbunial consisting of the Queen Of The Fairies, The Lord Of Misrule, The King Of Khaos and The Duke Of The Dolphins have created as a sort of walking bad-vibe magnet come anti-talisman, er, man?"

But he received no answer, for at that very second Crowley spotted a hand-painted sign saying:

" Ye Little Beezleycombe Folk And Crafts Festival (Ye Electrical Instruments & Un-Real Ale Ist Verboten!!!!)"

hanging on a gate.

"We're here!" he barked, savagely slamming on the brakes and the crustoids tumbled out of the transit van and piled into the Real Ale tent with their new found mates and got hog-whimperingly blasted on tons of stinking scummy beer with bits floating in it and then lay out on the grass and dug the genuine folk music being played by an arran sweatered Noel Edmonds style bearded ginger bloke who was sat on a stool strumming an acoustic guitar and singing in that hideously nasal mock-rural voice that folkies seem to think is the way everybody in Britain spoke back when the average life expectancy was 25, everybody slogged their malnourished guts out in the turnip fields all day up to their knees in stinking cow shit for some fat parasitic Norman bastard aristocrat and constantly stank like a dog's arse and had an IQ of about 12 and spent their entire diseased lives groping fearfully in the cold, fetid shadows of malodorous superstition.

"Yeah! Those were the days!" thought Juggling Jim, dreamily as he "dug" the totally authentic folk music of his Saxon ancestors.

"Those were the days," he ruminated, "when nobody pointed at crusties in the street and shouted stuff like - Get a bath, hippy! You fucking stink! - and stuff and took the piss out of folk music by sticking their fingers in their ears and going - Hey Nonny No! - in a crap pisstake of the way everybody used to talk back in the good old days before science ruined everything, because, back in them days, *everybody* was a crustie and had caucasian dreadlocks and smelt "natural" and was into folk music! Yeah! And soon (he thought happily) soon the good old days will be back! Soon ALL music will be ethnically pure folk music played on proper instruments by proper musicians and nobody will listen to artificial and ethnically impure manufactured shit like The Spice

Girls!"

"I'm the man, the very fat man, who waters the workers beer-uh!" warbled the real-ale-pot-bellied and woolly-jumpered ginger-beardo speccy twat folk singer on the stage, the rolled "aaaaars" of his authentic folk voice bouncing off the surrounding green hills and echoing all along the floor of the beautiful valley in which the concert was being staged, a valley which Mother Gia (in her infinite wisdom) had created as an acoustically perfect natural concert hall which thus rendered the hideously artificial concept of electronic amplification redundant - thought 49 year old real-ale-pot-bellied and woolly jumpered speccy twat folk singer Roger Finnegan as he lovingly surveyed the beautiful folk-fans who reeled and jigged in front of him as craply as only pissed white hippies can.

Roger had nearly slashed his wrists when Dylan had gone acoustic at The Isle Of Wight but had instead written an angry and brilliantly sarcastic letter to Folk Times asking why Dylan hadn't just cut his hair, started wearing a suit and joined the Nazi Party and "cut out the middle man, man!" Since then times had been hard for folk. Albion had succumbed to the hideously alien and horribly artificial mongrel moronicism of rock'n'roll as represented by caterwauling capitalist pawns like The Beatles. But there is hope, thought Roger, as he noticed the number of young people in the audience, like that dreadlocked young chap with the acoustic guitar slung over his shoulder who danced a jolly jig with a middle aged and incredibly fat hippy woman wearing a hessian peasant dress and sandals and flowers in her naturally greasy, stinking and unwashed hair, man!

"This is IT!" - thought pissed-out-of-his-tiny-hippy-brain Patchouli Pete as he frenziedly jigged and reeled with the fat hippy woman whilst desperately trying to keep his crow-feathered and extremely battered top hat on top of his head and stop the acoustic guitar slung on his back from swinging round violently and smashing other revellers in the face

"This is REAL!" he roared suddenly, buzzingly furiously with the wonderfully authentic farkin' workingclassyness of it all and the sure knowledge that the New Age Revolution which would herald The Age Of Aquarius was coming soon as evidenced by his recent fortuitous meeting with the strange but wonderful people who had given him and Juggling Jim a lift and revealed to them that they were in fact on a secret mission from Mother Gia at the holy bequest the Grand Druidic Quadbunal consisting of the Queen Of The Fairies, The Lord Of Misrule, The King Of Khaos and The Duke Of The Dolphins!

In fact, so folked-out of their tiny pissed up heads were Pete and Jim that they failed to notice that their new found chums had all sneaked off back to the van where they had broken open its vast arsenal and were preparing to charge into the field of jigging folk scum whilst screaming insanely and spewing flaming liquid death from state-of-the-art combat flamethrowers for a laugh.

"You don' wan' be doin' thar, young mizztrezez'n' marrzzterz!" said a ruddy cheeked old geezer dressed in an ancient tweed suit, cloth cap and muddy wellies just like the farmer from 1998's hilarious 'Ooh ARR!' TV ad for Ambrosia Cream Rice (which so deeply upset red-cheeked, mangel-wurzel munching and sheep-shagging English yokel types with its crass regional stereotyping).

"Yeah? An' wassit fackin' gotta do wif you, you yokel cant!? Chew1sam? Eh? You nosey fackin' **CANT!**" snarled Dagenham Pete as he emerged from the van and rammed the nozzle of his flamethrower in the farmer's ruddy face.

WHACK! WHACK! WHACK! WHACK! WHACK! WHACK! WHACK!

The farmer's gnarled walking stick flashed through the air inna speeded-up Hong Kong Kung-Fu movie stylee and the homo-phobic cockernee roadie crashed to the cowshit covered ground in a twitching, crumpled heap of partially paralysed and utterly unre-constructed sexist pig meat.

The old farmer stood calmly smiling as the rest of the Lung posse emerged from the van.

"Uh oh, like total weird!" exclaimed one the deaf yank cheerleaders, pointing at the sky where a crow in midflight hung motionless against an eerily still sky.

"Who dares disturb The Devil's work!" growled Crowley, hefting an automatic shotgun loaded with white phosphorous rounds.

"You fuckin' towniez makez oi fuckin' larf!" chortled the farmer, picking a big fat juicy green bogey out of veiny red nose and then chewing on it sloborously with the few baccy stained teeth that remained encased in his ancient old head before gobbing it out with deadly accuracy straight down the barrel of Crowley's weapon which fell to bits in his hands.

"Snot-fu!" gasped Animal, impressed.

"Why do you want to stop us, old man?" growled Stalin. "You a stinking folkie-lover?"

"Oh blezz oi no, young mazzer Stalin!" laughed the gimmer, raising his gnarled old hands in supplication. "Oi hatez zem caterwaulin' hippiz wiz zerrrr patronizin' fuckin' parody of a zhitty old way of loife zat zose of uz old enough to remberrrrz it iz fuckin' glad iz gone foreverz. I hatez zem juzt as much az much as orl dezent folkz duz! Woi duz zou zink oi invoited zem 'ere in zerrr firzt plaze, zou zilly young zorrrzage?"

"Your accent is becoming increasingly inconsistent, grandad!" pointed out Crowley, a curious smile of recognition on his blubbery lips. "Why don't you knock off the "oo-arr" bullshit and cut to the chase!"

"Arrr!" sighed the old man, "Yuz alwayz wuz an impatient little puppy, mazzer Aleister. But, if you inzizst..."

And with that he waved his stick, said "Izzy whizzy! Letz Get Bizzy!" and

b u m f!

the Lung Posse found themselves suddenly transported to the top of a hill overlooking the folk festival. They crowded behind the old man who was staring down at the frozen tableau of the folkies in mid-frolic.

"Fukkkkkkkkkkerzzzzzzzzz!" he growled in a voice so deep and dark and seeped in ancient malice that all who heard it shivered.

The tableau below suddenly unfroze. The bales of hay

stacked in the fields on either side of the festival site slowly
stirred. Shapes emerged from the shifting straw, staggering on
insubstantial legs like new born foals. And then the very ground
began to quake. A huge red giant slowly pulled itself from the
clinging earth. The Lung posse gasped in horrified amazement.

"I don't fucking believe it!" gasped Crowley.

"That's fucking....*outrageous!* " laughed Animal.

"That is absolutely totally punkrock!" giggled Stalin, who
went to slap the old man on the back but suddenly thought better
of it.

"That's....that's...." stammered the now recovered
Dagenham Pete openmouthedly, "That's...that's one of them wotsit
things, wostsit- called doo dah bollocks things?"

"It's a combine harvester!" gushed Animal, "But it's not
just any old combine harvester! It's the rural English manifestation
of the Hindu Juggernaut which, if I remember correctly, was first
described - in a rather garbled form, admittedly - in the deranged
writings of Old Mother Shipton and which was later unconsciously
and rather more specifically prophesied by the yokel-pop novelty
act The Wurzels when they bizarrely managed to have a Top Ten
hit with 'Oive Got A Brand New Combine Harvester', which, if I'm
not mistaken, was a reworking of the song 'I've Got A Brand New
Pair Of Roller Skates' which had previously been a novelty hit for
high-pitched American singer-songwriter, Melanie!"

"Oh yeah!" exclaimed Stalin. "I remember you droning on
about it the other day! But didn't you also mention that, in The
Last Days, the combine harvester would be driven by a dog-
hatred obsessed factory farmer ripped to the sunkissed ruddy tits
on cider and snorted insecticide?"

"Eggzcuze oi, boyz!" murmured the old man suddenly,
whilst snorting a pile of highly-toxic looking yellow powder up off
the back of his incredibly gnarled left hand through a rolled-up
greasy fiver rammed up his incredibly hairy right nostril "but -
ZNONK ! - oize got zum werk to do!"

And with that he produced an impossibly massive flagon
of scrumpy from inside his jacket, knocked it back in one gulp,
farted violently and set off down the hill towards the combine
 harvester, staggering slightly as he did so and stopping for a piss
at regular 30 second intervals. Dogs suddenly appeared from
nowhere and started barking at the pissed old git and then darted

in to nip his heels as he slashed.

"Gettafuckyabastardz!" snarled the gimmer, lashing out at the frolicking dogs with his stick and thus fulfilling another part of the prophesy

Eventually he reached the massive combine harvester and, with a surprising (not to say absolutely amazing if not down-right fucking impossible) speed, grace and agility, clambered up into the driver's seat.

"That thing's got to be half-afucking-mile wide!" noted Stalin.

The old man turned in his seat and waved back at the onlooking Lung posse before pulling a lever which caused The Wurzels' song "Oi Am A Zider Drinker!" (the smash-hit follow up to 'Oi've Got A Brand New Combine Harvester' and the last time the band would feast on the sweet nectar of chart success) to blast forth from the harvester's massive speakers.

With their music drowned out by The Wurzels and the oncoming combine harvester's throaty metaphysikal-mechanical roar, the folkies stopped frolicking and, as one, looked up and pissed and shat themselves and then tried to run screaming from the festival site but were stopped by an army of spooky looking straw men clutching rusty scythes who chopped several of the folkies off at the knees and shoved the rest back towards the oncoming giant combine harvester driven by a dog-hatred obsessed factory farmer ripped to the sunkissed ruddy tits on cider and snorted insecticide. The terrified mob then hysterically sprinted to the east where they were confronted by a crowd of cider-pissed locals who beat them back with bricks and cudgels and savagely snapping sheep dogs.

Not one escaped the combine harvester's thrashing blades.

"Reckon this year'll see a good harvest round these parts!" quipped Crowley as the transit van rocketed away from Little Beezleycombe nor'but 10 minutes later.

"I could've 'ad the cant!" snarled Dagenham Pete.

"Hey, any chance of sticking the anti-gravity on back here!" yelled Stalin from the back as the 50 sexmad deaf yank cheerleaders pulled a train on him wearing strap-on dildoes and Bobo the sign-language talking pygmy chimp sat thumping away randomly at the keyboard of Crowley's Apple Mac Powerbook and accidentally wrote the greatest novel ever written in the English language in 10 seconds flat.

"Yeah, OK!" laughed the blindfolded and empty socketed Crowley as he fumbled for the switch and accidentally pressed the auto-destruct button which blew the transit van into a billion pieces and killed the fucking lot of them.

CHAPTER 4

SQUADDIE!

'In the late 20th Century, the only valid artistic enterprise is the wilfully perverse development of a remorseless and numbing addiction to the concepts of extreme noise and extreme speed.'

Anon.

A smile flickered on Mad Mick's cruel lips. The fingers of a doe-eyed corporal from Barnsley flickered on his rock hard cock.

Mick looked through thick lashes at the grunting, sweat-soaked face of the camo-clad lad before him. Circle-jerking with squaddies had never been his fave way of getting his rocks off - he'd far rather kill them than fuck them but, all ideology brutally brushed aside, there was something undeniably sweet about a man in a uniform. Something boyish and vulnerable - something that shrivelled his massive scrotal sac to the size of a refrigerated satsuma and gave him a hard-on a cat couldn't scratch.

He tensed, spasmed and yelled profanities as his tightly tugged tummy banana stiffened still further and suddenly spat spunk, his own fist instinctively tightening around the mottled shaft of the para on his right. His ears sang with a primal male roar as his seven camo-ed comrades in copulation came simultaneously. Geysers of hot cum screamed through the air, splattering faces and clothes. The circle collapsed outwards, each man laughing gibbonously at the perfection of the moment, with embarrassment at the sudden puncturing of machismo and with guilt at the sheer naughtiness of it all.

With tears pouring down his flushed cheeks, Mick propped himself up on one elbow, weakly wiped away the string of glutinous semen that dangled from his dimpled chin and smilingly surveyed his equally shattered lovers. And then he screamed as each and every head of his recently milked squaddie chums simultaneously disintegrated into a fine red mist with a loud "pop".

Meanwhile..darn sarf

Cutting edge bad-boy enfant terrible novelist Hamish Martin (45) smiled patronisingly at the sexy young miniskirted student gurlie who was interviewing him for The Guardian.

"Can I offer you a drink?" he smiled, as the pretty little thing fumbled nervously with her Sony Professional Walkman, exposing a delicious flash of firmly muscled thigh as she did so. He felt his cock stir under his stylish brown corduroys and hastily concealed the bulge under a hardback copy of his latest novel - Hackney Marshes (the gripping story of a young (45-ish) and incredibly handsome though angst-ridden cutting edge novelist of whom everybody else is insanely jealous).

"Uh, yeah, thanks!" said the girl, giggling nervously and blushing. "Could I have a cup of coffee, please? Milk, no sugar?"

"Of course" said Martin, exuding an utterly irresistible air of relaxed enfant-terrible arrogance and potent Alpha male chutzpa. He noted the girl's widened pupils, her rapidly blinking eyes, the continual crossing and uncrossing of her superbly muscled legs. He noted how she sat with her shoulders back and her young breasts thrust provocatively forward. He pictured her bee-stung lips closing gently over his throbbing shaft. He shouted to the kitchen.

"Self! Here boy! Quick!"

The girl's huge eyes widened still further as a monkey, dressed in a purple bell-boy costume complete with a pill box hat, came sauntering through the door.

"Two coffees. Milk. No sugar. Chop chop!" barked the great novelist.

"Ook! Ook!" chattered the monkey, tugging its forelock as

it ran from the room.

The girl gaped. Her mouth a perfect "O". Thoughts of fellatio once again caused the book on Martin's lap to levitate

"That's Self" explained the novelist, smiling. "Got him from a circus. Actually, maybe it's him you should be interviewing."

"I'm sorry?" said the girl.

"Self's a novelist too."

The girl frowned.

"You think I'm taking the piss!" laughed Hamish, effortlessly slipping into the young persons' street slang of which he was such an undisputed master.

"You know the saying about giving a million monkeys a million typewriters?" he smirked, not wishing to make too many assumptions about the girl's education.

"They'd eventually produce the entire works of Shakespeare?" asked the girl, nervously.

"Exactly!" said Hamish, in the same tone of voice you'd use to congratulate a puppy which had just learnt to stop shitting on the living room carpet. "Well that's the subject of my next novel - it's about a young, cutting edge enfant terrible novelist, who all the other schmucks, dweebs, geeks and, er nerds are always "dissing" because they're jealous of him. Anyway, he has the absolutely far-out idea of training his pet monkey to write his novels for him! On a sort of po-mo, magical-realist, fin-de-siecle self-parody, no pun intended, "tip", seen?"

The girl looked dumbfounded.

"Lawks a mercy, guvnor! I can see that I'm just going to have to show you!" sighed the novelist. "Self! In here. Chop chop!"

Minutes later the monkey was sat in front of the state of the art Macintosh computer, chattering rapidly and using its tiny fists to hammer at the keys..

A tiny single skinner spliff dangled from Self's mouth, the ash dropping onto the clattering keyboard. The girl was amazed to see the screen rapidly fill up with blocks off text.

"But he can't possibly be typing that fast!" she gasped, girlishly.

"OK, I'll come clean!" laughed the novelist, now dead sure of a soon-come sure-fire shag scenario with the obviously overawed young beauty.

"It's a special word processing programme," he

explained, staring deep into her rapidly blinking deep brown eyes. "Professor KR Murray at Cal Tech fed all my writing into a main-frame computer which analysed my unique style and then synthesised over a billion uniquely Hamishesque sentences. Now, and here's the clever bit, she then created a programme that randomly produces a block of perfectly coherent and structurally sound text in my unique style every time a person - or in this case a monkey - hits a key, *any* key!"

"Oh, you mean the Autotext Project!" chirped the girl brightly.

Hamish froze. The girl, he noticed, was sporting an odd grin.

"You know about it?" he asked, suddenly confused

The girl giggled and nodded. And reached into her hand-bag.

Literary London was shocked by the news of Hamish Martin's sudden retreat into self-imposed literary exile. His publishers were startled by the author's somewhat eccentric written request that the advance for his next novel be paid in bananas, raisins and peanuts to the apes and monkeys of the world's zoos. The Retropolitan Police were baffled by the discovery of the headless and handless male corpse stuffed through a tyre suspended from a rope in London Zoo's chimpanzee enclosure. Martin's next novel - story of a female pygmy chimp in an alternate universe, parallel with our own, who wakes one day to discover to her horror that her husband has turned into an over-rated, upper-middle class, Oxbridge educated junkie novelist - sold millions.

CHAPTER 5

POPE!

'Cybernetic warfare is the ultimate weapon and we can't afford one nerve jammed child. Throw your Beatle and rock and roll records in the city dump. We have been unashamed of being labelled a Christian nation, let's make sure four mop-headed anti-Christ beatniks don't destroy our children's emotional and mental stability and ultimately our nation.'

Reverend David Noebel, Communism, Hypnotism And The Beatles: An Analysis Of The Communist Use Of Music, 1965.

Mick stared up into the evil, gimlet-eyed face of Monsignor Mikey "Boy" Mancini, an ex-Green Beret karate black belt who had decided to dedicate his life to the divine cause of International Papism after God had spoken unto him during a broken bottle'n'diamond tipped knuckle-duster fist fight with US Navy Seals in a Washington strip club in which he and his drag queen chums had kicked the fuck out of the sailor boys and then skullfucked them for laughs and free beer.

"Lash him, boys" murmured Mikey, pushing the foul memory of his previous existence as a cocksucking crossdresser from his now purified mind.

Mick instinctively curled into the foetal position and whimpered, his macho facade brutally smashed by the wrecking ball of massive traumatic shock and then pounded into gravel by latent physical cowardice. He did what any real hero would do when faced with the invulnerable might of God's Mighty Fist Made Flesh, he cried like a soft swot being tortured by the school bully and screamed for his mummy.

LASH! LASH! LASH! went the electrowhips which the R&D department of Vatco Inc had to designed to cause maximum pain for minimum gunk.

"HA HA HA HA HA HA HA!" cackled the circling celibates.

"MUMMY!" screamed Mad Mick The Needle.

"Hang on, son, I'm coming!" roared 47 year old mother of 7 Enid The Needle as she burst through the bushes stood in the command cupola of a Puma armoured car with water cannon attachment.

The cruel clerics ceased their lashings to stare at the intruder.

BUDDHABUDDHABHUDDHA! spat the armoured car's .5O calibre machine gun.

"Spang! Peow! Dang!" sang the huge bullets as they wanged off the Papal hit squad's tantric force fields.

"Woman!" roared Mikey "Boy" Mancini, "You di*AAAAAAAAAAAAAAAAAAAAARGH!* "

Mick, still whimpering, glanced up to see the venomous vicar melt into a pool of putrescent slime.

"Mama Mia!" screamed Mancini's lieutenant, "she must have loaded the water cannon with...."

"Unholy water, you dumb, arselicking sheetsniffers with your irrational and wholly debasing worship of the non existent and peculiarly psychopathic god, "God". You make me *sick!*" barked Mick's mum who had been rendered unusually articulate by a massive dose of combat strength amphetamines that she'd mugged off an RAF helicopter pilot during the previous week's Stingers vs Apaches melee in which the incredibly dumbly named Yorkshire White Rose Bastard Army (composed entirely of York

City fans) had taken 95 per cent casualties in a no holds barred dogfight with the cream of Britain's thin blue line but had taken 23 very expensive and cool looking attack helicopters and their crews screaming into hell with them. Mrs The Needle, who bore the rank of Colonel in the YWRBA, had limped off into the rubble of Bolton Abbey with her 2 surviving comrades, Ian and Richard. The last surviving helicopter, flown by the unfortunate Group Captain, had landed to assist "mopping up" and been seized by the YWRBA rump, flown to Harrogate and crashed into the suburbs because, as Mick's mum said at the time: "Harrogate is shite and everybody in Harrogate either wants or deserves to die."

Two hundred and thirty four delegates at a pharmaceutical sales conference died messily but not too horribly as most of them were so skullfucked on free samples that their pain barriers were thousands of feet high and several miles thick. Mrs The Needle should have died with them but didn't. A strange combination of blast forces and the protective influence of the demon William Green had thrown her clear to land unscratched but a bit shook up and stinking on a skip full of black polythene bags containing human body parts.

"Yeah!" snarled the mother of our hero, "Unholy Water! Cack your cassocks, popey boys! I've got 5000 gallons of the one earthly substance guaranteed to penetrate your allegedly invulnerable tantric force fields and reduce the flesh of truly believing Christians who practice extreme celibacy to the consistency of napalmed blancmange!"

"SHUT THE FUCK UP AND JUST KILL THEM!" screamed Mad Mick whose extensive self-indoctrination in the mores of shitfiction had bequeathed him the unshakable conviction that folk who had their enemies within range and defenceless but then waffled on at great length usually got topped.

"Don't shoot!" screamed the Soldiers Of Christ.

"Repent!" shouted Mick's Mum, "Renounce the Vicar Of Rome, Renounce The Nazarene, renounce the strange god "God" and all his works and I'll think about letting you live."

"We renounce!" screamed the Scourges of Satan. "Fuck God!", "The Virgin Mary Sucks!", "The Dev rules!"

"SHUT IT!" screamed Mrs The Needle, "and *WANK!* "

Trembling with fear and blubbing like gurlies, the allegedly rock Papal Paramilitaries gingerly tossed up their cassocks, pulled down their shreddies and mincingly touched lengths of virginal cockmeat which immediately leapt into turgidly steely fuckpoles and spurted great arcs of thick, stinking semen.

The 9 remaining hit squad members slumped to the gore-splattered ground as their tantric powered gravity units and force fields whimpered into oblivion.

"You've got spunk on me tank!" roared Mrs The Needle as she whipped out a cute little sub machine gun, flipped off the safety and blew the screaming Jesuits into flapping messes of utterly humiliated and slaughtered shit.

Back in his bunker, deep beneath the Vatican, the Pope muttered a terse "fuck" as he watched the nine little violet lights on his World Map flicker out one by one as, back in Bradford, Mrs The Needle delivered the coup de grace with the weapon from which her family had taken its name - a stainless steel knitting needle dipped in buffalo dung.

"Thanks, Mum!" said Mick as he attempted to simultane-ously wipe away a snaking column of snot from his chin and pull on his spunkstiffened black Levi 501's.

"**Shut it, puff!**" snarled his Mum as she dropkicked him with both of her size 15 cherry red 19 holer steeltoecapped DM's.

Mick rolled, sprang to his feet and attacked! Within seconds mother and son were a blurring mass of fists, boots, flashing teeth and butting heads which ended, as usual, in a brutally tender fuck in which Mick was rogered raw with the impressively proportioned strap-on dildo that Mrs The Needle wore at all times to maintain her place in the family pecking order.

Meanwhile, *dahn sarf*....

"Art is a bourgeois concept created and sustained by a self-perpetuating ponce oligarchy and specifically designed to denigrate the culture of the working clarses!" roared bespectacled and donkey jacketed Jane Sutherland through the tightly clenched megaphone as the dinner jacketed filth of the Turner Prize audience drifted into the Albert Hall beyond the protective screen of steely eyed coppers, the enigmatic smiles flickering about the rozzers' butchly pursed pig-lips being the only outward indication of the lower middle class English Male Tory Philistine cynicism which is the universal pig 'tude t'wards matters "arty farty". The pigs all thought, no, *knew*, that all "artists" were either coke-snorting pinkoid arse-bandit chancers or hairy legged vegetarian muff-munching lesboid freaks in big glasses who watched Channel 4, read The Guardian and shagged black men on the quiet but wouldn't dream of opening their legs for a white man, a real man, a honest, hard working BRITISH copper.

"Slaaaaaaaaaaaaaaaaaaaaaaags!" thought all the pigs simultaneously as their little curly cocks stiffened and their stunted minds seethed with a poisonous stew of social class envy, xeno-phobia, racism, puritanism, sexism and penis envy.

"Look at them, bloody bastards!" swore Jane Sutherland, ineffectually, referring to the pert nosed filth of the art establish-ment rather than the pigs.

"Yeah!" jeered her boyfriend, Oliver French, wankerishly. "Fackin' parasites!"

Jane trembled savagely as an ice cold thrill ran down her perfectly formed bourgeois spine. She loved it when Oliver swore! Their lovemaking was fuelled by a stream of extremely rude words which Oliver whispered in a growly, mockcockernee voice into her shell-like as he humped her like a shitting dog on their black cotton sheeted bed.

Jane and Oliver and the other "non-artists" who had turned up that night to "picket" the Turner Prize awards saw them-selves as "really radical" and on the "cutting edge" of "intellectual" debate. In fact they were all mediocre never-will-be's, every single bleating one of whom would have leapfrogged over the thin blue line of sneering pig rockery, donned monkey suits or gurly frocks and ponced into the Albert Hall in a flash if they were ever offered the chance.

The nominees for that years Turner were the usual collection of wasters, ponces and shitehawks, all with the usual predilection for slinging bits of old shit in the corner of a room and then writing ten pages of wanky gibberish in art-ponce code about it despite the utterly undeniable **FACT!** that you could see **REAL** art of the organic persuasion on several football pitches and many rock'n'roll stages every day of every week that shat heavily and from a great height on the festering corpse of the self-perpetuating ponce oligarchy's pathetically redundant and compromised con-cept of "art" which was, let's be totally fucking honest, basically just Duchamp's urinal gag repeated endlessly like some senile old pub bore with stinking teeth and yellow breath dribbling through

the same old joke again and again and again and again and all
the time giggling ninninshly at his own feeble wit like a hyena with
asthma until a pack of violence-addlcted gay bikers at the bar get
so pissed off that they motorbike boot him through the pubs olde
worlde stylee mock-Dickensian bow windows and into the car park
where they lash his glass porcupined body into artscum steak
tartare with their razor edged bike chains before stomping him into
the noon-day Summer sun-softened tarmac and then squirt gallons of recently recycled rough-cider piss laced with amphetamines down his still quivering throat through the apesnoutlike
mouth that protrudes from the Ribena-coloured tarmac like a prehistoric miniature of the Hollywood bowl done in old tombstones.

"And the winner is...." said Jeremy Galworthy, president
of the Turner prize committee, "Ali***AAAAAAAAAAAAAAARGH!* ".
His announcement suddenly warped into a bloodcurdlingly
inhuman scream as he simultaneously received a crossbow bolt in
each eye, flapped around for a bit like a decapitated chicken and
died, noisomely shitting himself in pain, shock and terror.

"**SHUNK!**" went a hundred crossbows, "**SHUNK!,
SHUNK!, SHUNK!, SHUNK!, SHUNK!, SHUNK!, SHUNK!,
SHUNK!, SHUNK!, SHUNK!, SHUNK!, SHUNK!, SHUNK!,
SHUNK!, SHUNK!, SHUNK!, SHUNK!, SHUNK!, SHUNK!,
SHUNK!, SHUNK!, SHUNK!, SHUNK!, SHUNK!, SHUNK!,
SHUNK!, SHUNK!, SHUNK!, SHUNK!, SHUNK!, SHUNK!,
SHUNK!, SHUNK!, SHUNK!, SHUNK!, SHUNK!, SHUNK!,
SHUNK!, SHUNK!, SHUNK!, SHUNK!, SHUNK!, SHUNK!,
SHUNK!, SHUNK!, SHUNK!, SHUNK!, SHUNK!, SHUNK!,
SHUNK!, SHUNK!, SHUNK!, SHUNK!, SHUNK!, SHUNK!,
SHUNK!, SHUNK!, SHUNK!, SHUNK!, SHUNK!, SHUNK!,
SHUNK!, SHUNK!, SHUNK!, SHUNK!, SHUNK!, SHUNK!,
SHUNK!, SHUNK!, SHUNK!, SHUNK!, SHUNK!, SHUNK!,
SHUNK!, SHUNK!, SHUNK!, SHUNK!, SHUNK!, SHUNK!,
SHUNK!, SHUNK!, SHUNK!, SHUNK!, SHUNK!, SHUNK!,
SHUNK!, SHUNK!, SHUNK!, SHUNK!, SHUNK!, SHUNK!,
SHUNK!, SHUNK!, SHUNK!, SHUNK!, SHUNK!, SHUNK!,
SHUNK! and SHUNK!"**

"**SplatTHUNK!**" dopplered a hundred artponce eyeballs,
"**SplatTHUNK! X 100!**"

The last thing that the collected monkeysuited and
gurlyfrocked posho scum of the art-earth saw was the

"demonstrators" from outside bursting into the hall roboticaly like Arnie in Terminator.

Within five minutes they saw **NOWT**, mainly because their brains had been pierced but also partly because they all had a crossbow bolt in both eyes.

And yet, when the Retropolitan Police Armed Response Unit burst into the hall not 15 minutes later, they were shocked and disappointed to discover, amidst the crossbowed-to-fuck corpses of the despised "art" establishment, a huddled mass of failed artists who had tossed aside their crossbows and gone into a spontaneous and utterly nauseating group hug in the middle of the hall.

Under interrogation the tearful, shit-scared and utterly remorseful demonstrators all told the same story. The "Anti-Art" demonstration planning meeting they had all attended the night before had been taken over by an extremely charismatic young woman who had, they now remembered, hypnotised them and then given them the secret command to go berserk, kill the pigs, burst into the hall and off all the "art" establishment scum. She'd also supplied them with state-of-the art combat crossbows which they had hidden under their long artstude stylee overcoats and they were very sorry but could they go home and get some therapy now, please?

"Hmmmmm!" mused Chief Superintendent of the Terrorist Squad, Charlie 'Slagkiller' Miller as he bummed his pet labrador dog, Goldie, with the same thrusting vigour that he had brought to all his twice nighty love sessions since his wife, Doreen, had run off six years ago with an 18 year old Riot Grrl with a tongue that could tie knots in cherry stalks. "Sounds like the work of that notorious terrorist bitch Karen Skull to m...*UUUUUUUUUUARGH!* **UH UH UH!** YES! YES! *AAAAAAAAAAAH!* **WHAT AN *ARSE!*** *UUUUUUUUUUUH!* **I LOVE YOU! I LOVE YOU! I LOVE YO...**" screamed Miller just seconds before Goldie finally got so fucked off with the interspecial rape buggery that he whirled round and bit the pig's face clean off before ripping his throat out, crashing through the front window and killing another 16 coppers before finally being cornered and shot in the back by the RSPCA after he'd surrendered.

Respect, Goldie.

Meanwhile....

"So, I've decided to take my work underground, to stop it falling into the wrong hands...." ...the old-skool manual typewriter clatter backgrounded intro-sample to track 1 of the Prodigy's 'Music For The Jilted Generation' chattered from the Mac's powerful speakers as 25 year old scientific genius Dr Lara Green tip-tapped the final paragraph of her report whilst clad in a "MORRISSEY IS A TWAT!" Viz-bootleg T-shirt, baggy black-dyed German paratroop combat pants and a pair of shiny DM hiking boots. She ran a hand through her close-cropped dyed-blonde hair and smiled at the utterly incongruous cultural synchronicity.

This synchronicity would kill her. The Prodge had punctuated the track 'Intro' with sampled sound of breaking glass. It camouflaged perfectly the sound of an artificial-fibre gloved hand smashing a window at the back of the laboratory. Unaware of the approaching danger, Lara grinned as she put the final touches to the report's final paragraph. Using 20,000 ferrets - all suffering from various artificially induced cancers - she and her team of substance abusing scientist chums had painstakingly sought the Holy Grail of medical science - the universal cure for cancer. And they'd found it.

Lara clicked onto the Apple logo, triggered the CD control window and punched the volume up to max whilst sparking a huge skunk packed spliff and grinning ecstatically as she thought of all the poor smacked-up slap-head cancer patients the world over who would now cease suffering and live. How many potential Beethoven's, Einsteins, Piccassos and Keith Prodigys were there amongst them? She pressed "SAVE' and boogied sexily (to the irresistible skippety-hippety robobop of the Prodigy's 'Voodoo People') across the gleaming white open plan laboratory to the stacked ranks of wire mesh cages in which the 5,000 remaining ferrets twitched and swayed hypnotically to the aural electro-soma. She whacked the ignition button and laughed girlishly as the flame rippled down the lines of cages, automatically sparking the tiny one-skinner E-laced spliffs which the baccy, weed'n'powdered discobiscuit addicted ferrets started sucking eagerly, filtering the smoke through their tiny little nostrils as their hideous little red eyes glazed over and their sinewy little off-white furred bodies spasmed uncontrollably as the E kicked their central nervous systems into automatic dancemode and the vast laboratory slowly filled with a dense fog of swirling skunk-smoke. Which meant that Lara was unable to smell the approaching hideous fug of patchouli, stale sweat and mungbeancurry flatulence that hovered over the black-balaclava clad forms of the animal "rights" terrorists who sneaked up behind her under cover of the throbbing apocalypse of the Prodge's 'Poison' and bashed her brains out with a metal pipe.

"*I got the poison!*" barked one of the Prodge.

"*I got the remedy!*" woofed another, ironically.

The music crashed to a halt as one of the vegans smashed the Mac into sparking wreckage. Other carrotmunchers placed explosive charges and set the timers. Still others sloshed petrol over the work surfaces and remaining computers.

"Mmmmf mmmf mmmmmf mmf!" mumbled one of the veg-nazis into a cam-corder held by a colleague.

"You're gonna have to lift the balaclava up over your lips, man!" shouted the adrenaline crazed cameraperson.

"Mmmmf! Mm...Oh, yeah, right!" replied 29 year old one-armed Cliff Lineker, spokesperson for the Anti-Speciesist Army - an ultra-militant direct violent action animal "rights" terror group which specialised in firebombing chemists shops which refused to stop supplying genocidal anti-bacterial and anti-viral products but which had taken on the job of destroying this remote rural medical research centre at the suggestion of an anonymous letter that Cliff had received at the donkey sanctuary where he worked along with a cheque for £50,000 plus a promise of tons more dosh should the laboratory be destroyed by a stated deadline. The patchouli-scented letter also stipulated that Lara Green should be murdered and was signed 'A Friend".

"OK, right, I am a spokesperson for all those poor, defenceless, speechless animals that the human race has tor-tured, maimed, raped, disfigured and murdered over countless aeons of fascistic speciesist oppression!" screamed Linker, as he waved the blood'n'brain smeared length of steel piping at the camera.

Cliff Lineker had been involved in the animal "rights" movement for yonks. At first he'd just been a vegetarian, occasionally involved on the "cuddly" wing of the movement - collecting money for the starving Ethiopian's pets during the famine of 1982 for instance. But then he'd become a full-blown vegan and, as his protein-starved brain slowly slumped towards the vegetative state common to all vegans, he became ever more militant in his hatred of his own species, even going so far as to amputate his own left arm with a chainsaw when he realised that the inoculations he'd received as a child were in fact weapons of genocide against other species that had just as much right to live as did humans.

The question, of course, was the same that faced all animal "rights" militants - where do you draw the line? Cliff's answer was that you didn't. His cherished dream was the destruction of the entire human race, but lacking the wherewithal for such a grandiose ambition, he instead concentrated his feeble, protein-deficiency wilted energies towards the murder and maiming of as many of the human scum involved in the evil industry of "medicine" as possible.

Cliff wandered around the wreckage of the laboratory, ignoring the irritating phantom itch in his missing arm, as his black-clad vegan muckers scattered rabbit food on the floor and opened up the cages.

He bent down and picked up the tattered sleeve of the Prodigy CD. It showed a long haired crustie youth backgrounded by a sunlit rave, bravely giving the finger to the massed ranks of pigs gathered on the other side a gaping chasm. In his right hand the hippy youth held a large machete with which he was about to cut the rope supporting a rickety bridge suspended over the gorge, which, Cliff's diet-damaged brain just about managed to work out, probably represented the gulf between The Man and The Kids. Cliff sneered at the ideologically flawed symbolism. The pigs were backgrounded by massive satanic chimneys spewing pollution into a darkened sky. But the rave on The Kid's side featured huge speaker stacks! So where did The Prodigy think the electricity to run the speakers came from if not from the pollution spewing power stations on the pig side? Eh!? Cliff knew that the only "real" music was ethnically pure folk songs about how all humans were scum sung to the accompaniment of acoustic guitars built out of trees that had fallen down in a storm or something and not been murdered by speciesist agribusiness.

"Er, Cliff, I think we've got a problem!" yelled 32 year old Sarah Lloyd, hysterically. Cliff turned. And violently shat himself.

The 5,000 liberated ferrets, having sniffed the offered

nuts, raisins and bits of chopped up apple and rejected them in disgust had gathered around the fallen figure of Lara Green and were drooling, licking their little lips and baring their hideously needle-sharp little yellow fangs whilst staring at the vegan terrorists with boggly red eyes that radiated a sphincter-looseningly terrifying combo of hunger'n'hatred.

"AAAAAAAAARGHAYEEEEEEEEEEEEE!"

squealed the ASA cadre as they were ripped to bloody shreds by the tidal-wave of drug-addled and munchie-frenzied ferret bastardry and violently eaten.

"KABOOOOOOOOOOOOO OOOOOOOOM!"

went the research laboratory mere seconds after the ferrets, their bloodlust barely satiated, steamed out into the surrounding countryside to commence a wildlife holocaust that would quite literally decimate the nation's stock of native fauna.

Three days later Justine Justice heard a frantic scratching at her front door and opened it to find the street awash with plump ferrets.

"In you come, my psychotic beauties!" she chuckled, throwing the door open wide.

CHAPTER 6

VEG!

'Scratch a vegetarian and discover a Nazi'
Common sense, late 20th Century

Mrs The Needle, mother of Mad Mick The Needle and international terrorist mastermind, munched eagerly on a refreshing bar of Tropical Source Sundried Jungle Banana All Natural Dairy Free No Refined Sugar Chocolate whilst gazing with pride at her son as he girded his loins to do battle with swans.

The swans were buried up to their necks in sand. Mick was naked apart from some cool black ninja underpants and a massive pair of oxblood steelie DM's. His obscenely muscled body gleamed with oil. You could almost hear nipples, clits and cocks stiffening amongst the huge proletarian crowd shoehorned into Odsal Stadium. For that afternoon, of all afternoons, Bradford played host to the grand finals of Jeux Sans Frontiers **SAVAGE!** - the massively popular international TV game show with a difference. The Lord Mayor had made his speech (about how the final was just what the great City of Bradford needed to help it forget the recent blight of demonic and zomboid activity and the ongoing martial law situation) and the crowd had been driven into an anticipatory frenzy when the marching band and cheerleaders stripped their absurdly Ruritanian kit off to reveal the impossibly proportioned bodies of sexual athletes and porn stars and fucked each other raw on the pristine pitch, assuming impossible positions and screaming like brainprobed lab dogs as they came.

Now it was time for the big event. Mick was blindfolded.

The crowd murmured. The swans honked. Their hideous little heads boggled about atop their long sensuous necks. Like weird alien plants. Like Triffids. Except whiter. And cooler.

The rules were simple. A blindfolded Mad Mick The Needle - a local lad made bad - had exactly 60 seconds to boot the heads off as many swans as he could without peeking. The Italian champion, a lithesome raven-haired teenage kickboxer, had just booted the heads off 47 swans - a new world record. If Mick could top her total (and it was a big "if") then he'd not only be the Official World Champion Swan Head Kicker Offer but he'd also make Britain the Jeux Sans Frontiers **SAVAGE!** Champions Of The World for the 4th year running.

The gong gonged. The crowd roared. Using his chi to locate the invisible (to him) buried-up-to-their-necks birds, Mick launched into his dance of death. ***BOOT! HONK! SPURT! THWAK! ERUPT! HONK! SCREAM! BOOT! RIP! SPURT! ROAR! BOOT! TEAR! SLASH! BOOT! HURRAH! SMASH! SPANG! OLE! SPURT! THUNK! THWAK! SPLAT! BOOT! YES! UH! UH! UH! BOOT! BOOT! BOOT! BOOT! HURRAH!***

GONG!

Drenched in stinking swan blood and festooned with scarlet feathers, Mick was dragged from the field of carnage by beblazered umpires while the the gory head count commenced.

The crowd bit its nails and murmured. The two senior judges put their head together and waved their arms about. Then they nodded and held up cards that read "4" and "9" meaning 49 meaning that Mad Mick had just booted the heads of 2 more swans than his Italian rival meaning that he was now the Official World Champion Swan's Head Kicker Offer meaning that Britain was the World Jeux Sans Frontiers **SAVAGE!** champions.

"HURRAH FOR US 'COS WE FUCKING RULE AND YOU SUCK!" sang the crowd to the tune of 'Kung Fu' by Ash because sportsmanship was for genetically freakish public schoolboys with floppy Princess Di fringes and no knobs.

But, suddenly, the sky darkened and the joyous roar of the crowd was drowned out by the ***THWAK! THWAK! THWAK! THWAK!*** of helicopter rotor blades and the ***SHRIKKY! SHRIKKY! SHRIKKY! SPANG! PEOW! AAAARGH! KABOOM! FUCK! AAARRGH!*** of mini-gun bullets and rockets smashing into the packed ranks of carnivorous humanity.

"**VEGETARIANS!**" roared Mrs The Needle, her face screwed into a rictus of hate.

"**ANIMAL "RIGHTS" SCUM!**" bellowed Mad Mick The Needle as the swanblood drenched sand around his steel toe-capped DM'ed feet bubbled with screaming hot lead.

Mother and son, puce faced and tearful, shaking with impotent rage, howled abuse at the departing choppers while all around them the victims of the savage terrorist attack writhed and screamed in agony.

Nine hundred and seventy nine decent, meat-eating citizens died that day. Thousands more were crippled for life.

Mick and his mum booted groaning survivors out of the way as they headed for the exit, both of them silently plotting revenge for this outrageous wrecking of the Needle Family's day of glory. Already, as word of the terrorist outrage was flashed around West Yorkshire, huge crowds were attacking and destroying veggie cafes. In Leeds an ***Animals Have Rights!*** conference in the Draganora Hotel was attacked by a crazed mob who forced meat pies and pork scratchings down the throats of the anemic and pasty faced delegates before crucifying them from billboards with stapleguns. Carnivores who just happened to be a bit sickly-looking hid indoors in fear of being mistaken for protein deficient swanhuggers by the screaming mobs that roamed the streets inna Quatermass And The Pit stylee. Mrs The Needle and her sprog Mick were pissed off because they thought that every veggie in kicking-to-death distance would probably be already well kicked to death before they could exact their own personal and much more imaginative revenge. Sickener or what?

But, as they turned left out of Odsal Stadium and onto Leeds road, an armoured Rolls Royce with tank tracks on the back instead of wheels pulled up. The black tinted rear window hummed down. A fleshy face fixed them with a piggy stare.

"What the fuck do you think you're looking at?" snarled

Mrs The Needle "And if you're thinking about saying anything clever then don't because if you do I'm going to stick that flashy motor up your arse, especially if it contains any Latin, alright, flabby boy?"

"Hang on, Mum!" exclaimed Mick, "That's Sir Andrew Taylor-Bjork of Bjork's Pork And Associated Meat Products PLC fame. Maybe he's here to offer us a deal like we get to storm the HQ of the veggie scum using a shitload of top hi-tech government gear that we get to keep and they drop all outstanding charges against the both of us and bung us 20 million sex vouchers each a year for ever!"

"Bang on, young man!" chortled the jolly fat capitalist, wriggling his incredibly bushy eyebrows through a cloud of very expensive cigar smoke. "I like the cut of your gib. Cards on the table. You think I'm an enemy of the human race, I think you're insignificant maggots that, under normal circumstances, I'd gleefully crush beneath the heels of my Patrick Cox calf-skin Chelsea boots. But we both have a greater enemy ie The Animals Are People Too Troop or APT for short. Top the bastards and I'll set you up for life. Deal?"

"Do we get to pick our own team of assorted mavericks and psychopaths from the gutters of British society? asked Mick.

"Yup," nodded Sir Andrew.

"And do we keep all film, book, press and video rights?" inquired Enid AKA Mrs Mad Mick The Needle.

"OK!" said the toff.

"Sorted!" snapped Mick, emphatically.

Meanwhile...darn sarf

> *Bent double, like old beggars under sacks.*
> *Knock-kneed, coughing-like hags, we curse through sludge*
> *Till on the haunting flares we turned our backs*
> *And towards our distant rest began to trudge*
> She kissed the cold stone.

The Albert Hall fizzed with lust. Males bucktoothed and flecklipped. Females long-necked and flushed. Union Flags gripped in rigid fists. Mouths frozen in perfect O's roar their refusal to ever be slaves. Breasts nosing out of taffeta frocks. Taut bollocks support a forest of slowly stiffening cocks.

> *GAS! GAS! Quick, boys! An ecstacy of fumbling.*
> *Fitting the clumsy helmets just in time...*

There are those who fantasise about bombs exploding amongst honking filth that patronise The Last Night Of The Proms. Who hear 'Rule Britannia' and think only of the Somme. Karen Skull is one such nutter. She thinks of Siegfried Sassoon - whose same-sex lover died before his eyes. Of stammering Wilfred Owen - who thought war too dirty and too vile to be the stuff of poems. Who mirrored ugly evil with angry, ranting verse and saw in every single slaughtered squaddy the body of Adonis. Packing muscle onto poetry. Pansies shooting up amongst the poppies and all that bollocks.

The Last Night Of The Proms. The first day of The Somme. Mustard gas seeps from sewers, muffling the marching feet of kilted, bandaged, frightened ghosts. They surround the Albert Hall. Bayonets and sharpened shovels gleam. The doors cave in. The patriotic singing turns to frightened screaming.

"So the spell worked then?" asked Justine Justice.

"Like a fucking treat!" laughed a gasmasked Karen Skull. "I'm outside the Albert Hall right now and...hang on! Something's happening! A dinner-jacketed public school twat has managed to escape! He's staggering towards me, screaming for help! He thinks he's going to get away! But wait! He's been followed by a couple of the Tommy-spooks! Oof! One of them just got him in the kidneys with a bayonet! Now another ones spanging him repeatedly in the face with a sharpened entrenching tool! Ooh, that's GOT to hurt!"

"Top one!" chortled Justine Justice, back in Bradford, "look, I've got to go now, the ferrets need feeding!"

"OK, seeya at Armageddon!" said Karen Skull as she gave the Tommy ghosts a hand by kicking the screaming posho in the nads savagely with the sharp end of her stylishly steel-toe-capped left monkeyboot.

'Yeah! See ya!" said Justine Justice. Ten seconds later the phone rang again. It was Mad Mick The Needle with an offer she simply couldn't refuse.

CHAPTER 6b

COKE!

'Let justice be done, though the world perish.'

God

So thus it was that Mrs Needle and her mad son Mick found themselves hurtling through the upper stratosphere in really cool battle suits equipped with enough hi-tech James Bond style weaponry to win a world war (all of which Mick experienced with a nagging sense of deja vu). They had with them a handpicked team of nutters scooped from the gutters of British society. Sir Andrew, despite being a Tory and thus one who lied as easily as he breathed, had so far kept his word - although neither Enid nor Mick was thick enough to believe that the bellicose bastard wouldn't doublecross them at some stage and thus require a severe killing which he deserved anyway just for being a bastard without whom the world would be a nicer place in the first place.

This team included Mad Mick's 6 brothers and sisters, none of them looking very much like Mick because Mrs The Needle firmly believed that any woman who had more than one child by the same man was a traitor to her sex. It also included the American DJ Eve Ofdestruction and the stunningly attractive bisexual warrior against crap, Karen Skull.

CHAPTER 7

DISCO!

'I'm not a fan of disco. I find it mindbending... It's a contributing factor to epilepsy. It's the biggest destructor in history to education. It's a jungle cult. It's what the Watusis do to whip up a war. What I've seen in the disco with people jogging away is just what I've seen in the bush.'

Harvey Ward, director general of The Rhodesian Broadcasting Company, 1979.

They were dropped from very high up, wore dead cool radio mikes and were all off their boxes on incredibly groovy synthetic battle-cocaine which speeded up all human activity by a factor of 150. Thus they were able to conduct quite long conversations with each other even as they hurtled towards the Scottish mountain HQ of the veggie scum who they were going to burn, shoot slice, stab, gouge, knee, fist and fuck to death.

Karen Skull was the most sexually desirable human being ever. Mad Mick could not but help notice that, even in her bulky battlesuit and helmet, she looked totally and utterly fit.

"Hey, Karen" he said, his voice weak and trembly with lust. "I think you're great. I think your Anti-Crap Jihad is ace. How did it get started?"

    "I think you're great too, Mick, and your Mum," said Karen in a husky yet slightly insane voice. "It's a long story and it all started way back in....."

whoooo....

whooooooo

oooooooooo

oooooooooo

oooooo....

CHAPTER 8

DIVA!

'**Fuck a mod!**'
'**Fuck A Mod' by The Exploited.**

Karen Skull's childhood had been conventional enough -
lower middle class, liberal North London parents, nice house, lots
of cool toys and stuff but then puberty raised its smiling purple
head and her life turned to shit. From the age of 11 onwards
Karen had been consumed by a blinding and inextinguishable
rage. She rebelled violently against her parents and lounged
around the house in gothgear smoking menthol cigarettes and
grunting. By the age of 15 she had twatted the odd teacher,
hospitalised a whole posse of Hare Krishnas on Oxford Street
(whilst out shopping for spangly tights) and conducted a campaign
of telephone harassment and letter bombing against a whole
range of organisations including The Viewers and Listeners
Association, The Animal Liberation Front and the Parachute
Regiment. Only an IQ of 240 and a crafty tactical shag with a top
policewoman kept her out of prison.

Stunned doctors discovered that Karen was locked into a
permanent state of righteous pre-menstrual tension and adoles-
cent angst from which no course of treatment or Morrissey record
known to mankind could free her. On her 16th birthday Karen was
committed to a mental hospital but had garroted the head nurse
and escaped within a week. Since then Karen had captured the

imagination of the world with her **Anti-Crap Jihad** - an all-out war on a society and an economic system that she knew intellectually, emotionally and instinctively was corrupt, evil and beyond redemption. Her modus operandi was simple. First she drew up a list of the 20,000 crappest people in Britain. Then she started killing them.

The editor of Loaded had been trussed, smeared with dog food and then dangled over a pack of starving Alsatians which had their teeth removed and their tongues covered in sandpaper whilst articles entitled 'How To Beat Up Your Girlfriend And Not Leave Bruises!' and 'Rape - How To Get Away With It!' had been surreptitiously inserted into that month's issue of the magazine, inciting a crazed mob of extreme-radical feminist nutters to storm the editorial offices and mass-castrate the mag's staff with menstrual blood smeared nail scissors. The Commissioner of The Retropolitan Police was force fed cream until his liver burst and a particularly obnoxious back bench Tory MP had been drugged, locally anaesthetised and then served up a delicious hot dish that he only later discovered consisted of his own meat and 2 veg etc in a Vincent Price in Dr Phibes make-the-punishment-vaguely-fit-the crime stylee.

By her 20th birthday Karen Skull had whacked over a thousand scumbags and was the most wanted crim in the world, ever. On her 22nd birthday she executed an un-toppable work of art. She lured to London over 50 of the worlds sickest and most demented serial killers (all Yanks, natch) and then, using black-mail, hallucinogenic drugs and the promise of top slash frenzy and sicko mental fun, she trained them into a superfit army of berzerkoid bastards. Then she turned them loose on the elitist and pathetically twattish world of High Opera.

That night the Covent Garden Opera House - an upperclass temple to elitist culture run by a self-perpetuating oligarchy of smug poshos and heavily subsidised by working class taxes - was playing host to Wagner's Ring Cycle. The utterly crap nature of the music and the ticket price of 90 notes apiece for even the cheapest seats more or less guaranteed an audience chocka with bastards who deserved to die horribly.

At 9.15, with the stage full of fat lasses in horned helmets screeching their way through the only good bit (ie The Ride of The Valkyrie as featured in Apocalypse Now ie the best movie ever made), all the lights went out. The fat lasses, like true pros, carried on singing. The 50 plus serial killers did their stuff in the darkness. At 9.20 the lights came on and the fat lasses were faced with an image so horrific that they all spontaneously vomited and fainted and needed psychiatric help for the rest of their lives. Not only had the loonies (who were all up in the balcony giggling like ninnies) decapitated and then switched the heads of the entire audience, they had also strewn the entire building with the gory purple entrails of their victims and let loose a tribe of torture-demented spider monkeys who swung from the reeking guts and tossed eyeballs hither and thither with gusto.

"Damien Hirst eat your fucking psuedy money-for-old-rope heart out *daaaaaaaaaaaaarling!*" thought Karen Skull jealous-ly as she watched the scene on a remote TV link. Because, let's face it, if sticking a dead cow in a tank of formaldehyde is "art" then shitting down the gaping throat of opera is **superart!** Like all intelligent people, Karen regarded the concept of "high" or "classical" art as essentially a racist construct. It is no coincidence, she realised, that the classical is defined as that stuff created for the European ruling class during its mid-imperial stage ie when they were waffling on about Liberty, Egality and Fraternity at home but still kicking the shit out of black and brown skinned people and nicking their land abroad. This meant that the European ruling class *had* to develop the modern concept of racial superiority ie they were allowed to nick stuff off Africans, aboriginal Australians, Asians and native Americans because the "savages" weren't "really" human, QED the culture of these people was also "inferior". Trouble was that all the decent art created in the 20th Century was not only inherently multi-racial and multi-cultural, it also appealed to working class types. Thus real art, proper art, high art, *classical* art was defined as a) stuff made by white folks and b) stuff that was made deliberately boring and complicated so's as to exclude from its audience those who lacked the education in its pretentious, wilfully byzantine and pathetically archaic codes ie the working classes. Thus, the dominant ideology concluded, anything which was either a) made by black or working class people or b) wasn't as boring as fuck, was inherently inferior. Opera was the flagship of this racist, snobbish bullshit ideology - a dead culture kept artificially alive (by money stolen from the work-ing classes) as "proof" of the allegedly inherent superiority of the white ruling class.

It was because she **KNEW** all of the above (and remember that Karen has a brain the size of a small planet so if you disagree with her about anything it's because you're not as clever as she is) that Karen had her lithe, muscular back tattooed with a repro- duction of the gaudy social surrealist classic "*Tower Of Avarice*: Explanatory Nomenclature: *Deficit Financing Is When You Have Secured A Loan With Exorbitant Interest From An Insatiably Greedy Loan Shark, Who After Bleeding You Dry Tells You His Golden Calf Is Pregnant, It Looks Like It's Your Offspring, And There Will Be A Child Support Surcharge.* Poolroom Title: *All Shylocks Feed From The Dun&Bradstreet Pooper Scooper.*" by the "art" loathing artist and ranting poet, Robt. Williams, complete with the hieroglyphicised paraphrasing of the genius's greatest quote:

"All these art critics are standing on a rail-road track and the fuckin' freight train is flying at them but they're so myopic they can only see the texture on the oncoming cow- catcher. The freight train is "low art" - fuckin' cartoons! And everybody else can see the fuckin' thing. When you get off in the distance from the 20th century and you look at the graph- ics that were *powerful* , that *moved* people, it was fuckin' cartoons. Not conceptual art or a few boxes in an empty room chained together..."

The point *being* , thicky, that the only legitimate great art of the late 20th and early 21st Centuries, when capitalism thrashes and oozes puss like some cornered and mutilated steroid-bound smiley-face Hitlerian super-rat (high on PCP and a nauseating nostalgia for a non-existent alleged golden age when the serfs willingly sucked its numerous and permanently limp little dicks and were pathetically grateful for the chance to do so) and sickeningly cynical Little House On The Prairie stylee expensive sentimentality in its seemingly never-ending, totally revolting but nonetheless utterly exciting pornographic death throes - is hate-driven, scream- ing eyeball-jabbing and eardrum bursting wangst that sucker punches the sedated, blinded, deafened, cottonwool wrapped and shat-on proletarian masses in the brains, heart, guts and gonads *at the same time!*

Motherfucker.

CHAPTER 9

TROTSKY!

'My name is Jimmy Greaves. I am a professional footballer and I am an ALCOHOLIC.'

Blurb from the front of the paperback edition of 'This One's On Me' by Jimmy Greaves, 1979

"Talk about a legitimate target!" thought Karen, as she surveyed her gory brainwork. Then, as one, the serial killers clutched their hearts, gurgled and died thanks to the slow acting poison that Karen had fed to the nutters earlier telling them it was top drugs because Karen was, after all, on an **Anti-Crap Jihad** and no-one is crapper than a serial killer (unless it's the trainspotting nerdy middle class scumboys who eagerly idolise them).

By her 24th birthday, Karen had revised her list to include another 20,000 crappos. By her 25th birthday, despite the best efforts of a fear-frenzied State, she'd topped the lot. It was the most depressing day of her life. Deep in the bowels of her secret underground London HQ, Karen stared blankly into the flickering green screen of the supercomputer that she built and designed herself and wept. The marching columns of figures told their own story. For every crappo she'd killed, another 10 had taken his or her place. Karen knew the essential truth of Trotsky's statement that "a terrorist is a liberal with a bomb" but felt that underlying ideological unsoundness of her actions was far outweighed by the *fun* involved. Except that it was no longer fun. She could kill another 20,000 and another 20,000 and not even make a serious dent in the legions of crapness. She was like a surgeon faced with a terminally leprous patient chocca with tumours on every organ. She could hack and slash till Kingdom Come and still not save the patient. The solution? ***DRUGZ!***

Thus it was that Karen Skull The Individual Terrorist retired and Karen Skull The Mad Scientist Mastermind was born. Using vast amounts of dosh that she'd nicked off her victims before sending them screaming to Hell, Karen became the world's greatest medical scientist and set about trying to synthesize an AIDS-like sexually transmitted virus that only killed crap people. And now she was close, very close. Close enough, in fact, to be able to take some time off from her research to join Mad Mick's top team of Anti-Veggie Commandos when the promise of an amnesty was issued simultaneously through all of Sir Andrew's many media outlets. She thought amnesties sucked, that they were for wimps who couldn't handle being shot in the back by the SAS after they'd surrendered. But a good ruck was a good ruck and this ruck promised to be the best ruck ever.

OFFICIAL!

Meanwhile....

Chog McGog - the monobrowed Frankie Howerd looka-like award winning songwriter for the top Manc Merseybeat revival combo, Dadrock - grunted through coke-caked snotpits as he broke the luxury tour bus's "no logs in the chemical bog" rule and then muttered a terse "fook" as he felt the wobbling bog's stinking blue liquid leap up and splash his arse and then trickle down his short fat hairy legs to stain his dead cool Joe Bloggs tracksuit keks.

"Hey! Chog! Was that a log?" shouted Gog's kid brother, Spog McGog - the monobrowed Sinead O'Conner lookalike lead singer for the aforementioned top Manc Merseybeat revival combo Dadrock - from outside the bog.

"Bog off, Spog!" coughed Chog McGog as he scraped the klingons from his wolfmanishly hairy log-chute with King Size Rizlas because Spog had nicked the bog-rolls to toss at last night's foggy clog-fest of a togger game where Chog and Spog's beloved Man City had been clogged 9-0 by top Frog togger team St Etienne - which was also the name of top pop combo that Chog and Spog thought sucked the cock of a dog with cancer of the cock 'cos they weren't Paul Weller or Ocean Colour Scene and therefore weren't modrock and, like Dadrock, bigger than God - or so thought Chog and Spog.

"Hey! Chog!" teased Spog, "You splashed your Bloggs?"

"I've splashed me Bloggs, me clogs, me socks, me Man City togger top and most of me other togs, plus me bollocks, me arse and me cock, our Spog!" admitted Chog as he clicked open the lock and emerged from the bog and savagely smacked his sprog in the clock with the a rolled-up copy of top rock rag Modrock which covered proper rock gods like Dadrock, the Ocs and The Troggs and had no truck with prog-rock, ponce-rock, puff-rock or any other dogscockgobbling mock-rock bollocks that Chog and his brother Spog thought fucking sucked.

"FUCK!" roared Spog as he failed to block Chog's slog at his fizog and took it full clog in the gob.

"Now just knock it off, young Spog and old Chog!" said Alan McGob, recoiling in shock as the Chog clobbered Spog rocked back on his clogs and dropped like Chog's log on the flobflecked ten-togs where the boss of the top modrock gods was having a snog with a female Frog goth who was frightfully posh and shouted out chunks of My Life As A Dog in the style and the manner of Roger McGough and frothed at the gob as she wobbled and bopped like a rubber-spined dog on the cosh-like knob-end of the rock-boss's lob.

But Chog and sprog Spog went at it like dogs as the Chog log blocked chemical bog of the rocketing Dadrock bus coughed like God when the top skunk packed spliff that Chog had dropped in the bog ignited the fog that whiffed forth from the bog (containing Chog's log, the top drugs in Chog's log and the chemicals in the bog into which Chog's top-drug clogged log had been dropped plus the drugs in the fag which Chog had dropped in the bog on top of the drug-packed log before clogging sprog Spog for mocking his bog-splashed Bloggs, socks, clogs, Man City togger top and other top togs) and blew up. Killing Chog, Spog, Alan McGob, the female Frog goth and all the other bods and poor sods who slogged like dogs for top modrock combo Dadrock. Thank fucking God.

    "FACKIN' HELL!" ejaculated homophobic cockernee roadie Dagenham Pete as he saw the luxury tour bus on the opposite side of the M1 motorway explode in a massive fireball which rained bits of gob, flob, knob, log, chemical bog, Alan McGob's pet dog Rodge plus, of course, chunks of bod - up into the air to rain down on the countryside for miles around. **PLIP! PLAP! PLOP! PLIP! SPLOT!**

    "BOOM SHANKA!" screamed blindfolded band manager and van-driver Aleister Crowley ecstatically as he thrashed uncontrollably and simultaneously farted through his nose, shat through his mouth and vomited through both his ears whilst his massive bald head rotated 360 degrees at 347 RPM inna Linda Blair stylee thanks to the karmic-feedback hellfireball which whiplashed through his allegedly spectral body like an army of miniaturised sex-masseurs each dedicated to vigorously wanking-off one of his billions of throbbingly rigid nerve-endings with gusto (a sensation that magickally if temporarily endowed the lucky dead satanist bastard with a 400 foot long semi-sentient penis which savagely uncurled like one of those party-blower things, osmosified through the windscreen and smacked through the rear window of a Ford Mondeo up ahead which contained a trio of Catholic priests returning from a Society For The Protection Of The Unborn Child rally in London which the knob tore to bits with its massive teeth and then noisily ate before curling back up and whacking into Crowley's lap with a satisfied **SLAP!**) when tendrils of the satano-tantric force-field surrounding the devil-worshipping rock band's insanely speeding transit van snaked out to grab the still screaming souls of Chog, Spog, Alan McGob (and his pet dog, Rodge, of course), the female Frog goth and all the other bods and poor sods who slogged like dogs for top modrock combo

Dadrock - and syphoned them into the Lungmobile's evergreedy screamingsoulpacked fuel tank.

"**Burp!**" said Crowley's cock and spat out a skull.

"OOK! OOK!" said Bobo the talking pygmy chimp in the back of the van as he pointed at the calendar clock in the top right hand corner of the screen of the Apple Mac Powerbook on which he had just knocked out the greatest novel ever written in the English language in ten seconds flat by accident.

"Oh no!" groaned the Lung's guitarist and resident expert on all things occult, Animal, as he saw the date, "It's yesterday once more!"

"Shooby dooby doo!" chorused all the impressively thighed and sexily ra-ra skirted deaf yank cheerleaders spontaneously, under the impression that the handsome young devil-rocker was, for some bizarre reason (probably connected with the like, really weird magick stuff that kept going on and shit?) quoting The Carpenters.

"No, he's right!" barked inter-specially&pan-sexuality clit, cock'n'nipple-stiffeningly pretty Lung drummer Daemonic Dave savagely. "It is, quite literally, yesterday!"

"Which means..." said equally incredibly handsome Lung singer, Stalin slowly "that tomorrow, after we'd just witnessed The Dog-Hatred Obsessed Factory Farmer Ripped To The Sunkissed Ruddy Tits On Cider And Snorted Insecticide thresh 2,332 folkies to death with his Satanic Combine Harvester and we'd left him and all his jolly scrumpy-slaughtered farmer chums slipping about drunkenly in the field full of slimy folkie guts to the headbanging techno-for-the-masses genius of 'No Limits' by 2 Unlimited that was blasting out of the mobile disco they'd hired in to celebrate the extermination of the creme de la creme of the British folk scene whilst they gleefully burnt the local bobby who was a virgin alive in a giant wicker man like what happened to Edward Woodward in that film and we got in the van and were heading up to tomorrow night's gig in Dundee, that...."

"That when we asked Crowley to stick on the anti-grav unit" sighed Animal, "whilst the strap-on-dildo wielding deaf yank cheerleaders were pulling a train on your arse..."

"That the stupid bastard must have accidentally pressed the auto-destruct button instead!" exclaimed HSGHKLKLKFFHFH-HT, the band's interdimensional alien-demon bassist (who, thanks to a bizarre and arcane law of occult science that is far too complicated to explain here and which you are probably too thick to understand anyway, is only allowed to utter one sentence - which must contain exactly 13 words and contain no more and no less than 90 characters - per millennium and had thus just shot his bolt for yonks).

"Blowing up the van and killing everybody on board!" continued Stalin, seamlessly.

"Which, thanks to the fact that the van and its occupants are protected by an invulnerable tantrick force-field" woofed Animal, smacking his fist into his palm, "set up an occult paradox/hyper-reality karmic-feedback loop cum Mobius strip...."

"Which the tantric force-field could, like, only resolve by ripping time-space a new asshole and sorta, like, shoving us back here to yesterday? Wow! Cool!" exclaimed the lip-reading deaf yank cheerleader who was vigorously bumming Stalin with the strap-on dildo that speared up sexily from underneath her incredibly short ra-ra skirt.

"AGAIN!"

typed Bobo the sign-language literate pygmy chimp in 72 point Machine font on the screen of the Apple Mac Power book by accident.

"Which, as we're now travelling North, presumably means" said Animal, glancing at his watch "that we're about to pass ourselves travelling south on the opposite side of the motorway towards the top party where we picked up the deaf yank cheerleader lasses and Bobo.."

"**FACK ME! WE JAST PARSED ARSE-ELVES!**" ejaculated Dagenham Pete from the front.

"Which means" roared Animal, hastily whacking various buttons on his extremely expensive occult computer-watch whilst simultaneously flicking through the "tour news" and "gig guide" sections of the New Musical Express and doing some hasty calculations in inhuman blood with a quill pen made from a singed feather plucked from the arse of the mythical bird, the Phoenix, on the back of an old fag packet, "that..."

"HEY LADS! GUESS WHAT?" roared Crowley over the hurtling transit van's internal PA system, savagely.

"WHAT?" roared back everybody in the back of the van simultaneously.

"WELL, AND YOU'RE GOING TO LOVE THIS!" teased Crowley, erotically, "ACCORDING TO MY SATANIC RADAR, THAT COACH RIGHT IN FRONT OF US...."

Everybody, including Stalin and the deaf yank cheerleader who was buggering his arse off, ran (or, in the case of the two young lovers, wheelbarrowed) to the front of the bus to see what the clumsy slaphead ghost driver was talking about.

"...IS ACTUALLY THE TOUR BUS OF THAT IRONICAL-LY MONICKERED SHITE-AWFUL MISERABILIST INDIE-SCH-MINDIE BAND, THE ZEST (YOU KNOW, THE BAND WITH THAT LANKY HIPPY SINGER WHO WROTE A WHOLE ALBUM OF FUCK-DREADFUL SONGS ABOUT HIS BIRD LEAVING HIM AND WHO WAS THE ONLY SURVIVING MEMBER OF THE KAREN SKULL/APOCALYPSE RECORDS MASSACRE THAT WAS IN THE MUSIC PAPERS A BIT BACK?) GOING UP TO PLAY THAT OPEN AIR BENEFIT CONCERT FOR THE SAMARITANS IN LEEDS!"

"To the Batmobile, Robin!" bellowed Stalin, bloodthirstedly as Crowley switched on the van's auto-pilot (taking extra-special care not to knock the auto-destruct button again) popped his eyes back in and rushed to the very rear of the transit van where Dagenham Pete had pulled out the band's huge wicker dressing up-basket and the Lung posse were furiously squabbling over the tons of clobber therein.

Smacked up lanky hippy wanker Ashley Richards was happy. Which meant, paradoxically, that he was incredibly sad. His girlfriend had just left him - a fact which made him incredibly depressed but which also meant (because he was one of them nauseatingly twisted emotional necrophiliac masochist wankers who get their rocks of by wallowing helplessly in melancholy, bleakness, defeatism and soul-sucking spiritual collapse) that he was now able to write yet another pisspoor albums's worth of miserably stunted shit songs that would sell in their millions to all the other twisted emotional necrophiliac wankers out there in the bleak intellectual wastelands of indie-schmindie hell.

The few intelligent music paper writers who actually possessed any taste whatsofuckingever had not only been utterly stumped by The Zest's incredible commercial success but were also totally baffled as to what it was exactly that made The Zest the biggest pile of stinking fly-blown dog-shit in the entire history of rock - **EVER!** It wasn't that your bird leaving you was necessarily shit lyrical subject matter - one only need listen to the incandescent glory of The Righteous Brothers epic 'Boo-hoo-my-bird's-left-me!' anthem 'You've Lost That Lovin' Feeling' (or any one of several dozen Beatles' songs) to realise that. And it wasn't even the fact the crap drug smack sucked talent, energy and originality out of an artist and usually left him or her a hollow, burnt-out husk within a decade - 'cos Lou Reed's 'Perfect Day' was proof enough that even fuck-ugly junkies could occasionally knock out a half-decent tune if they had to.

It was the simple, undeniable, overwhelmingly, self-evident and self-sustaining **FACT!** that The Zest were totally and utterly and unarguably and completely and irredeemably and without the slightest-shadow-of-a-ghost's-fart-of-doubt, utter and total and complete and irredeemable carved-in-fucking-stone

ABSOLUTE FUCKING SHITE -

O-FUCKING-FFICIAL!

"Well that's a bit bigoted - you bald, speccy, spotty fat bastard!" you sniff wankerishly, going on to explain in extensive and rather patronising detail the difference between *subjective* (which is to say "aesthetic") "opinion" and *objective* (and, one would presume, scientifically verifiable) "fact". To which I can only reply - **FUCK OFF HIPPY! THIS IS MY BOOK AND IF I SAY THEY'RE SHIT THEN THEY'RE SHIT, O FUCKING K!?! NOW SIT DOWN, SHUT THE FUCK UP AND DON'T INTERRUPT THE NARRATIVE AGAIN, ALRIGHT, WANKER!?!?**

What The Zest's puzzled critics failed to realise, however, was that a substantial part of the record-buying public were incredibly boring and emotionally crippled lower-middle class heterosexual white boys who considered themselves really right-on but were in fact so subconsciously infested with the racist, sexist and homophobic prejudices of their incredibly tedious gender, social class, ethnic group and sexuality, that they actually sought out and, *unfuckingbelievably*, actually found merit in, bland/safe/mediocre art made by incredibly dull people just like themselves. Which is why The Zest are massive - **FACT!**

Ashley Richards stared out of the coach window at the miserable, drizzly and mediocre English day and saw that it was good. And then he saw a semi-naked pirate with gunpowder twists burning in the ends of his Salvador Dali moustaches come padding down the side of the coach towards him with huge plastic sucker caps on his elbows and knees whilst being bummed by an impressively thighed lass in a ra-ra skirt who wore an eyepatch and had a white-spotted red hankie on her head.

"Far out" thought the smacknumbed lanky hippy fuckwit as he turned to look at the opposite window where an upside-down and incredibly fat cockernee pirate, obviously being suspended by his ankles by someone on the roof, was pointing and making faces at him whilst obscenely mouthing the word "**PAFF!**"

Just then a chimpanzee (which looked as if it had just wandered straight off the set of a PG Tips advert directed by Hannibal Lechter's evil twin brother whilst off his fucking face on magic-mushrooms marinated for a million years in the LSD laced piss of a thousand screaming maniacs) wearing huge boots and baggy leather trousers (and with a stuffed parrot on its hairy shoulder) waddled up the aisle of the coach with a bloody cutlass between its sharply fanged teeth, a skull'n'crossbones decorated tricorner hat on its head and a Apple Mac Powerbook under its hairy arm.

Ashley leant out into the aisle and stared after the chimp. Er. Wow. Nobody seemed to be, like, driving the bus, man. He looked towards the back seat. It was strewn with human entrails and someone had stuck the heads of the rest of the band and crew on poles and had reassembled their acid-bath bleached bones into a hideously realistic skeletal dinosaur. And the bus was on fire. Somewhere, deep in the very heart of the lump of desiccated dogshit that was all that remained of Ashley Richard's smackbattered little brain, a tiny little alarm bell started to ring.

He felt someone squeezing his bony arm.

"I can't find a fucking vein!" laughed yet another pirate.

"Mmm, mmmmm, mmmm, uh!" mumbled Richards, feebly, taking the syringe off the pirate with trembling fingers and whacking it into the skin between the big and index toe of his naked and utterly filthy left foot which was the only place left on his hideously skinny little hippy body that wasn't covered in scar-tissue encrusted smack-needle tracks. Except for his face, of course, but the sex-symbol was wisely saving that for his old age.

Ashley Richards awoke in the throes of a devastating cold turkey nightmare. He quickly surmised that he was in fact lashed to the front of the speeding tour bus by his own entrails. He screamed, attempted to shit and piss himself through organs that just weren't there anymore and was then crushed to agonising death as the driverless coach slammed into the back of an articulated lorry carrying dog food to Hull.

"That was a bastard trick!" roared Animal, tears pouring his incredibly sexy cheeks as he wiped hippy blood off his gleaming cutlass and savagely slapped Crowley on his broad, ripplingly muscled and obscenely tattooed back.

"Yeah!" agreed Stalin who was doubled up with giggling and rolling about on the floor like a limbless dog with rabies and a savagely bad case of parasitic worms which were making its bum itch like billy-o and thus kicking in to action the aeons old instinct to wipe its arse free of the irritating little invertebrate bastards by dragging itself across the grass on its buttocks whilst it was still helplessly in the frothgobbed and wobblesome throes of the visually exciting but excruciatingly painful hydrophobia.

"Your idea of sticking our auto-destruct mechanism and tantric force-field on the front of the speeding tour bus to which we'd tied that miserable hippy bastard with his own guts splayed out in the exact centre of magickal pentagram done in the fucker's own blood which means that the wanker's going to spend all of eternity waking up in the throes of a savage cold turkey nightmare mere seconds before being agonisingly pancaked up the arse of a truck carrying dog food to Hull again and again and again forever was *fucking brilliant!*"

"Cheers, me dears!" replied Crowley, modestly as he weaved the insanely speeding satanic transit van through the

southern English country lanes which the on-board satanic
computer had mapped out as the insanest route to the folk festival in the village of Little Beezleycombe where the band planned
to meet up with themselves tomorrow and investigate the
possibilities of tantrick-sex magick fuelled by the van's occupants
actually having sex with themselves (a concept which Dagenham
Pete, the band's homophobic cockernee roadie, found mind-
bogglingly disgusting, natch).

And that's what they did. And that's where they stayed -
psychotically yo-yo-ing between two rigidly fixed points in space-
time for ever and ever amen. Well - for a bit, anyway.

Meanwhile....

Ashley Richards awoke in the throes of a devastating
cold turkey nightmare....

CHAPTER 10

DEATH!

'The balance of our population, our human stock, is threatened....They are producing problem children, the future unmarried mothers, delinquents, denizens of our borstals, sub-normal educational establishments, prisons, hostels for drifters...If we do nothing, the nation drifts towards degeneration.'

Sir Keith Joseph, British Conservative intellectual, 1974

The carnivorous commando of assorted nutters that hurtled towards the veg-fash HQ smelled their enemy long before they saw them. At 1000 feet up the combined stench of mung bean curry flatulence and unwashed skin was nauseating. At 500 feet the 'chutes on the backs of their power suits ripped open. Twenty seconds later our heroes were on their feet, on the ground and splattering veg-scum left, right and centre. Karen Skull quickly located the chief dormitory and in 2.3 seconds gassed 398 veggies to death in their sleep. In 9.8 seconds all the veg-filth were dead except one.

Noel 'Rampton' Alban was what passed for an intellectual in veggie circles. Like all intellectuals he looked like shit with his kit off. In the 3.4 seconds before he was rudely awoken and slaughtered like a hog, he had a curious dream.....*whoooo whooooo*.....

INT. NAZI TORTURE CHAMBER

NOEL ALBAN is strapped spreadeagled and upright in a torture cell complete with iron maiden, rack, brazier with irons heating up etc. He is bruised and battered and being tortured by Nazis who are offering him bits of meat.

NAZI 1
(*Holding a plate of cold cuts and a fork*)
Vould you like eine kleine piece of roast lamb, hein?

ALBAN
Get stuffed, Nazi. I'm saying nowt!

NAZI 2
Eiser you spill zer beans or ve vill be making you eat zer flesch!

ADOLF HITLER walks into the cellar, cradling something within his tunic.

NAZI 1
Zer Fuhrer! Achtung!

NAZI 1 AND NAZI 2
Sieg Heil!

HITLER
Zo! Zis is der Englander prizoner who is refuzing to eat der meat?

NAZI 1
Jahwhol, mein Fuhrer!

NAZI 2
Unt he schtinks, mein Fuhrer!

HITLER
Zo, mein crusty little kamerad, I zink zat zis dizgrazeful behaviour vill SCHTOPP! I zink zat you vill eat zer meat, MACH SCHNELL!

ALBAN
Never! I'll never contaminate my body with the flesh of my fellow creatures!

HITLER
Zen you give us no choice. If you refuse to eat zer meat zen ve vill be forced to use - ZER CAT!

ALBAN
Torture me all you want, you Nazi scum, but not a sliver of the sacred flesh of Mother Gia's furred, feathered, wooled, scaled or otherwise organically encased animal, bird, fish or other being, nor the blood drenched dairy products that they produce, shall pass these lips. Or eggs.

HITLER
Zen it is time for - ZER CAT!

HITLER reaches into his tunic and brings out a cute lickle kitten. He then cocks his Luger pistol and puts it to the kitten's head.

HITLER
Now, eat zer meat or zer cat'z head iz zo much brain pûré schplattered on zer wall of zis fine torture chamber.

ALBAN
You fiend! You evil, rotten fiend!

HITLER
Eat zer meat, schweinhund!

ALBAN
Never!

HITLER
You haff five of your English zeconds and zen zer cute lit-tle kitty-kinz getz zer 9mm bullet in zer furry bonce!

ALBAN
You bastard!

HITLER
Ein!

ALBAN
Let the kitten go!

HITLER
SVEI!

ALBAN
Stop! I'll eat the meat! I'll eat the meat!

Alban leans his head over and wolfs the meat.

HITLER
Sehr gut! Now ve vill schoot zer kitty-kinz for sadistic fun reasons.

BLAM!

CUT TO CLOSE UP OF ALBANS'S FACE SPLASHED WITH CAT
BLOOD AND BRAINS AND BITS OF GINGERISH FUR

ALBAN

Noooooooooooooooooooooooooooooooooooooooooooooo!........

Being an intellectual and having once attended a New Age Dream Analysis Workshop, Damon 'Rampton' Alban was well aware of his dream's true meaning ie **GUILT!** Guilt because, deep down, Alban *knew*, that if you scratched a veggie you discovered a Nazi. Hitler had been a vegetarian. Animal Rights activist Bridgitte Bardot had married a leading member of the nazi Front National etc. This was the maggot that gnawed at the very heart of Morrissey fan Alban's ideology - the knowledge that the human-loathing veggies like himself, were, deep down, when push came to shove, smiley-face fascists who would prefer to see the human race in its entirety exterminated just to save worms and flies and shit like that. You only had to ask a veggie the perfectly rational question:

You are flying a B52 bomber loaded with high-explosive , HIV infected needles and nuclear waste. You have to crash this bomber onto one of two islands. On island A is one human baby. On island B are a shitload of baby seals, cute lickle chimpanzees, kittens and a rain forest. Which island do you destroy?

to see them flapping their kagouled arms around, going red in the face and harumph!ing about "typical omnivore tactics" and "rhetorical questions" to realize that vegetarianism/animal rightism hides beneath its insipid townie sentimentalist face, a heart of pure evil.

Then Alban awoke to discover himself cowering in a circle of power-suited carnivorous monsters and honked like a puppy as his body attempted to eject the sickening stench of burning human flesh.

Mad Mick picked him up by the nads and squeezed. Alban screamed that hideous, pathetic scream that intellectual veggies always make when you squeeze their bits with a kevlar-plated and titanium dust coated state-of-the-art combat power-glove.

"*W-W-W-Why?* " screamed Alban, blubbing like a twat.

"Because," said Mick, speaking as slowly as he could in case the superspeed that coursed through his boiling blood made him unintelligible to the evil veggiefuhrer, "because you tossers attacked the swans head kicking-off finals!"

"No we didn't! We nev..." squealed the veggie, his denial

aborting suddenly in a series of blood spluttering grunts as Mad Mick pulled his head off and held it aloft, dangling the spinal column - just like the alien did to the pig in the subway in Predator 2 - a cool movie.

Suddenly the entire building was lit up by the blinding flash of a neutron bomb.

Much to his atheistic astonishment, Mad Mick found himself floating, floating, floating towards a brilliant white light. Suddenly a choir of freshly scrubbed and brylcreemed choirboys wobbled out of the smoke on either side of the Spielbergian lighting effect, singing *"There is a green hill far away without a city wall/ where our dear Lord was crucified/ He died to save us all"* and then segue-ing seamlesly into the chorus of 'I Like To Go Awandering' ie *"Fare la lee/Fa la la/Fare la lee/ Fare la **HA HA HA HA HA HA HA HA HA!**/Fare la lee/Fare la la/He died to save us all"*.

"Cool!" murmured the spook versh of Mad Mick The Needle as he entered the white light. ***SPANG!*** Mick suddenly found himself in a waiting room. The walls were painted shit brown. Millions of humans sat on shit coloured plastic chairs. They all stared into space. They all clutched bingo tickets. At the far end of the waiting room a clacking clock thingy displayed the ticket number of the customer currently being dealt with by a bored looking angel who sat behind chicken-wire reinforced bullet proof glass in a little booth.

Since time immemoria,l man has tried to wrap his tiny little monkey brain around the concept of heaven. Some have visualised it as a massive garden where the chosen lounge around on deck chairs getting their huge cocks sucked by top totty whilst they chomp on Turkish Delight and slurp sherbet through liquorice straws. Others said it was full of gurly haired blonde blokes in nighties strumming harps and smiling like wanking chimps. The vikings claimed that the afterlife consisted of huge rucks with other vikings followed by massive piss-ups with tons of fried chicken legs of gargantuan size that you could just take a bite out of and then sling over your shoulder to the slavering wolfhounds without worrying about making a mess on the carpet before engaging in ace rumpy with buxom blonde orange sellers in low cut maxi-dresses with white frilly bits around the tits.

They were all right. What none of them predicted,

however, was that the waiting room to heaven looked and smelt exactly like a Sunderland DHSS Office circa 1985. Except bigger.

CHAPTER ELEVEN - ONLY GOOD BOYS GO TO HEAVEN

ALIENZ!

'The revolutionary youth hears your music and is inspired to even more deadly acts...We will play your music in rock'n'roll marching bands as we tear down the jails and free the prisoners...Comrades! You will return to this country when it is free from the tyranny of the State and you will play your wonderful music in factories run by the workers, in the domes of emptied city halls, on the rubble of police stations, under the hanging corpses of priests, under a million red flags flying from a million anarchist communes... THE ROLLING STONES ARE THAT WHICH SHALL BE!...ROLLING STONES - THE YOUTH OF CALIFORNIA HEARS YOUR MESSAGE! LONG LIVE THE REVOLUTION!'

Leaflets distributed by hippy nutters during The Rolling Stones 1969 American tour.

We must momentarily leave Mad Mick The Needle suspended in limbo and travel to the Planet Milkin, a lush, oxygenrich and green world on the other side of the universe.

Milkin differs from Earth in that it contains not just one sentient species but 2049, ranging from the hive-mind of the multi-segmented Flyingworm to the 24 ft tall 6-legged Limegreen-mohawked Bigmonkey. These various species existed side by side for millions of years and, by the Earth year 1957, were members of a peaceloving socialist utopian civilisation where all the physical work was done by machines, thus liberating every single individual (or collective hive mind) to devote its every waking hour to the pursuits of philosophy, pure science and art.

Every single one of these sentient species was innately herbivorous. The very concept of "violence" was considered to be the unique and exclusive province of those species who had yet to emerge blinking into the bright, invigorating fresh air of self-conscious intelligence. Thus the human poisons of exploitation, greed and selfishness had never raised their ugly heads on Milkin. All recorded history proved (and all archeology suggested) that the concept of **hur-rah-hu-huh-huhrah-hah-hahrarh-ah** (which literarily translated means; "being-nice-to-each-other-like-leaving-a-public-washroom-in-the-state-in-which-you-would wish-to-find-it-for-instance") was both a universal and natural state of being for *all* intelligent beings.

But all that went to fuck in the Earth-year of our Lord (ie the alleged son of the weird god "God") 1957 when, thanks to a massive disruption in the space time continuum involving some incredibly difficult sums and savage physics, all the TV and radio receivers on Milkin were suddenly and simultaneously bombarded with broadcasts from the planet Earth ie us. Most of this stuff, coming from the 1950's, was boring black'n'white bollocks but some of it was the first snuffling, sniffling, snarling blatherings of Rock'n' Roll. This gripped the Milkins by the nuts, metaphorically speaking. Later it would drive them, pinkfrothgobbed and spluttering through tightly clenched stainless steel-fangs, lemming-like over the cliff of ultra-niceness into the shrieking, stinking, squealing pit of total mega-barkingmaddogness, evilness and tee-hee-hee I'm-a-loony choppy-choppy slash-the-shower curtains

stylee, sharp-fanged giga-byte-your-facking-face-off- **YA-CANT !!!!**
mad cockernee inna rub-a-dub wif an 'ard-on, a sawn-off anna
broken bockle pressed urgently against your f-f-f-frobbing jugular
stylee

iNsAniTY!!!!!!!!!!

Readers who are good at sums and difficult science are
going to find this hard to swallow. They're going to wrinkle their
massive brows, boggle their blood-red little piggy eyes under "The
Wolfman" style meet-in-the-middle eyebrows and squeak on endlessly about "time/space" and "light years" etc. To them I say:
There is more in heaven or earth than exists in YOUR philosophy,
Horatio. **BESIDES WHICH** a previous supercivilisation of hyper-
intelligent 4 brained snails which ruled the universe billions of
years before the first lung-fish threw itself gasping onto the still
smoking volcanic Earth beach and evolved into a dinosaur, had
left very sophisticated radio and TV relay transmitters positioned
by all the black holes and it was these that were suddenly
switched on by very old but durable alarm clocks and thus
enabled the Milkinites to enjoy the Earth transmissions of 1957
simultaneously with the people of Earth despite the seemingly
impossible distances involved so stick that in the cap of your
leaking purple biro and stick it up your ass, bald-headed beardo
speccy good-at-sums science twat.

Under the sudden saturation of cheesily grinning and
badly acted Earth crap, all art, philosophy and science
immediately ground to a halt on Milkin and the massive planet's
entire population of over 987 billion sentient beings all became
savagely addicted trash-culture junkies. The previously tranquil
and homogenous culture of niceness that the Milkins had enjoyed
for endless and uncountable aeons collapsed as the Milkinites
divided into bickering tribes, each obsessed with the trivia and
extolling the virtues of, say, Mickey Dolenz in Elephant Boy or
Doctor Finlay's Casebook as Earth culture - the fizzing, flyspurting,
stinking blur of activity that is the speeded-up movie of the rotting

of the capitalist body politic - acted like a cancer-causing acid on the previously lovey-dovey niceness of Milkinite society.

The bickering turned into snarling and the snarling turned into sneering and jeering and the sneering and jeering turned into finger waving and pointing and the finger waving and the pointing turned into swearing and the swearing turned into spitting and the spitting turned into poking and the poking turned into pushing and shoving and the pushing and shoving turned into slapping and nipping and the slapping and nipping turned into punching and headbutting and shinkicking and the punching and headbutting and shinkicking inevitably turned into

WAR!

Like the ginger-headed swot at school with the thick-lensed glasses held together over the bridge of the nose with a filthy elastoplast, the Milkinites were crap at fighting but just try to imagine that ginger-headed speccy swot pushed *too far* and going into that invincible ginger swot berzerkoid flailing windmill arms fighting style and crying *FURY!* Now imagine 987 billion ginger-headed swots going boo-hoo-hoo windmill fury crazy at the same time. Someone call the teacher on playground duty, *NOW!*

The Milkinites kicked the fucking crap out of each other, progressing in a few years from milk crates and pool cues to jet aircraft, napalm, poison gas, tanks and machine guns. This degeneration was accelerated by the fact that each individual species seemed to be particularly prone to addiction to a different earth genre. The Mulletheaded Landsharks, for instance, dug horror movies. The Stinkingparrotheads fell head over heels in love with the I Love Lucy Show. The Insideout Jellykittens opted for continental art movies. The Eighteyed Pan-Ahsleyite Barkingcows became massive fans of the hard boiled cop genre whilst the Telepathic Gulls more or less made John Ford's westerns the basis of a religion.

None of them, however, was to prove to be a match for the

Limegreenmohawked Bigmonkeys. The Bigmonkeys latched onto war and science fiction movies big time. By 1972 they had copied and put into production all manner of real and speculative Earth weaponry including laser guns, robo-warriors, combat hovercraft armed with flame throwers, feet-seeking battle axes, electro-bolases and the supersonic bomber - all of which they used on their rival species with much vim, vigour and gusto.

The Bigmonkeys had several other advantages. For one they were the Milkian species which most anatomically and psychologically resembled the human race and were thus able to adapt to human weaponry with far greater ease. But, even more importantly, they were absolutely gagga about rock'n'roll.

In this they were not alone. Milkian culture BEWAFM (Before Everything Went Absolutely Fucking Mental) being class-less and therefore a stranger to racism (never mind speciesism) was perversely and utterly vulnerable to the core features of rock-'n'roll - its proletarianism and multi-cultural nature. So pernicious was the influence of rock'n'roll and so widespread its popularity, it seemed at first as if the music would serve as the glue that would hold Milkian culture together. If everybody agreed that Elvis was King, for instance, what was there to fight about, *really?* **Dream on, liberal!** The broadcasts from Earth had a devastating effect on a major flaw that had hitherto lain dormant at the heart of the Milkian psyche. The Milkians, for all their achievements and apparent maturity, were revealed as massive latent trainspotters, anoraks and saddos. The Grinning Duckwolves, for instance, were fanatical about the music of Eddie Cochran and fought a genocidal war to the death against the Chuck Berry obsessed Gliding Molefish. But the Bigmonkeys seemed to be uniquely blessed with a crucial anti-trainspotting gene which enabled them not only to recognise the underlying spirit of rock'n'roll (of the strung-out, stringy, snake-hipped and bee-sting lipped seedling chancers of 1950's R&B - of that rancid slice of the fluffy, white All-American Wonderloaf which erupted with fizzing green mould when the primitive Rock Music Industry (despite its inherent ten-dency towards castration, homogenisation and blandness) made savage, unrelenting and beautiful love to a bunch of swivel-pelvised, speed-crazed black culture-vandals and guilt stricken idiot savante white-negro trash hicks, idiot savantes and mumbling godfearing mummy's boys with hellfire in their bellies who, in a red-raging amphetamine psychosis, staggered from town to town in pink Caddies with Buck Rogers rocket-tailfins and trunks stuffed with $100 bills pursued by posses of outraged Fundamentalist Christian Mcarthyite racists convinced that the dangerously addictive jungle-noise these scum peddled was hypnotising their beautiful, peach-skinned and blue-eyed daughters into reefer addiction and from thence into sucking the massive cocks of cocaine crazed and wild eyed negroes - a time when a 4/4 beat, a leopardskin jacket and a greasy haircut meant you were a threat to democracy, decency and the American Way of Life on par with (if not greater than) that presented by the Red Chinese Army. This the Bigmonkeys instinctively knew and, knowing this, they also, *crucially*, knew how to move with the times, daddio.

In the late '50s - when things were still at the stage of nipping and namecalling - the Bigmonkeys were uniformly dressed in classic British Teddy Boy gear, their limegreen mohawks dripping with lard. By the early '60s - when the fighting had progressed to the level of knives, ninja sticks and steel toecapped DM's - the Bigmonkeys could be distinguished form the constantly rucking mass by a) their superior tactics b) the fact that they nearly always won and c) their immaculate mod suits and rocketlaunching scooters. In 1970 the Bigmonkeys finally cleared Milkin's largest land mass (98 times the size of Asia, North America and Europe combined and then some) driving huge battle tanks and dressed in kaftans and sandals, their limegreenmohawks allowed to grow to ridiculous lengths and off their fucking little furry monkey boxes on synthesised speed, acid, coke, acid and smack.

It didn't all go their way. The Amphibious SnakeElephants, for instance, were also big time on rock'n'roll and war movies and in 1971 launched an invasion of the Bigmonkey homeland using landing craft, attack helicopters and suicidal berzerker killer robots that spat acid. More than that, they came dressed in glitter suits that were glitterier and platform boots that were taller than those worn by the Bigmonkeys. For the next five years the Bigmonkeys gave ground steadily. And then punkrock happened. The Limegreenmohawked Bigmonkeys adapted. The Amphibious SnakeElephants didn't and, as usual, Chuck Darwin gouged out the eyeballs of the slow, clumsy and redundant and unzipped and inserted his massive sexsword into their gaping sockets to spit hot liquid killerDNA into their screaming brains like the kickass mothernaturefucker he **IS!**

The SnakeElephants looked increasingly sad in their gaudy face make up, frizzy bassist-out-of-Mud wigs and bacofoil jumpsuits as they were crushed to death (with their huge brains spurting out of their prehensile trunks) beneath the tracks of the laser spurting sex-tanks driven by the Big Monkeys in their tartan bondage trousers, Seditionaries style "wanking cowboys" ripped T-shirts and ironic Ted style blue suede shoes.

But whilst the Limegreenmohawked Bigmonkeys were kicking some serious Amphibious SnakeElephant arse, victory was far from a foregone conclusion. Other species, including the Spaghetti Western obsessed Furry Bikinitrolls and the superhero worshipping Whinsome Biglippedcorgis had meantime taken advantage of the Limegreenmohawked Bigmonkeys distraction and invaded the supercontinent from the North. And if that wasn't enough, the robot slaves who had loyally served Milkinkind for endless aeons finally had enough, declared themselves an independent species and went to war dressed as Gary Numan from his 'Are Friends Electric?' period. The weapons wielded by each warring faction were by now way above and beyond those actually used on Earth - the entire arsenal of the Science Fiction genre having been "invented" and ruthlessly applied with disastrous results. Most of the surviving factions thus had vast stocks of atomic, bacteriological and chemical weapons plus space ships, vast armies of zomboid mutants and other totally demented stuff that they only refrained from using for fear of retaliation and mutually assured total destruction.

Milkin teetered on the edge of oblivion. The time was 1 nano-second to midnight. The shit was but the merest micromillimeter away from hitting the fan. The fat lady was stood up, clearing her throat and clearly about to sing. Something had to give. And it did.

The more efficient species had hundred of thousands of their members glued to tellies and radios, desperate not to miss a single nugget of information from Earth which might tip the interspecial struggle in their favour. The casualty rate amongst these "watchers" was horrific. Hundreds would go totally and utterly insane on each shift. Those that survived were the hardest of the hard, desensitised to such an extent that they became the Milkinite equivalents of psychopaths. These survivors, after a mere 12 days of blanket exposure to earth culture, were utterly fucked and were only of use in shock-troop suicide assaults. Amongst all the armies that battled on Milkin, the ex-watcher battalions were the most feared. Unfortunately for the Milkinites, suicide missions have a habit of leaving survivors. Soon Milkin was awash with thousands of potential Hitlers, Pol Pots, Papa Docs, Thatchers and Stalins and it became horrifically obvious that sooner or later one of the Milkinite empires would topple into the hands, claw, pseudolimbs (etc) of one of these utterly ruthless bastards and it would only then only a matter of time before the nutter started spraying the planet with all manner of incredibly deadly genocidal weapons and fucked everything big time and for ever.

Milkinite culture AEWAFM (After Everything Went Absolutely Fucking Mad) was thus hoist by its own petard. No individual Milkinite species could afford to cease "watching" but neither could any species afford to ignore the damage that the watching inflicted. Dulled by alien culture overload and numbed by three decades of accelerating barbarism, the Milkinites were none the less fully aware of the oncoming crisis. So they told their watchers to keep an eye out for "a sign".

Thus, when, in 1980 BBC Scotland transmitted a "jokey" news item about the utterly shit 4th generation studs'n'bristles punk rock band The Exploited, the effect was shattering.

The Exploited were lumpen lagerlouts whose xenophobia, stupidity and crap music alienated them from all but the most retarded and scabrous of the earth-punks. Unfortunately there were several hundred thousand earth pseudopunk scum thick enough to provide the band with a substantial and moderately profitable fan base.

The Milkinite "watchers" knew none of this. They only knew that singer Wattie, with his lime green mohawk, was a dead ringer for a Limegreenmohawked Bigmonkey. Only a lot smaller. And with only one set of arms. And smellier.

Militarily, several of the Milkinite species were at a stage where they could have kicked the crap out of Darth Vader, the Klingons, The Borg, The Mekon, Ming The Merciless, the Daleks, The Romulans, The Men In Black and the Cybermen singlehand-ed. Psychologically they were a pathetically easy lay, ripe for incubation with any metaphysical bollocks that you tossed their way. Except, of course, Earth religions, which the Milkinites knew all about but thought so silly and specious, that they misinterpreted them as high comedy.

Thus was found the cultural glue that re-united the Milkinites. Thus was born the Religion of Wattyism. The other species, upon learning of Watty and after gazing upon His countenance, laid down their arms and pledged allegiance to the Limegreenmohawked Bigmonkeys. For surely they were the chosen species. For were they not indeed made in the image of Watty? Thus was Limegreenmohawked Bigmonkey hegemony established over the entire vast planet. Thus was 'Fuck A Mod' adopted as the Planetary anthem. And thus was the destruction of Earth made an inevitability.

CHAPTER 12

HENDRIX!

'El
Iod
Eheieh
Tetragrammaton Elohim
Eloah va - Daath
Elohim Gibor
El Adonai Tzabaoth
Elohim Tzabaoth
Shaddai'

The 'nine mystic names' needed to summon up The Dev according to The Key of Solomon.

"It's what you expected it to be, Mad Mick," murmured a figure in the next seat.

Mick swivelled and stared deep into dark brown puppy-dog eyes.

"You have me at a disadvantage, sir...No! Hang on! It's you! It *is* you!" gushed Mick "You're Jimi Hendrix ie the greatest musical performer of the 20th Century! Every 'She's Leaving Home' style white girl's wet dream and every racists' screaming, sheetsoaked nightmare! The Cock God whose eclectic electric strap-on dildonic scrabblings, whinings and mewlings drenched the crutches, blew

the minds and fuelled the dreams of a entire decade as it stumbled from boundless hope into eternal despair!"

Jimi Hendrix smiled that dead famous supercool smile that
made him look like a cat that had just drunk a pint of brandy laced
cream and was now having its little ginger cock sucked by an
expert cock gobbler with a PHD in making cats come slowly. He
was dressed in the black leathered and gaudily feathered glad
rags of fin-de-siecle Kensington Gore me-generation radical chic
piggery circa 1968 and cradled in his bulging lap an impossibly
beautiful electric guitar which he strummed, stroked, strangled and
choked with long and sensuous fingers causing mutant notes to fly
like psychedelic spunk in zero G - sparse and tingly, primitive in
their vitality but Mozartian in their cosmic potentiality.

Hendrix slapped the fretboard. The music died. He handed Mick the guitar.

"You know what you've got to do, Mick..."

Mick looked down at the instrument. It seemed to be
nestling into his lap. He felt the first stirrings of an erection. When,
at last, he looked up he saw that the entire waiting room was now
empty. The angel behind the chickenwire and bullet proof glass
was staring at him pointedly and impatiently. The clock thingy
above his head read:
874,683,938,278,192,837,291,327,188,2791.

So did the bingo ticket that Mick suddenly discovered in
his left hand.

CHAPTER 12a

KITTEN-RAPER!

'Say YES to International Socialism'

Popular song title, late 20th century

"Christian or given names?"

" Mad Mick."

"Family name?"

"The Needle."

The Recording Angel, caged by rusty chicken wire and scratched-to-fuck-by-the-nails-of-the-damned bullet-proof plexi-glass, sucked on the chewed-to-buggery lid of a cheap biro as he single-fingeredly computer scrolled. It was a vulgar little off-brand PC, noted Mick with some alarm (he had expected Macs in Heaven).

The Angel looked crap too. He was cursed with a

meanness of lip, a sallowness of complexion and a cruelty of eye which, when combined with gelled hair scraped back into a Steven Segal style pony-tail and a neatly trimmed black Noel "The Anti-Punk" Edmonds style beard, screamed "**GIT**" violently. In fact, if it hadn't been for the pristine white robes and the huge swan wings, Mick would have assumed that the bastard was a geography teacher or a state subsidised provincial poet paid to patronise the working classes by some shithole of a "community arts centre" or something.

"According to our records," said the Angel, fixing our hero with the sort of smugly magisterial sneer that middle-class wankers who couldn't fight their way out a wet paper bag even if you gave the paper bag an extra long marination in a diluted hydrochloric acid solution and poked lots of little holes in it first, usually give counter-culturally inclined working class sinners when they feel secure from any threat of physical retaliation, "you've been a very, very bad boy, Mr The Needle. A very bad boy...".

"Yeah, yeah, yeah" spat Mick, impatiently, "so how about you tell me what the fuck's going on here, eh? Am I in heaven or what?"

"You are indeed, laddy. But not for long. For an evil little bastard like you there's only one place you're going to spend eternity and that's **Hell!** That'll wipe the smile off your face, aye laddy? Chained to a rock in a sea of eternal fire? Suffering the eternal torments of the dammed? Think you'll be such a "hard man" after a couple of millennium of that, do you, aye? Sunny Jim? Hmmmmm?"

"**DON'T CALL ME SUNNY JIM!**" roared Mad Mick The Needle, leaping out of the incredibly uncomfortable grey plastic chair and smashing it half a dozen times against the chickenwired plexi-glass in one incredibly fluid and breathtakingly beautiful movement.

For a couple of seconds the Angel lost his clerkish cool and flinched.

"**KITTENRAPER!**" screamed Mick, impotently tossing the shattered chair over his superbly muscled shoulder.

"Sit down **NOW!**" barked the Angel, in the same tone of voice you'd use to scold a new dachshund puppy that had just shat in your new trainers for a laugh.

"**SIZE OF AN ELEPHANT!**" erupted Mick hopefully as

he leapt up onto the desk and proceeded to give the screen that frustrated his attempts to boot the slimy seraphim's smug head off and shit down his neck a damn good kicking.

Spang! Spang! Spang! went Mad Mick's swanblood encrusted combat steelies.

"Aroooga! Aroooga! Arooooga!" went the incredibly loud alarm. Mick was blasted off his feet by the noise and crashed to the ground with blood spurting out of every hole in his face. How loud was this alarm? Well, if the car alarm is indeed the kookaburra of the urban jungle then imagine a jungle with incredibly good acoustics populated by a million small-elephant sized kookaburras equipped with extremely powerful electronic megaphones and off their beady eyed and beaky faces on extremely strong drugs that make you scream all day and then imagine that these large and utterly skullfucked birds were very, very frightened by an 17.9 on the Richter Scale style earthquake. It was like that. Only louder. And more annoying.

Mick writhed in agony under the acoustic assault'n'battery. So shattered was his spectral central nervous system by the blitzkrieg of undopplered cacophonic terror that he failed to notice the clubs that rained down on his quaking foetal form. Clubs with 20,000 volts of shrieking, leaping white electric **DEATH!** running through them, wielded by 9 foot tall angels in state-of-the-art white riot-pig gear. Dozens of them. Battering. Beating. Bashing. Belting. Bruising. And booting. Powdering bone. Pulverising pelvis. Shattering skull and jellifying internal organs. Metaphorically tossing Mick off the cliff of life to land with a sickening thud in the cold arms of...

DEATH!!

CHAPTER 13

GOD!

'Please don't be waiting for me....'

John Rotten, 'Holidays In The Sun'

"Here's the evil little cunt!" barked Hammer Of The Sinners Archangel Gabriel as he snapped Mad Mick's head back by his curly locks so God could get a good look at him. This worried Mick because A) when he'd been alive he'd kept his head permanently shaved because life was too short to worry about combs and hairdryers and stuff like that and B) because he'd just been killed and brought back to life for the second time in one day and the constant resurrections were doing his fucking head in. And thus it was that Mad Mick stared into the face of God.

Predictably enough God was a hundred foot tall multi-armed Father Xmas faced old white man with a disgusting hippy beard, long, fluffy white hair and mad boggly eyes. From under-neath each arm sprang a leg. On each of these hundred legs protruded a muscular and knobbly knee and on each of these 100 knees lay a screaming baby Jesus. In each of his 100 hands God held a Dennis-The-Menace's-Dad style slipper. In a truly awesome display of physical co-ordination, God spanked the red raw arses of the screaming baby Jesi whilst whistling the bass line to Talking Head's 'Psycho Killer' and bopping his hideously hirsute head like a in-the-back-of-a-car-window nodding corgidog on E.

Mad Mick was far from unsurprised to note that the

animated zomboid horrorcorpse of Peter Suttcliffe sat on God's right hand side whilst James Anderton, ex-Chief Constable of the Manc pig force, sat on the other. For was not this The God, thought Mad Mick, that on hearing the pitiful whinings of some old slaphead who had been teased by some kids who'd shouted "Get thee hence, baldhead!" on his way to the synagogue, had sent down some frothgobbed and bogglyeyed she-bears to rip the cheeky wee kiddiwinks to bloody fucking shreds? Yes it was. The bloke was a ruddy **NUTTAH!** Never mind the poor bloody hedonists and samesexers of Sodom and Gomorrah that the utterly insane motherandfatherfucker had nuked to slag, this dickhead had run up a old-testament body count that made Hitler, Mao, Stalin and Pol Pot look like kiddy-kuddling social workers. The geezer was **POTTY!** A 24 carat, solid gold, splish-splash-I-was-having-a-blood-bath, certified, genuine, accept no imitations, head-the-ball, raging Cadbury's fruit'n'nut head-case **BARM POT!** And no mistakin'!

"Hiya, Mad Mick!" burbled God, drooling vast slicks of stinking acidic dribble out of both corners of his mighty mouth at the same time like some massive metaphysical mucous machine.

"Hiya, God!" replied Mick, giving the King Of Kings the respect that, as eternity's No.1 all-time, undisputed heavy-weight CHAMP-EEEEE-ON! of motiveless, mindless "Nurse! Get me a cattleprod, a straitjacket and 5000 cc of rhino strength superProzak NOW!" slaughter, torture and sheer bloody-mindedness, He deserved.

"Uh, does the cunt's name appear in the book?" asked God, as his massive eyes span rapidly in different directions.

"No, Lord." replied Gabriel, looking at Mick with malicious glee, "Shall we send him to Hell so he has to spend eternity chained to a rock in a lake of fire **4 EVAH!!!!???**"

"Uh, could do!" said God, teasingly, as he simultaneously slung 100 slippers over his mighty shoulders and proceeded to gingerishly buttfuck the baby Jesi up their 100 ring-pieces with 100 holy fingers, causing the previously screaming 100 wee bairns to now holler in celestial orgasm.

"Or shall we have him chained to a rock and have an eagle come along every evening and rip his liver out without anesthetic like Zeus did to Prometheus just for giving mankind the secret of fire?" asked Gabriel with a relish that Mad Mick thought probably bordered on the sexual but didn't because, unknown to Mad Mick, angels were nadless.

"Nah!" spaketh The Lord as He removed 100 babyJesishitencrusted fingers from 100 babyJesiringpieces and sucked them feverishly in 100 drool dribbling Godgobs that suddenly and miraculously appeared all over his fantastically immaculate body.

"Nah! Nah! Nah! Nah! Nah!" barketh The Lord as, with 100 Mighty Joe Young style fists, he crushed the fragile skulls of the 100 recently digitally buggered screaming baby Jesi and tossed them over his two incredibly muscular shoulders. "That would be too easy by **HALF!**"

He suddenly sprouted a million eyeballs (topped by a million ferocious Dennis Healey style eyebrows) all of which stared at Mad Mick with an intensity that would have had crazy Chuck Manson doing spunk-spurting anti-tantric cartwheels of appreciation.

"This little toerag" spaketh God, jabbing at Mick with 100 index fingers rudely "has *really* pissed me off, and I mean ***REAL-LY*** pissed ***ME***, ie <u>**GOD!**</u>

OFF!"

CHAPTER 14

MARTINAMIS!

'The new groups/don't understand/what there is to be learnt/They got Burton suits/HUH!/They think it's funny/turning rebellion into money...'

Joe Strummer out of The Clash in 'White Man In The Hammersmith Palais' ie the second best pop song ever - *OFFICIAL!*

SUDDENLY, without any warning what-so-***EVAH!!***, God's neck stretched violently until it was at least a 100 ft long and wiggled all over the place like electrocuted sentient spaghetti, only thicker. God's head bopped seductively for 4/5ths of a second and then **WHAM!!!** It was in Mad Mick's ***FACE!!!*** Literally! As in God's face was **IN** Mad Mick's face ie we are talking metaphysical facial osmosis and top horror spesh FX that haven't even been invented yet.

Mad Mick could feel God stomping around his brain like a gang of cockernee 1970's folk devil skinheads let loose in a stately home by a East End loan shark in order to teach the absent aristo not to fack arahnd wiv the moolah, savvy? Kickin' in windahs, drawink 'itler moostashes on ver Gainsboroughs, shitting in ver suits hof harmour an' generally 'avin' a LARF, innit? **OI! OI! OI!** Wot chew lookin' at, ya ***CANT?!?!*** as described by Martin

Amis (whose command of the English Working Class vernacular is legendary).

"**OOF!**" Mad Mick grunted like a pig on a platform suddenly and sharply shafted up the arse without the benefit of vaseline or foreplay by a particularly well endowed shire horse (ie the noise made by 17 stone of prize pork as it is savagely split in two by a throbbing length of purple-headed equestrian cockmeat that would need a condom the size of seven black plastic bin bags glued together to cover its mighty girth - which sounds nothing like "**OOF!**" really, but you get the idea) as dozens of 4 inch tall little skinheads came bursting through his every orifice (plus a score or so of other holes that the tasty lickle bleeders had decided to kick in his flesh in their impatience). For about 20 seconds the tiny bovver Gods (for They were He and He was They) ran riot all over Mad Mick's spasming spiritual body singing *"I like punk/I like Sham/I got nicked outside West Ham"* by Martin Amis's fave band - Ver Cockernee Rejects.

"**Oi!**" sharted God who had now adopted the appearance of Ron Moody **IS** Fagin in Oliver ie the 5th best film ever made and tons better than the book which sucks the cock of a ginger dog with highly contagious cock cancer even more than Martin Amis's The Rachel Papers - which is *really* saying something.

"Oi! Ger ovah 'ere, you bleedin' lickle toe-wags!" sayeth The Lord, thereby continuing the Martin Amisesque theme of acutely observed cockernee street argot.

"Geezer!" roared the small army of small skinheads as they leapt off a stunned Mad Mick and hurled themselves like tiny shavenheaded exocets into the beard of The Lord God AKA Ron Moody IS Fagin.

Whilst most of the tiny skins clung onto God's beard and made "wanker" signs at Mad Mick with their free hands whilst singing *"My old man said be a Luton fan/I said - Fuck awf! Bollocks! You're a CANT!"* to the tune of 'My Old Man's A Dustman', one skinhead, the smallest and the most agile, clambered up onto God's shoulder and proceeded to shout into His h'ear -'ole whilst gesticulating violently at Mad Mick.

"'As 'e nah?" spaketh God in his Ron Moody IS Fagin persona.

"'E did wot? Caw blimey! Nah! Did 'e weally? Coo! Well hi h'neffah!"

Now Mad Mick was no top expert lip reader but he could tell that the violently gesticulating little skinhead, like the proper cockernee he was, was saying "cant" every other word which, Mad Mick surmised, was probably the vowel-mangling Thames Estuary mispronunciation of "cunt" rather than either a philosophical reference or the popular contraction of "can not".

"EEEEEEEEEE-**NUF!**" shouteth the Lord.

SUDDENLY the Lilliputian skinheads were no more. The angel Gabriel was gone as well. There was just a bollock naked and disgustingly curly haired Mad Mick The Needle on one side of infinity and The Lord God Almighty on the other.

"Hubbah hubbah!" slobbereth The Lord, fixing our hero with a look of pure evil. "Boy, am I gonna have fun with you or **WHAT!!!!!!!?**"

God clicked his fingers...and then there was nothing at all...

Meanwhile...in Ibiza...

"And this is a rat on speed!" barked the illegally sampled voice-over from a TV doc about E over a stomach-churning cacophony that sounded like an air-raid on a zoo. The 3,987 shaven headed, nose-pierced, semi-naked and utterly skullfucked occupants of the Oi!Gabba room in Ibiza's packed and sweaty AaAaAaAaAaAaAaAaAaAaAaRgH! club crashed, smashed, bashed and thrashed their strychnine'n'ecstacy rigidified bodies together in a deranged and extremely physically dangerous mix of the traditional rave robo-twitch combined with the demented ritual violence of the "mosh" copied from the "straight edge" devotees of mid-80's hard core yank punk rock.

Most youth cults have a drug of choice that defines them just as much as their clothes, their music or the length of hair. The straight edgers had been unique in that their chief distinguishing characteristic had been their refusal to consume *any* drugs - including caffeine, nicotine and alcohol. As a result the straight edgers were immediately identifiable by the mad staring eyes, rigidly taut muscleature and permanently clenched teeth that were only the most obvious outward signs of a state of psychosis that was the inevitable result of defying over 2 million years of human evolution. Because, of course, homo-sapiens have grown up with drugs - one need only look at the deranged psychedelic paintings of Heronomus Bosch or read of the nightmarish effects of St Vitus Dance to see the effects that a diet of mouldy rye bread had on the occupants of medieval northern Europe, for instance. 'Cos human beings **need** drugs and without them become something less than human.

The straight-edgers then compounded their psychosis by also adopting veganism and a refusal to engage in casual sex with the result that their social lives, inevitably, thus centred around "moshing" - which can loosely be defined as smashing the fucking shit out of each other to extremely loud punk rock music (the lyrics of which extolled the virtues of the straight edge lifestyle and preached anti-violence).

Oi!Gabba was the dance equivalent of straight edge punk rock. Except with drugs. The Oi!Gabba-heads had made the amazing discovery that combining non-lethal amounts of strych-nine with copious quantities of Ecstacy was exactly like doing no drugs whatsoever ie exactly like taking tons of drugs. Lord Buddha meets Lord Krishna in a brainwreckingly ironic cultural feedback loop cum Mobius strip and the result is a psychotic dance phenomenon that makes the homophobic 'Disco Sucks!' mass burning of dance records at Chicago's Wrigley Field baseball stadium in the late '70s (on the assumption that dance music was lame, limpwristed faggoty slop compared to the ripplingly muscled and testosterone spurting heterosexual perfection of "real" RAWK! played by "real" men on "real" instruments) look like the wankiest event in the entire history of yoof kulture bar none -**OFFICIAL!**

In the AaAaAaAaAaAaAaAaAaAaAaRgH! club's Handbag room 5,876 E-addled teens wobbled to Handbag. In the Techno Room 3,356 cokestiffened 20 somethings borged-out to Techno. In the Speed Garage Room 2,631 SpeedGarageHeads speedgaragebobbed to speedgarage and in the Ambient Room 4,962 soft wankers who couldn't handle their drugs "chilled out" to whale noises. And then the Handbaggers went collectively mEnTaL, whipped out their nail files and steamed en-masse into the ambient room and stabbed, gouged and disemboweled all of the ning-nang-nonged-out whale-huggers to death in 1 minute 34.562 seconds flat. Then they whipped out their hairspray cans and bic lighters and steamed into the Speed Garage Room where they flamethrowered all the SpeedgarageHeads into screaming, liquid-fat spurting human candles before crashing like a multi-won-derbra'ed juggernaut into the Oi!Gabba room where, after they'd booted, fisted, knee'd and headbutted the thrashing mob of E'n'Strickheads into piles of still twitching deadflesh, they turned on each other with much gusto with the end result that at exactly 4.15 am the last of the 20,812 British ravers left alive on the island was seen staggering down the road from the club - spurting blood from numerous wounds and missing both her arms - shortly before she was totally hedgehogged by an articulated lorry.

The investigating Spanish police were completely baffled by the carnage that they discovered in the smouldering wreckage of AaAaAaAaAaAaAaAaAaAaAaRgH! and admitted to being completely stumped as to the reason why 20,812 presumably typical British kids should suddenly go completely doo-lally mental and start slaughtering each other with gusto. They should have read this book. Particularly the next chapter.

CHAPTER 15

E!

'They told me that you had gone totally insane and, uh, that your methods were unsound.'
'Are my methods unsound?'
'I don't see any *method* at all.'

Martin Sheen and Marlon Brando giving it large in Apocalypse Now .

A BRIEF INTERLUDE IN WHICH THE WORLD OF MAD MICK THE NEEDLE IS PLACED IN SOME KIND OF CONTEXT AND A FEW QUESTIONS WHICH MAY BE NIGGLING AWAY AT THE BACK OF THE MIND OF THE MORE INQUIRING SORT OF READER ARE ANSWERED IN FULL.

QUESTION: When is the action in this book taking place?
ANSWER: Exactly ten years into the future from the second that YOU, nobody else, just YOU, first heard about this book. This conveniently avoids one of the major pitfalls of speculative fiction ie it dates so quickly. I mean, if you first read George Orwell's 1984 in 1985 then you'd know it was just made-up bollocks. But if George Orwell had been dead clever like me then he wouldn't have let himself get pinned down like that. The dozy twat.

QUESTION: Oh come on! Do you seriously expect us to believe that the world of Mad Mick The Needle is in any way, shape or form a possible near future?

ANSWER: Get a grip. This book is **not** fictional. It is an exact representation of **EXACTLY** how the world will be **EXACTLY** 10 years from the very first second you first heard about this book. **OFFICIAL!**

QUESTION: Oh yeah? Sure! So Britain's going to be full of psychopathic terrorists like Mad Mick and Enid The Needle and Justine Justice and Karen Skull in just 10 years is it? So how come we haven't heard of all these people already?

ANSWER: An evil conspiracy shields you from the reality of the world in which you live. *Many of the things described in this book are already happening!!!!*

QUESTION: OK, that makes sense. But can you explain why the world of Mad Mick the Needle is so different from our own? Why everybody is so violent and how come human beings are going to become capable of acts of violence that seem to defy the laws of both physics and biology?

ANSWER: Those are very good questions but to answer them you will have to read the next chapter which is a potted history of Acid House.

CHAPTER 16

ACID !

'While it is clear that God is the source of music, Ezekiel 28:13 implies that Satan was the first musician. But his song, which once resounded about God's throne, turned into a dirge of death when he rebelled against the Almighty. Since that day the devil has had the world dancing to his tune.'

Larson's Book Of Rock, 1980.

A POTTED HISTORY OF ACID HOUSE

Acid House was music which swept Britain in the 1980's. Young people would converge together in fields and jiggle about to **thumpalonga disco music** for hours fuelled by a drug called **Ecstacy.**

The grown ups were very worried about Ecstacy or **"E"** as the kids called it and gave it to some rats. These rats marched up and down in straight lines for hours and hours and then died of dehydration because the scientists had forgotten to give them any **Lucozade**. From this the scientists concluded that E makes you want to dance.

Other side effects of E were that it a) gave you Parkinsons

Disease, b) gave you irreversible brain damage and c) made you like and hug and kiss everybody and feel all **lovey dovey huggy kissy feely**.

The grown ups were very worried about a) and b) and the fact that in a few well publicised cases middle class kids died of dehydration because they forgot to drink Lucozade or because they couldn't afford to pay a fiver for bottles of tap water that the cockernee gangsters who ran the acid house "scene" charged because they'd already spent their money on **"disco biscuits"** as the kids called E's which cost £15 pound a time and were usually cut with aspirin, speed or **rat poison** anyway.

Little did the grown ups know that the real reason E was an evil drug was c) (it makes you like and hug and kiss everybody and feel all lovey dovey huggy). Scientists of the future will discover that the human brain is only capable of producing so much of the lovey-lovey-huggy-huggy-kissy-feely chemicals that induce "niceness" in a lifetime and that gobbling E's means that you use up these chemicals damn fast and sooner or later become a **screamingly violent nutcase** who goes round killing people for fun. Scientists worked this out exactly ten years from the very first second that you first heard about this book. This is the world of Mad Mick, Justine Justice and Karen Skull. This IS the future - one never ending summer of

HATE!

There is **NO** escape. Even if you have only ever taken one half of one E **YOU _will_** go doolally psycho smash-your-mum-in-the-face-with-a-chainsaw-for-looking-at-you-funny **mEnTaL**. YOU **will** skin Snoopy, the family dog, and wear him as a hat despite the fact that he saved your life when you were a kid by dragging your pram from out of the way of a speeding bus, the driver of which had just had a heart attack caused by too many "straight" drugs like beer and bacon.

There is **no escape** even if you haven't even ever so much as sniffed a bleeding E! You too, Mr and Mrs Dead Straight, you are doomed to madness. This is because very few sewage filtration plants are capable of weeding E out of the water. So think about it, every weekend you've got millions of twathatted kids gobbling E's like **Smarties** (sort of like M&M's for our American readers) and gulping down gallons of fizzy Lucozade to stop themselves dying like rats from dehydration. Now a lot of this E infected Lucozade is going to be sweated out but millions and million of gallons of **E piss** are none the less pumped into the Ecosystem. Soon the seas will all be infected. Scientists will notice that fish are a lot nicer than they used to be and are moving a lot more **rhythmically** that you'd expect. But this will only be the calm before the storm - a storm of **fish violence** that will shock and horrify an entire generation of marine biologists into early retirement. But they will find **no refuge** on the land. Here they will be savagely attacked by bees, crows, cows and other land based species.

And the stuff that is sweated out - that stuff has a half life of 500 years - we are all of us breathing in microscopic amounts of E with every breath we take - not enough to make us huggyfeely-loveydoveynice maybe, but it all adds up. There is **no escape**, oh no. The world of Mad Mick is **OUR** world and it is coming a lot sooner than you think (unless you think it is coming exactly 10 years to the second after you first heard about this book in which case it is coming **exactly** as soon as you think it is).

Aha! - you say knowingly, wagging a finger and peering at the author over the top of a pair of Norman Tebbit style intellectual half-moon spectacles - Aha! That's all very well **BUT** it doesn't even start to explain all the weird supernatural stuff that also seems to be going on in the incredibly violent world of Mad Mick and his mates. What about these demons and the **physical impossibility** of many alleged acts of violence which we have read about in these pages? Your E theory doesn't even **START** to explain these.

Look, OK, for a start nothing in this book is "alleged" - it **WILL** happen and secondly, what about all the **LSD** that's been taken since the 1950's, eh? Ha! Gotcha! Where do you think that's all gone? Eh! Why do you think the world's been getting stranger and stranger? Where do you think all these UFO's and **showers of fish** and stuff are coming from? We have opened up portals to alternative and parallel realities with our increasingly drugged-to-buggery little monkey brains. **It is obvious.**

So there you have it - proof positive that you are reading a book of prophecy. Everything is going to go sick, mental and **weeeeeeer-DUH!** very very soon whether you **"just say no"** or not so you might as well **just say yes** and get down the disco and boogie until your internal organs are shaken loose of their moorings and you projectile haemorrhage **great geysers of boiling blood** from every orifice because we're all going to die anyway - **FACT!** Now, back to the narrative.

CHAPTER 17

NUTTAH !

'These Spice Girls have not been brought up - they have been allowed to grow up like animals.'

Vivienne Westwood, 1997

Eleanor Harper pulled her shiny red electric car into Leicester East service station on the M1 motorway in central England exactly 50 years to the second after Mad Mick The Needle, Enid The Needle, Karen Skull and a load of other people including some savagely wounded but still barely breathing vegetarians had died instantly after a neutron bomb had been dropped on a castle in the remote Scottish Highlands.

She paid for a cold chicken salad and a pot of darjeeling tea in the Julie's Pantry and sat down to read her Daily Mail whilst she ate. A lot had happened in the previous 50 years. After Mad Mick and his terrorist muckers had been killed, scientists (given near lethal doses of the same experimental Combat Strength Battle Cocaine that Mad Mick's posse had been whacked out of their tiny skulls on when they attacked the Scottish castle HQ of the vegetarians) had not only diagnosed and discovered chemical cures for the Drug Madness but had also stumbled across a way of removing all drugs from the environment for ever. Right wing authoritarian nutters had then swept to power in every country in the world and stayed there. All the junkies and dealers and casual drug users (plus anybody who used slang or wore strange clothes) had been rounded up and shot. The portals to alternative universes healed up and the demons that were stranded on this side of the reality/screaming fucking nightmare interface were hunted down and then the history books were Stalinisticaly rewritten to make it look as if they'd never existed. Youth culture was officially banned and the kids were forced to act like young adults ie wear incredibly dull clothes and have crap haircuts etc until they were old enough to get married and have children of their own which more or less all of them did. Children were once more soundly beaten by their parents and coppers were once again allowed to give you a good solid clip around the ear hole for being cheeky or scrumping apples. Capitalism managed to resolve all its internal contradictions and life got incredibly dull and boring. Eleanor Harper ate most of her chicken salad but left a little bit on the side of her plate for Mr Manners.

"Thank you," said Mr Manners who suddenly sat down in the seat opposite her and scooped up the remains of her meal.

Mr Manners was the only demon left this side of the reality/screaming fucking nightmare interface and had managed to escape being hunted down and written out of history chiefly because he was a uniquely middle class demon but partly because he looked like everybody's favourite male relative ie the jolly uncle with the twinkly eyes and pockets a jingling and a jangling with shiny half-crowns which he'd give you after entertaining you briefly with some clever magic tricks and piggy back rides. He was also one of the very few demons who did not rely for his corporeal sustenance on the nightmares, drug hallucinations and insane ramblings of the more deranged members of human race. No, Mr Manners was rather the physical manifestation of the table manners which lower middle class parents have drummed into their unfortunate offspring for endless generations. He almost blinked out of existence in the famine conscious 1960's and '70s when it was voguish for bourgeois parents to order their children to eat every last little scrap on the plate because children were starving in Biafra/India/Bangladesh or whichever nation had recently had their pot bellied, big eyed and matchstick-limbed kids plastered pornographically over the pages of that week's Sunday colour supplement but there had always been enough traditionalist parents to keep him ticking over as a sacrifice dependent metaphysical entity on skeleton rations, so to speak.

Trapped in Leicester East service station, Mr Manners wanted his mates back. More than that he wanted to turn the clock back 50 years to when the environmental overload of drugs in the eco-system had pushed the planet to the very verge of what promised to be an incredibly interesting armageddon of intertwisting realities, unrealities and downright impossibilities. But time was running out. Mr Manners knew that the Milkinite invasion fleet, led by the Wattie out of The Exploited look-a-like Limegreenmohawked Bigmonkeys, was nearing Earth after having hopped across the galaxy through a series of intergalactic relay stations built into black holes by the 4 brained snails that used to rule the universe way back in the good old days millions of years before the first lungfish first flapped ashore on the prehistoric Earth beach and evolved into a dinosaur. PLUS he knew that the Milkinites were coming tooled up and ready to ruck ie to **EXTERMINATE** the human race for showing disrespect to The Lord God Creator Of The Universe And Master Of Everything aka Wattie out of The Exploited.

Mr Manners knew that he and his demonic muckers relied for their existence on the continuing existence of the human race. He also knew that the human race stood no chance against the Milkinites unless they stood shoulder to shoulder with the now effectively exiled demon legions. **PLUS** he also knew that unless history itself was changed ie Mad Mick and his terrorist muckers (ie the top 200 hundred crusaders of Khaos whose extremely deranged anti-social naughtiness was the grease on the front wheels of the day-glo florescent paint spattered nuclear powered battle tank of the fun version of human history as opposed to the kneechewingly dull grey smelly version which had in fact prevailed) were somehow saved from being nuetronbombed to death 50 year back, like, then that was it, as in finito, as in **Aliens 1 - Human Race 0.** As in no more Mr Manners who would be replaced on Earth by some weird Alien god or demon which, thought Mr Manners, would suck the painfully distended anus of a skyscraper sized shitgibbon with arse cancer. **THEREFORE** something had to be done. Mr Manners wasn't exactly sure what but he knew that Eleanor Harper was the key because despite looking a like a braindead, Tory voting, desiccated, sexless old bag, she was in fact the immediate reincarnation of Mad Mick The Needle who had been punished by the weird god **"God"** by being sent back to Earth as the female child of an extremely conservative middle class couple who'd brought her up to be a total and utter stiff.

Eleanor Harper aka the reincarnated Mad Mick The Needle, had been born of parents who both possessed the **"Gummer gene"** ie the gene found in all incredibly dull, boring, conservative, sad people with zero sex appeal, crap politics and the dress sense of the dead . This thought God, was hilarious and, to make Mad Mick suffer all the more, he'd kept the evil little bastard "alive" but locked helplessly in the most tedious and mediocre corner of Eleanor Harper's knucklesuckingly tedious and mediocre soul.

Mad Mick was thus forced to endure years of a seriously torturous megasuckfest in the most hideous prison imaginable. He felt himself to **be** Eleanor Harper (which, in a way, he was), to share her stunted, crippled world view, to be a walking fun-free zone and, most hilariously of all (thought God), to actually believe in the strange Christian god, "God". Thus was the soul of Mad Mick The Needle - possibly the coolest human being ever apart from Lenin, Che Guevara, Jimi Hendrix and me - wracked with selfdisgust of an intensity that would have driven a lesser mortal screaming into uncurable gouge-your-own-eyes-out-and-insert-the-arid-stems-of dried-sunflowers-in-the-sockets-for-fun insanity. Fortunately, however, Mad Mick was already insane and had been so since birth. Since both his births. Or since his birth and her birth, maybe. Don't think about it too much, monkeyboy, your brain isn't big enough.

This wasn't the first time God had punished a mortal in this way. After Adolf Hitler had splattered his brains all over the Berlin fuhrerbunker wall in 1945, God had punished the evil Austrian with a diabolically nasty set of crap reincarnations - not because He wanted to punish Hitler for being the crappest human being who had ever lived (which he undoubtedly was) but because He recognised in the lunatic vegetarian couldn't-handle-his-drugs speedfreak operaloving wanker an evil that almost matched His own and, remembering the unfortunate incident with the Angel Lucifer AKA The Dev, decided to take no chances.

Thus had The Lord God Almighty AKA **God The Ripper** serially reincarnated a fully conscious Hitler as a series of seriously shit animals including one of the butterflies that were released on stage during the Rolling Stones tribute concert to

Brian Jones in Hyde Park where all the insects had dramatically and hilariously piled on to the ground in front of the stage, stone cold dead but still twitching hideously thus badly damaging the karmic consciousness of the thousands of watching hippies and thereby paving the way for Altamont and death of the so called **Age Of Aquarius** which God thought was cool because he'd always been a staunch believer in short back and sides and suits for everybody except himself and had indeed considered making "Thou Shalt Dress Appropriately" one of the 10 Commandments but had changed his mind because He realised that the more people dressed like Him (ie long hair, huge beard and long flowing hippy robes) then the more jealous and pissed off He'd be and thus the more likely He'd be to act like a total bastard because it was only when He was being a total bastard that God felt entirely happy.

What a

NUTTAH!

Chapter 17 b

PUFF!

'Let's kick out the Tories! (dang de-dang dang dang dang) The rulers of this land! (dang de-dang dang dang dang) For they are the enemy! (dang de-dang dang dang dang) Of the British working man! And woman!'

Kick Out The Tories by The Newtown Neurotics (revised non-sexist version)

Meanwhile, back in the present AKA exactly 10 years from the very first second that you first heard about this book...

By now, of course, the entire country was firmly held in the slavering jaws of the bog-eyed E-beast.

"ORDER! ORDER!" screamed Madam Speaker hysterically.

"The trouble with the honourable members sitting on the benches opposite" yelled Tory home secretary Michael Suttcliffe, "is that they are **soft** on crime and soft on the **causes** of crime!"

"Fuck off we are!" snarled New Labour shadow home secretary Eric Manson as he leapt angrily to his feet

"You're shit/and you know you are!" chorused the Tory back benches to the tune of Go West by The Pet Shop Boys, covering The Village People, gleefully, as they waved their order papers and made vigorous wanker signs at the honourable and right honourable members on the benches opposite.

"If the Home secretary wants to look at my DM's," said the New Labourite, hoisting up his foot, "then he'll see that they're covered in the dried blood of a fucking beggar who tried it on with me just this fucking morning!"

"FUCK OFF! FUCK OFF! FUCK OFF! FUCK OFF! FUCK OFF! FUCK OFF! FUCK OFF!" roared the Tory back-benchers to the tune of 'Amazing Grace' as they pulled down their pinstriped trousers, turned around, bent down and exposed their hairy, heroin-needle pocked arses to the New Labourites whilst scowling over their shoulders and flicking them the V.

"ORDER! ORDER!" screeched a puce-faced Madam Speaker, uselessly.

"He fucking come up to me!" screamed the opposition spokesperson over the Tory barracking, "and he goes - Copy of the Big Issue, sir?"

"YOU'RE A CUNT! YOU'RE A CUNT! YOU'RE A CUNT!" bellowed the Tory back benches to the tune of 'Be Kind To Our Fine Feathered Friends' by Edward de Souza.

"Sexist! Sexist!" shrilled the assertively confident New Labour womyn members, angrily but non-confrontationally.

"So I says," continued New Labour front bencher Eric Manson, bravely, "I says - **TOUGH ON CRIME! TOUGH ON THE CAUSES OF CRIME!** - and I smacked the twat! I did! I smacked him and he started crying! So I smacked him again! Dead hard! And then, and then, right, then I kicked his fucking head in!"

"Did you fuck, you soft **CUNT!**" roared Tory Prime Minister William Crippen, leaping to his feet and snarling like a dog. "You probably gave him fifty quid and then dragged him back to your fucking Islington puff-palace and got him to suck your fucking cock until his scabby lips frayed, you fat fucking Northern arse-bandit cunt!"

"Sexist! Sexist!" shrilled the padded-shoulder suited New Labour chick MPs, furiously.

"ORDER! ORDER!" screamed Madam Speaker.

"And then, right," said the Prime Minister, half-turning to milk the applause of his own back benches, "he probably got on the phone and invited his good friend, the leader of the opposition, around for what I believe is known amongst the homosexual fraternity as a "shit sandwich"!"

"That is utterly **OUTRAGEOUS!**" stormed New Labour

leader Tony Eichmann, as he leapt to his feet. "I am appalled, Madam Speaker, to hear such sickening and utterly appalling homophobic bigotry in this house!"

"Hear! Hear!" chorused the New Labour back benches, nodding profoundly.

"Especially coming from the Prime Minister," continued Eichmann, smugly, "who, if my memory serves me correctly, was himself more than a little bit partial to the occasional portion of juicy cock back when he was my fag at Eton!"

"Ah-*haaaaaaah!* " chuckled the New Labour benches whilst nodding knowingly.

"W-w-w-what?!" spluttered the Prime Minister, almost exploding with rage, "Are you calling me a ***fucking puff!?*** "

"**PUFF! PUFF! PUFF!**" roared the New Labour benches, pointing at the Prime Minister gleefully.

"ORDER! ORDER!" thundered Madam Speaker, "Can I remind honourable members that pointing is **UN**, I REPEAT, **UN**parliamentary behaviour and ask them to cease forthwith?!"

"ARE YOU CALLING ME A FUCKING PUFF?!" demanded the Prime Minister, who was now actually having to be physically restrained by several of his front bench colleagues.

"ANSWER! ANSWER!" roared the Tories.

"I am sure that the Prime Minister is familiar with the expression - if the cap fits, wear it!" smirked the New Labour Leader.

"**CUNT! CUNT! CUNT!**" chanted the Tory back benches, spitting at the benches opposite and tossing coins.

"Or perhaps, in his case," continued Eichmann, in the smug manner of one who is about to deliver a devastating parliamentary bon mot so witty and droll that it will assure his place in every Dictionary of Quotations ever henceforth published anywhere in the entire English speaking world, "it might be more appropriate to say - If the ***cock*** fits, (smug pause) **SUCK** it!"

"FUUUUUUUUUUUUUUUUUUUUUUUUUUUUUUUUUCK AWFFFFFFFFFFFFFFFFFFF!!!!!!!!!!" roared the Tory back-benchers, leaping to their feet and pulling off their pin stripe jackets and cold turtle-soup stained ties.

"HA HA HA HA HA HA HA HA HA!" exploded the New Labour MPs, giving the Tories the universal "come-and-have-a-go-if-you-think-you're-fucking-hard-enough" two handed finger-wiggle.

"**LADIES AND GENTLEMEN!**" roared Madam Speaker suddenly in a voice so devastatingly loud that it crushed the childish cacophony stone cold dead.

"I have **never**, in all my years as Speaker of this house," she said, lowering her voice and spitting each acidic word into the cold vacuum of embarrassed silence that now gripped the chamber in its icy maw, "been witness to a more childish, boorish and, I might add, utterly offensive display of discourtesy, abusiveness and downright unparliamentary nastiness than that which it has just been my displeasure to have witnessed here in this chamber this afternoon."

She seemed to be staring at each member individually. They all shuffled their feet and stared at the ground, desperately trying to avoid her penetrating laser-beam gaze.

Did I say all? For their was one Tory back bencher so off his face on crack that he didn't give a fuck.

"Suck my cock till yer lips fray, *slaaaaaaaaag!* " he bellowed, unoriginally, whipping out his tiny cock and waving it magisterially in Madam Speaker's general direction.

"Sexist! Sexist!" cooed the expensively hair-doe'd New Labour womyn MP's in perfect unison.

"GET YOUR TITS OUT FOR THE LADS!" screamed the Tories, "GET YOUR TITS OUT FOR THE LADS!"

"OK, if that's what you want!" snarled Madam Speaker, leaping to her feet and unzipping her incredibly convincing full-body prosthetic Madam Speaker costume to reveal that she was in fact - **JUSTINE JUSTICE, TERRORIST SHE WOLF, BRITAIN'S TOP WITCH AND BARKING MAD BLOODSTAINED CLAW-HAMMER OF THE BOURGEOISIE!**

"PARP!" barked over 600 MP arses as our elected representatives collectively terrorshat.

CLICK-CLUNK! SHNIK! The MPs, paralysed with fear could only stare in horror as the Anarcho-Nihilist-Leninist-Satanist Punk Queen Bitch Of Total Disorder assembled the "mace" and the "woolsack" into a fully functional mini-flamethrower that woofed flaming liquid death over the Tory back benches.

"Uh, three cheers for Justine Justice!" cried New Labour leader Tony Eichmann over the screams of the flaming Tory scum, desperately. "Up the revolution! Huzzah for the workers! Huzzah!"

"Suck flaming liquid death, grinning stooge hyena scum

puppet of the fascist boss oppressors!" snarled Justine casually as she turned the flamethrower on to the opposition benches and squirted.

"AYEEEEEEEEEEEEEEEEEEEEEEEEEEEE!" screamed the grinning stooge hyena scum puppets of the fascist boss oppressors as Justine's top-team of Bradford council estate gutter-rat terrorist muckers abseiled into the chamber from the public gallery and offed the screaming human candles with sharpened shovels whilst still others trussed up and gaffa-taped the still gaping-gobbed members of the government front bench.

Suddenly a huge hole appeared in the middle of the chamber floor.

"Aye up, our Justine!" woofed a coal-dust roughened Barnsley accented voice from the depths of the gloomy hole.

"Aye up, Uncle Tony!" laughed Justine Justice.

The terrorists cheered as they were joined in the heart of the Motherfucker Of All Parliaments by a score of brawny miners.

"Has tha' got Tory bastards all trussed, lass?" asked Uncle Tony, leader of the unemployed Yorkshire miners who had spent the best part of the last decade secretly digging a tunnel all the way from Bradford to London in preparation for this glorious day.

"All trussed, gaffa'ed and fully sedated, Uncle Tony!" chuckled Justine, gleefully waving a syringe.

"Well fuck off wi'em back t'Bradford then, lass!" spat the miner, savagely. "'Cos me and lads have tekken a vote and've decided to rig this place up wi'high explosive and have a glorious last ditch stand 'gainst pigs 'fore we blow fucking dump up, like!"

"If that's your democratically-arrived-at decision, Uncle Tony?" snapped Justine, suddenly serious as the last trussed up and sedated Tory cabinet member disappeared into the gaping hole.

"It is, lass!" said Uncle Tony, quietly. "No tears now. Go on, just fuck off."

Exactly 13.23 seconds later the tips of the stubby black machine gun barrels carried in the combat-coke stoked hands of the advance guard of the hastily scrambled armed bodies of men who compose the state tentatively poked into the smoke and debris filled wreckage of the chamber.

"This one's for Orgreave!" roared a grimy, stripped to

the waist proletarian hero as he tossed a fragmentation grenade whilst simultaneously firing a sub-machine from the hip.

Ten pigs were immediately slashed into shrapnel studded chunks of screaming dog food. Four hours later another 82 cops had died and over 200 of their colleagues were lying in huge shrieking heaps of humiliated pig-flesh. It took another 40 minutes and a further 48 cop-casualties before the last severely wounded miner was finally shot in the back after he'd surrendered.

And then the Houses Of Parliament, packed to the rafters with another 1,241 cops (and every single member of the House Of Lords), erupted in a massive fireball, killing the fucking lot.

CHAPTER 18

YONKS!

'Encyclopedias represent a vital part of many school libraries...(They) represent the philosophies of present day humanists. This is obvious by the bold display of pictures used to illustrate painting, art and sculpture. ...One of the areas that needs correction is immodesty due to nakedness or posture. This can be corrected by drawing clothes on the figures or blotting out entire pictures with a magic marker.'

Ray Martin, Christian School Builder, April 1983

So thus it was that Mrs The Needle and her mad son Mick found themselves hurtling through the upper stratosphere in really cool battle suits equipped with enough hi-tech James Bond style weaponry to win a world war (all of which Mick experienced with a nagging sense of deja vu) (all of which Mick experienced with a nagging sense of deja vu).

"AAAAAAAAAAARGH!" screamed Mick suddenly as his physical body whiplashed under the savage impact of the blunt

end of a major karmic feedback loop.

"OK!" he screamed, "Attack aborted! Repeat! Attack aborted! Everybody hover over to me using the Iron Man style jets in the soles of your state of the art combat boots **NOW!**"

When he was sure that his well tasty team of tooled up top terrorists were all gathered around him, Mick proceeded to explain the reason for his sudden change of mind.

"You're not going to believe this but I've just made a 50 year karmic round trip from the future and, trust me, you do **NOT** want to go attacking that veggie castle down there because there's going to be a neutron bomb dropped on it just after I've ripped the top mungbeancurrymuncher's pointy little head off and we all get instantly killed which is really weird because I had a dream this morning which was sort of a premonition but anyway after we've all been killed this acts as a some sort of a brake on all the really weird and unnatural stuff that's happening at the moment which incidentally is apparently caused by all the E and LSD in the environment or something and what happens is that the Tories rule the world for ever and everything gets seriously crap and I meet God and get punished by being reincarnated as a stiff but fortunately I'm rescued by the nice demon Mr Manners who sends my soul screaming back to now ie about 2 minutes before the neutron bomb goes off so that I can warn you and we all live and thus enable the imminent and impending inter-reality armageddon to take place plus the human race'll stand a chance against a soon-come planetary invasion by a bunch of nutters from the Planet Milkin who worship Wattie Out Of The Exploited in exactly 55 years time from now so what I suggest we do is that we do *not* attack the veggie HQ but attack the plush Docklands sky-scraper HQ of Bjork's Pork Scratchings And Assorted Meat Products PLC instead because it was obviously that bastard Sir Anthony Taylor-Bjork who set us up for a nuking and I reckon we should go around there now and give him a good pre-emptive kicking and save the entire human race at the same time!"

"Yonks!" roared the rest of the elite terrorist team. "What are we waiting for!"

So they all roared back up to the orbiting space shuttle that they'd jumped from (using the Iron Man style jets in the soles their state of the art combat boots to propel them back through the heat barrier from which they were well protected by their state of the art combat suits) from whence they tossed the NASA astronauts who formed the crew into merciless cold vacuum without space suits so that they imploded messily (partly as punishment for being dumb slaves of the Military/Industrial Complex but mostly for fun) and set the controls for London, England. On the way there (and remember that they're all still buzzing out of their terrorist gourds on experimental Combat Strength Battle Cocaine and thus moving and thinking many times faster than you are - unless you too happen to be buzzing out of your gourd on experimental Combat Strength Battle Cocaine in which case **YOU ARE A FUCKING LIAR** because it hasn't even been invented yet) they spotted the neutron bomb warheaded cruise missile heading towards the Scottish castle HQ of the veggies so they took the missile in tow with a tractor beam and dropped it on Windsor Castle as they flew over. Fortunately the Queen was not home that day because the very existence of the British Royal Family was as much part of the "key" which opened up portals to other dimensions as was the existence of Mad Mick and his terrorist muckers who, had they succeeded in their spectacularly spontaneous attempt to bring the House of Windsor to a rubble-free but very radioactive end, would have closed the aforementioned interdimensional portals and thus would have doomed the human race to bloody extermination at the hands of the Milkinite invasion fleet in 55 years time anyway.

Phew! Close shave or

WHAT!?!?

CHAPTER 18 b

LITERATURE!

'It will completely engulf him with its loud, driving beat, its repeated chords and phrases, its wild, sensuous sounds and its sadistic, neurotic, sensual and even obscene words: and it will bend his mind and body until he no longer has any control over any of his actions or thoughts...Rock'n'roll is one of the "weapons" that...revolutionaries are using to tear down everything that Christianity has built up in the United States of America ...Rock music is the devil's masterpiece for enslaving his own children. By the grace of God, let's keep him from enslaving the children of God so that they are powerless to win this generation to Christ!'

Frank Garlock, The Big Beat - A Rock Blast, (Bob Jones University, Greenville, South Carolina, 1971)

*"Oi caaaarnt read an' oi caaaaaaarnt wroite but it
don't really matturrrrrrr!"* bellowed the demon known to
mankind as The Dog-Hatred Obsessed Factory Farmer Ripped To
The Sunkissed Ruddy Tits On Cider And Snorted Insecticide to
the tune of 'One Man Went To Mow' as he flolloped around the
bonfire made out acoustic guitars in his battered old baggy wellies
whilst clutching a massive flagon of stinking scrumpy and a dog's
head on a stick. *"Coz oi comes fram Zumerzet - and' oi
caaaarn droive a trrrraaaactorrrrr!!!!!!!!!!!!"*

*'NO NO, NO NO NO NO, NO NO NO NO, NO
NO - THERE'S NO LIMIT!"* thumped 2 Unlimited's brilliant 'No
Limits' from the demonically enhanced speakers of the mobile
disco.

"How long have we been at this party now?" asked Helen
Keller's Iron Lung guitarist Animal as he dismounted from his
steaming dragon and accepted a huge skunk-packed spliff from
the rosy-cheeked and totally naked farmer's daughter who
pranced past wearing huge elk antlers on her head and shrieked
hysterically as she was chased by a dozen rabidly priapic satyrs.

"I make it about, let's see, 895 years, 4 months, three
weeks, 2 days, 7 hours and 15 seconds.....precisely!" said Animal
(2) as he tonked about with the buttons on his incredibly
sophisticated satanic computer-watch.

"I'm bored!" roared an utterly pissed Animal (3) as he
staggered up clutching two viking-style rams horns full of delicious
alco-nectar.

"Yeah, 895 years, 4 months, three weeks, 2 days, 7
hours and 15 seconds is too long to spend at any party!" moaned
Animal (97) as he teknolinedanced in perfect formation with 180
naked deaf yank cheerleaders whilst munching the mammoth-
tongue and Dijon mustard sandwich on rye that he'd scooped up
from the vast pile of ace grub that constantly spewed forth from
the massive Horn Of Plenty.

"Especially when the only record they've got is 'No Limits'
by 2 Unlimited!" agreed Animal (4,982) between grunts as he
wrestled naked in a vast vat of slippery Elf brains with an ancient
fish-headed river-god.

"So why don't we harness the magick created by the
combination of our super-scientifick tantrick force-field and our

satanic transit van's auto-destruct device in alliance with the arcane weeeeeeer-DUH!-ness of our strange mate The Dog-Hatred Obsessed Factory Farmer Ripped To The Sunkissed Ruddy Tits On Cider And Snorted Insecticide plus the incredibly powerful tantrik-magick we have unleashed by shagging ourselves?" asked Animal (345, 987) between loudly grunted "**UH!**s" as hevigorously slithered the entire hot steaming length of his pulsating pork python in and out of the well greased shit-chute of Animal (11) with gusto, "and collapse all the various doppelganger clone selves that have been created by the mind-bogglingly fast fluttering of the new arsehole in the space-time continuum that the resulting Yin-Yang ping-pong cosmik-feedback loop cum Mobius strip cum daemonic domino effect has ripped in the very fabric of the universe, back into hyper concentrated Super-versions of ourselves and then get back in the transit van and fuck off into the temporal sun-set for an ace Josey And The Pussycats style adventure in the distant past that will no doubt result in the imaginative but utterly gratuitous slaughter of a bunch of people whose only crime is that they just happen to get on our incredibly bigoted and utterly pig ignorant little tits?"

And so they did.

And thus it was that the super-concentrated Lung posse found themselves artfully plastered with tons of prosthetic make-up to make them look really boring, middle class and prematurely middle-aged so that they blended in perfectly with the audience attending a Literary Festival taking place in the draughty village hall of a posh southern English village where they listened with intense boredom to a "proper" novelist droning on and

on and on and on and on and on and on and on and on
and on and on and on and on and on and on and on and
on and on and on and on and on and on and on and on
and on and on and on and on and on and on and on and
on and on and on and on and on and on and on and on
and on and on and on and on and on and on and on and
on and on and on and on and on and on and on and on
and on and on and on and on and on and on and on and
on and on and on and on and on and on and on and on
and on and on and on and on and on and on and on and
on and on and on and on and on and on and on and on
and on and on and on and on and on and on and on and
on and on and on and on and on and on and on and on
and on and on and on and on and on and on and on and
on and on and on and on and on and on and on and on
and on and on and on and on and on and fucking boring bastard

ON !!!!!!!!!!!!!!

And then on and on and on some more in a dead wanky voice as
he read a long and utterly tedious extract from his new book which
was, by an amazing coincidence, about a dead wanky voiced
Professor Of Literature from Oxford who found himself reading a
long and utterly tedious extract from his new book in a draughty
church hall in a posh village somewhere in southern England. The
novel had won that year's prestigious Taylor-Bjork's Pork
Scratchings And Associated Meat Products PLC. sponsored
Taylor-Bjork Literary Prize hands down and was **SHITE** -

OFFICIAL!!!!!!

"Thank you, Alan!" cooed hot, happening literary she-
bitch and living feminist icon 57 year old Alison Dribble (whose last
warmly-reviewed-by-her-mates "magic-realist" novel had been
about a young (57-ish year old) woman who left her boring husband and kids and became a hot, happening home-counties
literary she-bitch and living feminist icon with her finger firmly on
the throbbing pulse of swinging modern Britain) when the
prematurely middle-aged speccy beardo novelist bore finally

droned to a close.

"Now, as you doubtless know," she smiled, smugly, "we have on the platform here today the entire judging panel for this year's prestigious Taylor-Bjork's Pork Scratchings And Associated Meat Products PLC sponsored Taylor-Bjork Literary Prize and I'm sure that there are those amongst the audience who have a few questions for the panel about how they finally arrived at their decision to award the prize to Alan's simply delicious literary masterpiece. Yes, the short hairy gentleman in the pirate costume at the back?"

"Ook! Oook oooooook OoOk OooooOOOOoOoK!" snarled Bobo the famous American deaf-language talking pygmy chimp, stabbing a short fat hairy finger at the platform.

"He says - Thanks to a new arsehole ripped in the fabric of the space-time continuum by evil satanic magick" translated Crowley, approximately, "he was able to send you lot a copy 'Claws Of The E-Beast' - the best novel ever written in the entire history of the English language that he's going to accidentally knock out on my Apple Mac Power book next week - and that you fuckers didn't even shortlist it and he wants to know why?"

Consternation froze the faces of the tight-circle of mutually arse-licking stunted bourgeois 4th rate half-talent wankers who represented the self-appointed and self-perpetuating oligarchy of constipated brain-dead zomboid posho fuckwits in charge of the fetid walking corpse with incredibly bad breath and a tendency to shit its own hideously unstylish brown corduroy trousers at irregular intervals that was the Modern English Novel.

"I think I remember that particular entry, Madame Chairperson!" snarled bushy-eyebrowed and foul-smelling pipe sucking Professor of English Literature Stephen Horatio Ignatus Tucker through clouds of vile smelling shag smoke, evily.

"It was - if I remember correctly - a piece of exciting, entertaining and linguistically cutting-edge pornographic trash!" he sneered. "A hideous hodge-podge of sub-literate moronicism which seethed with violence, sex, drugs, pop music and temporally impossible plot twists plus, if my memory doesn't fail me, a piss-poor plethora of poorly-researched "magick" which the imbecilic and obviously non-Oxbridge educated author tossed about willy-nilly whenever he was faced with the proper author's chores of character development and plotting!"

"Boo! Hiss! Shame! Gasp!" moaned the horrified audience.

"And, furthermore," continued the pipesucking bore "this alleged - and I use the term loosely - "novel" contained one particulary hideous section wherein the author, in the company of a satanic pop band called, I believe, Helen Keller's Iron Lung..."

"No! Say it ain't so! Tut!" gasped the appalled crowd.

"....attend a literary festival..." continued the creepy Prof, "where they hog-tie, slowly torture and then gruesomely butcher the entire judging panel of the prestigious Taylor-Bjork's Pork Scratchings And Associated Meat Products PLC sponsored Taylor-Bjork Literary Prize committee as some sort of barbarically clumsy failed satire on the stuck-in-the-mud, head-in-the-clouds redundant upper-middle-class snobbishness, effeteness and rank crapness of the aforementioned alleged tight-circle of mutually arse-licking stunted bourgeois 4th rate half-talent wankers who allegedly represent the self-appointed and self-perpetuating oligarchy of constipated brain-dead zomboid posho fuckwits supposedly in charge of the fetid walking corpse with incredibly bad breath and a tendency to shit its own hideously unstylish brown corduroy trousers at irregular intervals which the author contends *is* the Modern English Novel!"

"Bad show! Ridiculous! String him up!" muttered the offended assembly.

"Which indicates that the alleged - and I use the word loosely - *"author"* "" smugged the Prof, jabbing the stem of his pipe in Bobo's general direction, "is one of those misguided souls who actually regards readability, visceral excitement and balls-out, cutting-edge and in-your-face, down-your-trousers, and-up-your-arse-like-a-shit-eating-rabbit-on-speed **ExCiTeMeNt!!!!!!** as positive qualities of which, he no doubt assumes, the festering and incredibly dull zomboid horrorcorpse of The Modern English Novel is much in need! In fact, Madame Chairperson, I'm willing to bet that he's the kind of moronic philistine who actually believes that the writing of the late 20th Century should actually attempt to reflect the breathless, gibbering, breakneck pace of the braintrashing sex-fest of pop-kulture against which those of us who have an education rightly regard it as a bulwark of moderation and tedious decency, preserving forever - as if in fetid aspic - a set of self-evidently correct and utterly conservative ideals which mean that The

Modern English Novel is so boring, dull, self-referential and wonderfully utterly up its own arse that very few people actually want to read it and instead turn in their unwashed, stinking, non-Oxbridge and non-public school educated millions to the flash, glamorous, fast, moronic and typhonically titillating trashy joys of American 'genre' fiction which, of course, is a state of affairs to be warmly applauded because the last thing that we literary types want is for our books to be read by an audience of stinking prole scum who aren't dead- from-the-neck-downwards no-nob stiffs stuck in the 19th Century!"

"Huzzah! Stuff the oiks! Keep excitement and modernity out of The Modern English Novel!" roared the partisan audience, ecstatically.

"OOK! OOOK! OOOOOOK OOK! OOK!" replied Bobo angrily.

"He says - Fuck you, you patronising pipesucking cunt! He says - I'm gonna kick your fucking Oxbridge-educated head in, but only after you've been hogtied, tortured and then gruesomely slaughtered like the pig ignorant cultural dead-weight pile of decaying fucking pig shit you are, you braindead wanker!" translated Crowley as he led the Lung posse towards the platform with a massive battery operated and satanically enhanced Black&Decker power drill screaming bloodthirstily in all six of his pudgy hands.

And then Dagenham Pete, the homophobic cockernee roadie of satanic rock band Helen Keller's Iron Lung, awoke with a start. It had all been a dream! - dreamt mother-of-4 Julie Jones as she tossed and turned under a crisp, warm duvet in the tastefully decorated master bedroom of her recently bought new Barratt home in suburban Newport - typed Bobo the American sign-language talking pygmy chimp accidentally - read disgusted Taylor-Bjork's Pork Scratchings And Associated Meat Products PLC sponsored Taylor-Bjork Literary Prize committee member Stephen Horatio Ignatus Tucker angrily - wrote the lobotomised ex-music hack serfslave strapped to word processor in a dank, rat ridden Glasgow cellar furiously - dreamt Dagenham Pete the homophobic cockernee roadie of satanic rock band Helen Keller's Iron Lung, before suddenly awaking with a start - insanely acidflashbacked Professor Stephen Horatio Ignatus Tucker repeatedly as he made pathetic *"MMMMMMPH! MMMMMMPH! MMMMMMMMMMMM-*

MMPH! " noises through the gaffa tape that covered his beardy gob and stared with mad boggly eyes at the pirate-costumed pygmy chimp who jiggled about to 'Stuck In The Middle With You' by Stealers Wheel with a bloody cut-throat razor in one paw and one of the Prof's incredibly hairy ears in the other (a cultural reference which, of course, went straight over the Prof's head).

Chapter 18c

THATCHER!

'Anti-Rock Pledge: CONFESSING my faith in Christ and desiring to communicate his love and truth to my generation, and RECOGNIS-ING that many of the songs and singers of rock express and promote a morality and life-style contrary to the highest of Christian principles, I HEREBY PLEDGE MYSELF TO THE FOLLOWING:

　　　1) I will abstain from voluntarily listen-ing to rock music so that I might adhere to the admonition of the Apostle Paul to "Think upon those things which are pure, honest, just, lovely and of good report!" (Philippians 4:8)

　　　2) I will destroy all rock records and tapes in my possession as an outward, symbolic act of signifying my inner dedication to conscientiously discriminate as to the records I buy and listen to. (1 John 5:21).'

The Rev Bob Larson, Rock and Roll: The Devil's Diversion, 1967.

MEANWHILE, IN LONDON......

The sphincter-looseningly lifelike 9 foot tall "Margaret Thatcher" sex-mannikin (6 orifices and a sperm-sensitive voice box that roared **"THERE IS NO ALTERNATIVE!"** at 200 decibels each time one of its genuine baby seal fat greased vibrating love-holes electronically detected spunk) had cost Chief Home Office Hostage Scenario Negotiator Pete Ringer a cool 180K's worth of Class A drug vouchers but had been worth every single bastard gramme. And now the metal-boned sexfrankenstein thrashed, sparked, bucked and gyrated in a nightmarishly cyborgian parody of the female orgasm, the massive claws attached to its 14 foot long, quadruple-jointed hydraulic arms viciously scraping the expensive wallpaper on either side of the violently churning water bed, its evil, hawklike eyes blazing red as its incredibly life-like roast-chicken skin textured arse vigorously squeezed the last few drops of sushi'n'cocaine'n'champagne'n'pâté de foi gras flavoured cum out of the top civil servant's firmly gripped and still incredibly rigid little love truncheon.

"HEIL HITLER!" screeched Ringer ecstatically as he cracked open two ampoules of amyl-nitrate and sniffed viciously whilst the robot swiftly dismounted, brutally flipped him onto his front and proceeded to bang his heroin-needle pocked arse off with the massive black vibro-dildo that suddenly speared from its savagely thrusting groin as its pre-programmed voice box suddenly started spewing great chunks of Professor Milton Friedman's epic work 'The Road To Serfdom' (bizarrely back-grounded by 'Rule Britannia' overlaid with the sound of 20,000 nazi jackboots crunching gravel which Ringer had sampled off a copy of an underground Estonian neo-nazi gabba remix of Joseph Goebbells' infamous post-Stalingrad 'Total War' speech) at a central nervous system shredding volume that caused blood to bubble out past the genuine baby seal-fur plugs in Ringer's ears as the cripplingly huge amount of laxative chocolate the ecstatically writhing Home Office Hostage Scenario Negotiator had wolfed down not but 20 minutes ago kicked in and caused a great geyser of hot liquid shit to spit savagely out of his robotically rogered red raw anus, splattering the frenziedly bumming sex doll, which, electronically detecting the presence of pooh, automatically switched into Psycho-Dominatrix mode and proceeded to tie

Stringer up with electric flex, stick an orange in his gob, string him up from the ceiling and violently thrash his body with a public-school style cane whilst singing 'Der Holle Rache kocht in meinen Herren' from Mozart's awesome opera Die Zauberflute in a chillingly authentic electronic approximation of the voice of Dame Kiri Te Kawana.

LASH! LASH! LASH! went the cane as it carved great gouts into the scar-tissue covered torso which thrashed and twisted like an electrocuted salmon on a hot tin roof, splattering the shit-spattered and ripped-to-fucking-shreds wallpaper with flecks of tons-of-top-drugs adulterated blood whilst the robot simultaneously wrapped a silk scarf around the mutely screaming Tory pervert's neck and proceeded to strangle him with one hideous claw whilst violently wanking him with the other. Ringer's eyes bulged in his purple face like pickled eggs displayed on a velvet covered silver tray for the amusement of The Queen (in response to her recently expressed desire to occasionally be served samples of genuinely disgusting pleb-tuck in order that she might, as it were, "be as one" with the common folk and never ever again be seen to be as totally out-of-touch as she allegedly was during the insane and regrettable events of Dead Diana Week) as he trembled with terror because, although he knew *intellectually* that the sexandroid was programmed to cease strangling him long before it either crushed his windpipe or caused permanent brain damage through oxygen depravation, the lizard stem part of his cerebal cortex that ruled his emotions like a cruel feudal lord driven insane by tertiary syphilis and centuries of aristocratic inbreeding was convinced that he was about to die and thus flooded his tortured body with the adrenaline of primeval **FEAR!**

SPLOT! coughed the Tory's tiny knob, pathetically. SPLUT! SPLOOT! SUR-PER-PLAT! The roboThatch, electronically detecting that its owner had again spat spunk, segued seamlessly into Matron Mode, debondaged the bastard, replaced the orange with a dummy, wiped off the shit, wrapped his steak-tartare textured arse in bandages and a giant nappy and then cradled him in its monstrous arms while gently humming a lovely lullaby.

Ringer sighed. "This," he thought, "is heaven!". Through heavy-lidded pupils made anthropomorphic-Disney-cartoonishly massive by a potentially lethal combination of copious amounts of upper-class quality illegal drugs, tons of top nosh and spine-melting post-orgasmic euphoria, Ringer looked up lovingly at the now gently cooing SexGolem, made smugly contented sucking noises on his bright red dummy and internally chuckled at the thought of all those poor unwashed cunts who had never been to public school and were thus cut off forever from the skykissingly blissful joys of upper class sex!

"Time for your, beddy-byes, Master Peter!" billycooed the RoboThatch.

"But Matron" slurred Ringer from behind his dummy, "you haven't read me a story yet!"

"Oh very well!" cackled the hideously visaged android maternally, "But just *one* story and then its sleepy time or I know one young man who will be all yawny tomorrow when he should be negoshy-oshy-waiting!"

"Hmmmmmmm!" sighed Ringer ecstatically, nestling even further into the hard, metal expanse of the cyborg's massive yet incredibly firm chest.

"Once upon a time" purred the multifunctional fuckmachine "there were three little piggi…

SQQQQQQWAAAAUUUUK- IGKUCK-AAAAAAAAARKKKKKKKKK!"

The SQQQQQQWAAAAUUUUKI-GKUCK-AAAAAAAAAARKKKKKKKKK!" noise was a accompanied by a ferocious

KERBLAM!

and a spectacular shower of multi-coloured sparks that showered down into Ringer's disbelieving eyes as the head of the incredibly realistic Baroness Thatcher lookalike sex toy disintegrated under the savage impact of a titanium-tipped high explosive dum-dum shotgun charge fired from extremely close range, causing the now headless torso of the spunk, shit, blood and lubricant smeared android to spasm violently, lose control of its arms and toss Ringer up into the air to smash into the ceiling from whence he crashed savagely into the massive shit, sperm and blood smeared waterbed, causing it to burst and send 7,000 gallons of foully stinking water tidalwaving through the luxurious Mayfair flat whilst Ringer, brutally ripped from the bosom of his post orgasmic state of blissful euphoria by a savagely violent alteration in his physical circumstances that he was in no fit state to even begin to comprehend, croaked, spat rancid water and flapped amongst the soaked wreckage of his boudoir like a violently strobed epilectic frog spat suddenly from the eye of a blisteringly ferocious hurricane and surviving thanks only to the stupid laws of physics which unfairly discriminate in favour of smaller creatures in situations involving insanely violent acts of nature, totally unaware that, at that very nano-second, the mini-tidal wave was picking up his much treasured conversation piece "The Foreseeable Future Is A Dimly Lit Cul-de-sac Littered With The Loutishy Discarded Salt'n'Vinegar Crisp Packets Of Kosmic Karma And The Slipperishly Decayed Remains Of The Cadbury's Chocolate Orange Gorged Rottweiler Shite Of An Insane God's Sense Of Humour" by Damien Hirst (ie the heads of 235 animals from the World Wildlife Fund's official "endangered species" list pickled in formaldehyde and suspended in a large glass case) and had sent the artwork crashing through the now totally fucked flat's front windows from whence it fell savagely onto the unsuspecting head of an acoustic guitar strumming busker who was exactly halfway through the second chorus of Elton John' s especially rewritten versh of 'Candle In The Wind', splattering the arselicking forelock tugger muso bastard into the greasy London pavement with extreme prejudice and impeccable musical taste.

Amazingly, however, the busker did not die! No, even though his head had been traumatically impacted into his chest and both his eyes had been knocked clean out, the lucky bastard still lived, his hideously contorted broken arms still flailing blindly at an acoustic guitar that was now matchwood and his glass shredded lips still flapping as he sprayed the air with lung-blood and bits of broken tooth. For busking was more than just a hobby for 47 year old father of 3 Peter Baker - it was more than just an obsession! It was **his life!** So much so that his body now stubbornly refused to succumb to injuries so hideous that you would die of shock yourself were you ever to read about them in anything like their full and amazingly horrific detail. Even though his brain was half-hanging out through a fist-sized hole in his savagely fractured skull and even though he was spewing out a pint of hot blood a minute from every one of at least a half-a-dozen hideously gaping wounds, ultra-busker Peter Baker carried on busking *on pure instinct alone!* Like the true **super-trouper** he was! Stunned witnesses (all of whom are at this very moment shockvomiting with disgust at the recurring memory of the hideous spectacle) later reported that the traumatically foreshortened, empty-socketed and glass-porcupined plucky street performer was gamely grunting what sounded like a savagely brain-damaged medley of lines from such cheeringly familiar busking classics as 'Streets Of London' and 'Where Do You Go To My Lovely?' (while the heads of the endangered species from the now wrecked Damien Hirst artwork still bounced around him on the blood-'n'brain'n'formaledehyde'n'bits-of-acoustic-guitar splattered pavement) with a stiff-upper-lipped "the show must go on" and "business as usual" attitude reminiscent of those cheerful cockernees who refused to blub when they were singing "Knees up Mavver Brahn!" dahn ver chube durin' ver Blitz and made them proud to be British. Indeed, so impressed by the busker's stead-fast refusal to succumb to his nightmarish wounds were the aghast onlookers that several of them had already started to applaud and toss coins when the still bravely busking Peter Baker was suddenly seized and ripped to bloody shreds by what looked strangely like the Queen Alien that Sigourney Weaver offs with a forklift truck at the end of Aliens (except without a head) but what was in fact Peter Ringer's decapitated Margaret Thatcher lookalike hi-tech sex-doll gone berserk and commencing to run amok. The frankensteining android would later be blown to tiny bits in Hampstead by a massive air-fuel bomb dropped from a hastily unmothballed Vulcan supersonic bomber (also killing 9,874 totally innocent civilians and hideously burning or grotesquely maiming a further 67,980) but not before it had carved a swathe of carnage through the capital's terrified denizens that made the Great Fire Of London, Jack The Ripper, The Luftwaffe, Dennis Nielsen, The Retropolitan Police and The Black Death combined look like a buncha kindhearted amateurs whose hearts weren't really in it.

"What the fuck...?" spluttered Home Office Hostage Scenario negotiator Pete Ringer uncomprehendingly as he blinked moronically up at the automatic weapon toting black-balaclavaed figures that loomed ominously over him. *LIKE DEATH!*

"Colonel Dan Daniels, SAS!" barked one of the figures by way of introduction, brutally. "Rang doorbell. No reply! Kicked door in! Just in time! Destroyed terrorist android with minimal use of lethal force! Just doing job! **SAH!**"

"B-b-b-b-b-b...." shockstammered the cripplingly traumatised and utterly heartbroken Ringer, pathetically.

"No time! Cop this!" spat Daniels, expertly whacking a huge syringe full of top smack and government issue Combat Cocaine into Ringer's shockporcelained arm.

"Entire cabinet kidnapped by Northern terrorists!" woofed Daniels as his men shoved Ringer's now corpse-rigid body under a cold shower, towelled him off and dressed him in the only Armani suit they could find that hadn't been utterly fucked by the rancid tidal wave. Stringer suddenly spasmed savagely. Then he growled grotesquely through gritted teeth and violently shrugged off the helping hands of the squaddies.

"Terrorists!" he hissed horribly as the potent smack'n'-coke pick-me-up rapidly restored him to his senses. **"Let's kill the cunts!"** he added, insanely, whilst punching a hole in the sexan-droidclawshredded and blood'n'shit'n'machine-oil smeared wallpaper covered wall with his fist. "But first - gimmee more of them drugs, **NOW!**"

"Cop **THIS!**" bellowed Colonel Dan Daniels, sticking a pristine £50 note up each of Ringer's nostrils, opening up a suit-case full of top quality Royal Family strength coke and ramming the civil servant's head into it with brutally efficient gusto. Like in Scarface.

Ringer snonked instinctively and experienced the blind-ingly intense whiteness, depth of perception and chillingly cold enlightenment that IS Instantdrugnirvana! *BOOM SHANKA!* His evil Tory head was suddenly filled with sickeningly grotesque images of working class babies impaled on bayonets! *UREKA!* He was once again filled with sneering contempt for both the proletariat (who had to make do with shitty watered down and adulterated versions of the ace drugs he saw as his birthright) AND all those deluded ning-nang-nongy pillocks like Buddhists who spent years fasting, praying, chanting and contemplating their navels to achieve an "enlightenment" that the stupid fucking mugs didn't seem to realise could just as easily be achieved by having a line of Diana-strength charlie and a quick wank! He was restored! He was once again a brutally efficient and utterly evil catspaw of the dominant ideology!

"**HA!**" he roared, internally, as he suddenly realised in a blindingly brilliant piece of chemically assisted and culturally acute auto-analysis that would have had your average Professor of Cultural Studies wanking like a chimp with glee that his current circumstances were uncannily similar to those of Charlie Sheen at the beginning of Apocalypse Now when the military pigs come to get him to go off the insane Colonel Kurtz. Except cooler! MUCH cooler!

"Held hostage up North. Somewhere called Bradford!" continued Daniels with frighteningly brutal military efficiency. "Normal procedure. You keep 'em talking. We steam in. Shoot Johnny Terrorist in back after he's surrendered! Retire! Write book! Make millions! OK! Woof! Woof! *LET'S GO!*"

Suddenly the roof of Ringer's Mayfair flat was ripped clean off by 4 Harrier jump jets using chains and huge hooks and Ringer and the SAS troopers all grabbed hold of lengths of rope and were winched into the gaping bellies of hovering jet helicopters which then screamed off up to Bradford to kick some fucking terrorist **ARSE!**

In the hi-tech weaponry and sweaty trained-killer squaddie packed guts of the throbbing chopper, Pete Ringer smiled a cruel smile. And came again. Quietly.

CHAPTER 18d

PIG!

'Much of the violence is near Uvira. It has long had an air of menace but the mobs of young men parading through the streets waving machetes, metal bars and wooden stakes are new. They believe they are invincible, magically shielded by the twigs and leaves sprouting from their pockets and stuffed into headbands.'

The Guardian, 1997

"Hold your fire!" barked top pig Frank Stank. Two hundred flack jacketed elite combat cops reluctantly eased their twitching fingers off the hair triggers of their oiled and gleaming Heckler-Koch semi-auto slag-slaughtering sub machine guns. They were like machines, these men, tensed and turgid terrorist-terminators trained to take out the enemies of the state with extreme prejudice. Four hundred eyes squinted hawkishly at the dilapidated council house that contained their prey. Two hundred stunted libidos screamed for the subliminal sexual release that could only be achieved by the savage, slashing penetration of human flesh by thousands of titanium tipped explosive dum-dum bullets.

"Fuck me, vers farsands of 'em" chirruped cheerful cockernee costermonger-stylee rent boy cum judge stabber cum punk performance artist, Ricky Tickytimebomb as he twitched aside the dust caked lace curtains to stare nervously at the assembled forces of Law, Order and Decency.

"Today is a good day for someone else to die!" spat anarcho-psychopath Justine Justice as she heaved a bandoleer of heavy duty crossbow bolts across her massive yet amazingly firm breasts. "Hang on, what does *she* want?"

A mini-skirted woman with massive blonde hair was teetering up the drive clutching a cracked tea-cup. The top pig's megaphone spluckfustered and squawked liked an electroduck spitting spunk into a 3 bar electric fire and spasming like a twat hatted techno raver at the very peak of an E laced with domestos overdose heart attack as the voltage thrashed its cyborg body into a pulsating shitfest of blood, wire and sparking metal feathers. The boss pig told the lurching leopard-skin-tighted and low cleavaged lady that she was in great danger and ought, for her own sake, to retreat to a safe distance.

"FUCK OFF, COPPER!" shouted the heavily made up and come-to-bed-eyed woman, pivoting on one high-heeled foot and giving the assorted swine a Kes-style two-fingered salute.

Inside the knackered council flat the assorted besieged terrorists adrenally spasmed as the doorbell chimes rang in a chintzy versh of 'The Internationale'.

"Oh bugger!" ejaculated black belt karate master and ex-army demolitions expert Aki Khan as he fingered the 560 year old Himalayan throwing knife that his grandfather had bequeathed him with the wheezily requested deathbed wish that the youngster only use said weapon to slash the throats of fascists and bureaucrats.

"It's Mrs Harris from number 15!" explained Aki, "She's a ruddy nutter who relentlessly pursues a lifestyle of stereotypical Northern slapperdom which mainly consists of getting off her face on gin every afternoon before attempting to shag her way through the 289 most sexually desirable men in the greater West Yorkshire conurbation. She's been after me for years!"

"Hmmm!" murmured Justine, stroking her Arnie-style steroid-swollen jaw. "Is she the same Candice Harris who was rejected by the Turner Prize committee last year because her art wasn't middle-class, poncey and utterly fucking shit enough?"

"The same!" grunted Aki.

"Better let her in then! We could always do with more hostages!" laughed Justine, nodding over her shoulder to the corner of the room where the entire inner cabinet of the current Tory government sat trussed-up like the one-eared pig in Reservoir Dogs in stinking pools of their own shit, piss, blood and sweat.

It's really annoying the way Tories always void both bladder and bowel when you slash their throats open, thought Justine (who was a bit of a hygiene nut on the quiet) as she surveyed the pile of still twitching Tory corpse meat.

"Hang on, I'm coming!" shouted Aki as he ran down the stairs two at a time.

"You soon will be!" laughed Candice Harris, gingering her cleavage and feeling her clitoris stiffen in anticipation of the soon-come furious fuck-fest.

"What do you want?" yelled Aki as he threw the front door open wide in the cocky knowledge that the assorted heavily armed pigs wouldn't dare fire whilst they thought the creme-de la creme of Tory scumbastardry were still alive and rescuable.

"Have you got a cup of sperm, I mean sugar?" purred Mrs Harris seductively, pushing her pert breasts into Aki's face.

"For fuck's sake, Candice!" screamed Aki, suddenly coming over all hysterically eloquent. "Your behaviour is extremely inappropriate! Have you not noticed that we're engaged in a thrillingly tense hostage stroke siege scenario here!?"

"Oh shut up and fuck !" snarled Candice contemptuously as, in one fluid movement, she tossed the now redundant tea cup over her naked left shoulder, pushed Aki down onto the doormat, whipped out his impressively proportioned and heavily veined purple headed yoghurt squirter, mounted him and proceeded to milk him with her incredibly strong vaginal muscles whilst slamming the door shut.

"Aaaaaargh! Aroooogah! HeeeeeYAH! AaaaaaRUMPH!" screamed Aki as he was brought to the very brink of mindmushingly intense orgasm again and again by the most incredible cunt in Christendom.

"My **GOD!**" wailed Stank as the inhuman hollering reached his hairy and mole spotted ears. "They're torturing the poor woman! OK, lock and load everybody, we can't afford to wait for the SAS, on my command, we're going IN!"

"You're going **NOWHERE!**" roared a lean and muscular figure clad all in black with his face covered in sexy dark green camouflage paint (like Arnie in Commando and again in Predator) who appeared wraithlike at the top pig's side.

"Who the fuck are you?" squealed the boss pig as he stared into the clear blue eyes of this obviously well bred apparition.

"Colonel Dan Daniels, Special Air Service!" woofed the man in black, threateningly fingering the knuckleduster handled combat knife that dangled from his Sam Browne Belt. "I'm taking over this operation before you flat footed plods make a pig's ear out of it!"

"Wha? Y-you can't just ...." spluttered the king of the pigs seconds before Colonel Dan Daniels silenced his pathetic lower middle class whining with a snake-like strike on the jaw with his manly left fist that sent the blood-spurting pig flying back in slo mo to land with a sickening and spine cracking thud on top of the roof of a panda car from whence he rolled to land with a audible flump in a crumpled heap of humiliated pigflesh.

"What's going on?" bellowed Justine Justice as she finished dipping her blow darts into a an old-skool style round gold fish bowl full of highly toxic buffalo-snake urine that she'd bought in a bulk order with a stolen credit card from a Chinese herbal remedy shop in London's Gerrard Street.

"Strewf!" spat Ricky Tickytimebomb as he leant on his bloodrusted genuine samurai sword and surveyed the bickering forces of corporate bastardry through the filth smeared council house bedroom window. "Wot appears to be h'occuring is that ver top rozzer is 'avin' is blinkin' noggin bashed in a no 'old's barred demarcational dispute wiv some SAbleedin'S geezer whilst, mean-while, in the 'allway of this very cancil rat an'marse, our mucker Aki is getting 'is tubes cleaned by that bird from number 15!"

"So! The SAS!" snarled Justine, contemptuously as she rolled a stogie from side to side between her utterly seductive collagen enhanced lips like Clint as The Man With No Name in all them cool spag Westerns. "That means that they'll pretend to negotiate whilst planning a night-time attack with stun grenades where they'll shoot us in the back after we surrender..."

"Coo, larve a fackin' dack!" babbled the cheerful cockernee shittrouserdly. "We're facked and no mistake! What we gonna dooooo! What we gonna doooooo!"

KRAK!

Justine backhanded the fearful cockernee with a Mighty Joe Young style fist and started barking out orders.

"Bring up the catapult! Prepare the petrol bombs! It's time to cook some **PORK!** HAHAHAHAHAHA!"

"OK, Lieutenant, you know the drill?!" inquired SAS Colonel Dan Daniels of the dapperly dressed posho with the mobile phone and the steel-rimmed Himmler specs who stood in front of him.

"Yes, sir!" said Pete Ringer, government hostage scenario negotiator-in-chief silkily. "I keep them talking, make a few minor concessions and generally soften them up until it gets dark and you and your highly trained team of assassins can barge in, rescue all the hostages and shoot all the terrorist in the back after they've surrendered just like you did in the seige of the Iranian embassy way back in the good old days when Maggie was in power. **SIEG HEIL!!!!**"

"Make it so!" smiled Colonel Dan Daniels who modelled himself on Captain Jean Luc Picard out of Star Trek: The Next Generation - except without the woolly liberal emotional blancman-geness.

BRUP! BRUP! brupped Justine's mobile phone.

"Hello, Justine Justice, terrorist shewolf!" answered Justine, politely.

"Hi, Justine!" slurred Pete Ringer in his best let-it-all-hang-out social worker voice. "My name's Peter Ringer, I work for the Home Office. Now, look, I'm sure we can work this out so that nobody gets hurt. Why don't you tell me what it is that you want and I promise you that I'll do my very best to...."

"DIE, PIG!" screamed Justine, puce-facedly and broke the connection.

THWONGHAH! thwongahed the catapult.

"What the bloody hell!?" murmured Pete Ringer as he stared at the clumsy missile that was hurtled high into the air above him by the giant catapult that suddenly jutted from the bedroom window.

The slick gobbed professional liar stared in horror as the mis-sile broke up in mid air and divided into a score or so of individual projectiles which, with their momentum lost, now crashed down onto the forces of piggery like the multiplied fists of an angry and righteous God.

"**AYEEEAH!**" "**AAAAAAAAAARHG!**" and "**FUUUUUUUU-UUUUUUUUUUCK!**" screamed a score or more of coppers as they were suddenly and spectacularly turned into fat spitting human candles by the deadly rain of napalm and white phosphorous molotov cocktails.

The surrounded terrorists, surveying their handiwork, laughed their cocks and cunts off.

"Music...." roared Justine above the competing cacophonies of pig squealing and terrorist hilarity, "...**ON!**"

The jovial sounds of the classic recording of 'The Laughing Policeman' bellowed out from huge speakers in the council house living room. Watching TV crews pissed themselves with excitement. Burning filth plus top soundtrack! Ace footage! Arriba! Arriba! Sex on a fucking stick minus the fucking stick or **WHAT!**

"**BONG!** Death and destruction on a Bradford council estate! **BONG!** The cabinet hostage crisis takes a new and savage twist! **BONG!** Fifteen police officers dead and another 27 injured, several of them severely! **BONG!** Good evening, we're going straight over to the scene of the cabinet hostage crisis in Bradford, West Yorkshire, where this already bloody conflict looks set to take another and possibly even more violent turn...."

Justine, Aki, Ricky, Candice and the gaggle of wild eyed teenage scum known collectively as The Pudsey Posse were huddled around a tiny battery powered TV.

"OK!" roared Justine, her eyes alight with the bloodlust of imminent battle, "We can expect the trained killer dogs of the SAS to come blasting through the walls firing submachine guns from the hip at any second! ACTION STATIONS! MUSIC...**ON!** "

Outside, behind the barrier of armoured cars and tanks, the forces of the state felt their Jungian collective sphincter tighten as their Jungian collective ears were blasted with the defiant tones of 'Men Of Harlech' (Zulu movie soundtrack versh).

"**GO GO GO GO GO GO!**" screamed SAS Colonel Dan Daniels.

KARUMPH! Huge holes appeared in the walls of the council house. **BRAAAAKA! BRAAAAAAKA! BRAK!** barked the snazzy fired-from-the-hip sub-machine guns of the SAS troopers as they emerged wraith like and running at full tilt from the surrounding murk. **KARUMPH! BRAAAKA! BRAAAAAAKA!**

BRAK! KER-ASH! Tinkle tinkle! Ker-UMPH! BRAK! BRAAAA-KA! BRAAAAAAKA! BRAK! OOF! AAAAAAAAARGH!
screamed Mars, God of War, as yet more heavily booted absailing
SAS men smashed through the upstairs windows tossing stun
grenades willy nilly and firing at anything that didn't look like a
hostage.

Silence.

The front door of the spookily quiet and smoking council
house flew open. Out walked an erect SAS trooper. *"HUZZAH!"*
roared the watching pigs and squaddies spontaneously. ***SPLAT!***
went the body of the SAS man as it fell full length on its face to
reveal a hideous array of home made spears, crossbow bolts,
knives and hatchets sticking out of its highly trained and utterly
dead back.

"EAT HEAD, PIG FASCIST SCUM!" bellowed a blood-
caked Justine Justice triumphantly as **(THWONGHAH! THWONG-
HAH!)** her comrades in extreme direct action for its own sake
catapulted the decapitated heads of the slaughtered SAS men
straight back at the watching forces of repression.

"WOW!" ejaculated ITN cameraman Bruce Babbington as
he caught one of the oncoming SAS heads in a freak close-up
and noticed that it gripped between its tightly clenched teeth a
fizzing stick of red dynamite.

**KER-BLAAAAAM! AAAAARGH! OH MY GOD! MY
FUCKING LEGS! NOOOOOOOO! AAAAARGH! KER-UMPH!
AYEEEEEAH!**
Chunks of white hot machinery and even harder to replace
expensively trained ragged ended bloody body parts whizzed
through the air as the hastily improvised heads of death exploded
savagely behind the piggish barricade.

"Coo, lumee!" chirruped Ricky Tickytimebomb, nursing a
hard-on a cat couldn't scratch as he surveyed the spectac pork
barbecue with relish. "H'oive nevah seen so many pigs
a-screaming in h'agony in all my blessed loife, blow me if it does-
n't warm the cockles of yer blinkin' 'art, so it does!"

"OK, my babies" murmured a similarly excited Justine
Justice, "let's get out there and finish the bastards off whilst
they're still traumatised!"

"ZIGGER ZAGGER, ZIGGER ZAGGER!" chanted half the
teenage scum the tabloids called The Pudsey Posse.

　　　"**OI! OI! OI!**" replied the other half, slamming the shafts of their crude but wickedly effective home made spears into the carpet with gusto.

　　　"Um, hang on a minute" interjected Aki, "you've got us all bollock naked and smeared in archaic scribblings done in red paint augmented by the blood of the Prime Minister. Are you sure this is going to make us invulnerable when we ton out of here in a hooting, hollering Lord Of The Flies style mob!"

　　　"Oh ye of little faith!' laughed Justine, grabbing Aki by his ears and planting as huge slobbery kiss on his perfectly formed forehead. "Look, I'll explain it all one more time. One of the more interesting features of 19th century imperialism was that the fight-backs against the technologically superior Europeans invariably involved some attempt to use magick. The best known example is, of course, the Ghost Dance of the Plains Indians who thought they could make themselves bullet proof by ripping their nipples off and painting themselves with doo-lally doodlings but other examples include the so called fuzzy wuzzys of the Sudan and the Boxers in China. Now, then, those mugs bolloxed it up and got their heads kicked in. We, however, have got it sussed. When we go out there with our teeth gritted, waving our gleaming weapons aloft like fucking maniacs, the pigs will let fly with every gun they've got and the bullets will just spang off our magically invulnerable bods. And if you want proof, ask the 20 SAS muthas we've just offed without any of us getting so much as a scratch. Did that fucking rule or what!? With your bubbling teenage enthusiasm for gratuitous violence and my massive in-depth knowledge of arcane magick, we are unstoppable! There are psychopaths still abed in England who will **rue** the fact that they were not here this night! Onward! My cherubs! Deadpigcity awaits! **HUZZAH!**"

　　　"**HUZZAH!**" roared everybody else in the room, suddenly frothmouthed and boggle-eyed as the magick viking berzerker serum they'd taken earlier was kicked into action by the code word **"rue"**.

　　　"**IWANNAKILLEEPIGEENOW!**" howled bollock naked and wild haired recent recruit Candice Harris as she leaped around the room like an electrocuted salmon on a hot tin roof whilst clutching two massive meat cleavers and pissing herself violently in a savage bloodlust frenzy of **HATE!**

　　　"OK!" screamed Justine at a magickally enhanced head-in-the-bass-bins at a Motorhead gig style 456 decibels. "Let's kick pig **ASS!**"

"AYEEEEEEEEEEEEEEEEEEEEEEEEEEHAH!" screamed the terrorist collective as they threw themselves out of the shattered windows and hurtled to the attack.

It was just like the bit at the end of Butch Cassidy and The Sundance Kid where Butch and The Kid, surrounded by tooled-up pigs, decide to go out in one final blaze of suicidal glory! With one difference!

"**BUDDA! BUDDA! BUDDA!**" roared the pig machine guns.

"Don't shoot!" whined blood caked Home Office negotiator Pete Ringer pathetically, "they've got the PM with them!"

"Ha! Fooled you! I'm not really the Prime Minister" said a figure who it had to be admitted did look an awful lot like the PM. "Actually I'm teenage terrorist Carol 'The Cat' Williams, leader of the so called Pudsey Posse and I have disguised myself by flaying the PM's corpse and wearing his skin as a disguise. Eat spear, scumbag!"

"**Urgle gurgle urgle!**" grunted Pete Ringer bloodsplutteringly as the home made assegai punctured his lily white throat.

"**Die, bitch!**" giggled Colonel Dan Daniels who had been pushed to the brink of insanity by recent events as he levelled his snazzy sub machine gun at the horrific figure of the teenage lass dressed in the skin of the dear departed Prime Minister and squeezed the trigger, sexily...

"**DAKKA DAKKA DAKKA!**" shat the machine gun.

"**SPANG! SPANG! SPANG!**" went the bullets as they ricocheted off harmlessly.

"Whoops, was that your cock?" queried Candice Harris archly as she smashed the top squaddie in the nads with a hefty meat cleaver, spitting the cunt in two and killing him instantly.

The rest of the battle went pretty much the same way. End result - Terrorists 567, pigs and SAS - O! Live on prime time TV!

Result or **WHAT!?**

CHAPTER 19

FATCAT!

'For a long time, as I have said, the strong feudal habits of subordination and deference continued to tell upon the working class. The modern spirit has now almost entirely dissolved those habits, and the anarchical tendency of our worship of freedom in and for itself...is becoming very manifest...All this, I say, tends to anarchy.'

Matthew Arnold, *Culture & Anarchy*

The building thrust forth from the Docklands earth like the phallus of a buried giant.

KA FUCKING BOOM!

went its rounded bell-end as it suddenly disintegrated in a massive fireball.

"Right! We're in, we're tanked up on battle-strength super-cocaine, we're kitted out in state of the art combat armoured exoskeletons and we have at our disposal enough James Bond

style hi-tech weaponry to destroy a large army. Let's do it!" barked
Mick over the in-suit intercom.

"WOOF!" barked back the elite 200 strong squad of ultra-
terrorists as they fingered the triggers of their assorted hi-tech
weapons, unleashing a tidal wave of flame, metal and laser beam
death straight into the crowded ranks of the lobotomised £2-an-
hour security guards who ran full tilt towards them like lemmings
on angel dust and collectively died like dogs with hard-ons for
excruciating pain and traumatic amputation. Heads exploded,
super-heated internal organs slapped against the walls, arms and
legs detached themselves from flame-encased torsoes to be sent
skidding along corridors slick with blood and shit where they
collected in the corners, forming weird and gruesome sculptures
which would have had Damien Hirst tugging his tiny todger at the
utterly gratuitous and unadulterated art-wankyness of it all had he
but been there. Which he wasn't. The wanker.

Corridor by corridor, room by room and floor by floor, the
200 top terrorists shot, punched, kicked and headbutted their way
through the mangled flesh of the running dogs of corporate
security. But there were not 200 now, not nearly half that number.
Some fell victim to the weapons carried by their peaked capped
and glassily smiling foe, others to the building's fully automated
laser defence system, still others to craftily concealed hi-tech
booby traps.

On and on fought the 100, clearing floor after floor, killing ten,
twenty, a hundred times their own number - on ever downwards
towards their ultimate destination - the private sanctuary of Sir
Andrew Taylor-Bjork buried in a bunker almost 20 stories beneath
the increasingly manked-to-fuck building.

By the time our brave band of heroes reached the ground
floor there were but three score of them left alive. By the time
they'd fought down a further 20 floors that number was halved and
halved again.

And by the time the last of Sir Andrew Taylor-Bjork's
incredibly well trained posse of eunuch orphan superninja personal bodyguards had been eviscerated they were down to one - Mad
Mick The Needle.

Mick realised that he should be really, really upset. He'd
just lost his mum, his 6 brothers and sisters and the bird he really
fancied (ie Karen Skull) plus another 191 really good chums to the

forces of oppression. But he wasn't. "Perhaps I'll cry later," he thought as he booted open the gold-hinged heavy oak door that was the last barrier that remained between himself and his prey, "but for now I've got to concentrate on offing Fascist Numero Uno, The Top Tory, Mr Evil himself, the one and only Sir Andrew Taylor-Bjork and....and there he is......"

"Good evening, Mr The Needle, do come in, I've been expecting you!" gushed the fat bastard sat stroking a fluffy white pussy cat.

"No talk, you die!" pidgined an overadrenalised Mick as he raised his laser rifle and squinted down the sights at the fat Tory bastard who sat smirking in a plush black calf leather swivel chair only 10 meters in front of him.

"I don't think so, pleb!" spat Taylor-Bjork as he stuck his right index finger into the cat's eye. Too late Mick realised that the "pussy cat" was not in fact a pussy cat at all, it was a craftily disguised remote control device and what it controlled was a hypodermic needle concealed within Mick's state-of-the art battle suit which had just jabbed 300cc of extremely potent paralysing drug straight into his superbly over-muscled arse with the end result that he could no...longer....*move*....

"One nil! **KGHGHGHGHGHGHH!**" yelled Sir Andrew Taylor-Bjork as he leapt to his feet, punched the air, threw the fake cat over his shoulder and attempted to imitate the roar of a stadium crowd.

"Total victory is **MINE!**" thundered the fat man, his spittle flecked lips now mere centimetres away from Mick's rigidly staring eyes. Every fibre of Mick's very being ached to smash the corpulent corporatist cretin straight between his porcine eyes. But he couldn't. He couldn't do anything. He just had to stand there like a twat whilst Taylor-Bjork ranted and raved and breathed caviar breath all over him.

"So you thought you'd got the better of me when you aborted your attack on the Scottish castle HQ of the mungbean-currymunchers, did you? HA! I'm disappointed with you, laddy!" chortled the capitalist shit as he lit a huge and very expensive cigar and wiggled his bushy eyebrows.

"OK, so you've destroyed my corporate HQ! So what? Big deal! We were insured! So you've killed over 30,000 of my employees? HA! Downsizing by terrorist action! When I think of all the money you've saved me in the redundancy payments I was going to have to shell out tomorrow when every single employee was going to be replaced by a super efficient robot, why, I could kiss you, in fact, I think I will!"

Suddenly Taylor-Bjork's blubbery Tory lips were on Mick's, tongues and everything! **Yuk!** Unfortunately for the snog crazed meat mogul, however, the deadly paralysing toxin with which he had injected our hero had not paralysed the lad's vomitory system and thus it was that Mick, without a single voluntary muscle movement, managed to puke straight down Sir Andrew Taylor-Bjork's Tory bastard throat.

"BHJJJHJJHHYYuuuuuuuuuRGHHHHHHHHHHHHH!" gargled the shocked Tory snogger as his body reacted violently to the diced carrot invasion by throwing him backwards in a flailing armed fury fest of ferociously fucked up fat bastardry ago-go.

"BORK-HOOOOOEY!" exploded the Thatcher-worshipping sub-human as his own vomit rose to meet and mingle with Mick's.

"WhiiiiiiiiiiiipSPLAT!" went the mingled vomfest as it lashed around the lavishly decorated boardroom, pebbledashing every surface with an inch-thick parmesan cheese reeking gunklayer.

"EuuURGH! HarARarArRLPH!" vommed his sirship violently. *"ARK-huuuuuuuuuuRKbLUuuuuuuUUUUUFHKAPAuh-BLORGK!!!!!".* At last, when the projectile vomiting and the shaking had ceased, Sir Anthony turned to the frozen Mad Mick with fury blazing in his evil Tory eyes.

He whipped out a gold plated Colt Magnum Python loaded with high explosive **DEATH!** and back handed Mick savagely across the forehead. Bits of scalp and skull spattered insignificantly amongst the Jackson Pollockesque backdrop of mixed proletarian and plutocratic vomit.

"For that" screamed Sir Andrew in a puce faced rage, **"YOU DIE, CUNT!"**

Sir Andrew raised the gun until it was level with Mick's eyeline. Slowly he started to squeeze the trigger....

"UUUUUUUURGH!" roared Sir Andrew, suddenly clutching his chest, **"Uugahgahgahgah...."**. The fat man wobbled forwards and having wobbled forwards he then wobbled back. But the massive gun, held firmly in his right hand, never wavered from its target. Mick, dazed, in massive pain and still feeling a tad nauseous, looked on fascinated. He knew that his life now hung by a gossamer thread. If only the bastard would just hurry up and die of the heart attack or whatever it was before he summoned up the energy to pull that trigger. If onl

KERBLAAAAAAM!

SPLAT!

CHAPTER 21

VAMPIRE!

'The last dragon king left a daughter
who winged her way here over water
            So, for sport, so we
thought, we bought guns and we sought her.
      We hunted and hounded and cornered
and caught her.
A lumbering, cumbersome, fiery old snorter,
            She turned out far tougher than
we had first thought her."

Nick Toczek, The Last Great Dragoness

Up until the moment the hated terrorist she-wolf Justine Justice had kidnapped the entire Tory Cabinet, trussed them up, offed them and then used their blood to concoct a weird, magickal all-over body paint which made pig ammunition ping, spang and spad-ow harmlessly off the wearer's body, the 666 members of the secret and sinister cabal who really ran the world had little reason to know the word "Undercliffe".

But now the word was branded deep into the ancient, wrinkled forebrains of all 666 of the vice-rotted vampiric viceroys of sheer evil who gathered that evening in a crumbling castle in the fetid heart of an ancient forest hidden deep in the misty midst of the Carpathian mountains.

Outside the castle - smoking crack, injecting each other in the eyeballs with heroin or just running naked playing a strange game of tig with sharp sticks, were the 666 Igors who had driven or flown their 666 masters to this most unholy of meeting places.

Inside the great keep of the sinister castle sat the black clad ranks of the 666 vampires who really run t'ings, seen? So strong was the collective reek of evil that stunned rats toppled out of the rafters overhead and imploded in mid air. The vamps were all British, of course, all founder members of the organisation now known as The Conservative Party, naturally, and they were all at least 10,000 years old, some of them three or four times that.

They had been herding the humans towards their current state of alienated wage slavery under the savage rule of planet raping multinational corporations for millennia, fighting an utterly ruthless and brilliantly effective long term counter-insurgency campaign against the human race's instinctive and utterly natural yearning for communism, fun and dossing.

They had sabotaged the revolution in Russia and subverted or simply crushed every working class revolt ever since. If bribery, terrorism or coercion failed they would use brute force and could sleep soundly at night in their luxury, humanbabyskin covered beds - safe in the knowledge that, should push ever come to shove, the sheepdogs would always have more (and sharper) teeth than the sheep.

But Undercliffe had changed all that. **Undercliffe!** *AAAAAAAAARGH!* For the past two weeks the ruling-class pariahs had been waking up screaming whilst tangled up in the stinking folds of their piss soaked and shit caked humanbabyskin sheets. **"Undercliffe!"** they screamed, **"Undercliffe! UNDER-CLIFFE!** *UNDERCLIFFE!!!!!!!!!!!!!!!!!!!!!!!!!!!!* "

So, outside the castle the Igors, all 666 of them, ramble, puke and fight in an orgy of lobotimised dwarf-serf overindulgence whilst inside the gothic fortress, sat in rank after rank of deep, plush humanbaby-skin covered armchairs, lounge the creme de la creme of late capitalism's secret masters - The Vampiric Elite! Some of them resemble toads, others shaven whales. There is more than a touch of the simian about most of the rest. The general level of hygiene is low (by current world standards). Between them these "men" control 97% of the world economy and over 89% of its media. Each one of them is a mass murderer many times over. Most are also rapists and paedophiles. All of them bum dogs.

A heavy pall of cigar smoke hangs over the murmuring crowd. The murmuring increases as a figure in a massive dog costume mounts the spotlit podium.

Within seconds the murmuring dissipates to be replaced gradually by a plosive symphony of rabid barking.

The costumed figure waits patiently until he has the room's undivided attention.

"Gentlemen" says the Top Dog, "I hereby call to attention this, the second emergency meeting of The Grand Masonic Order of Aryan Supremacist Dogbummers (Conservative & Unionist)."

"Get down, Shep" murmur the crowd collectively.

"All hail Akra, he who gripped the mane of the she-bitch Albion! All hail Mutra blah blah blah blah blah etc" waffles the vampire in the giant dog costume.

A chorus of burps, farts and grunts erupts from the restless audience, most of who were eager to commence with the animal sex and child rape orgy that inevitably follows such meetings.

"The danger we face today is greater than any we have previously faced!" shouts the Top Dog. The sudden increase in volume has the desired dramatic effect. The burping and farting levels drop significantly.

"We have enslaved our foes. We have destroyed their leaders. We have kept the rest drugged, bribed or frightened. And if all else fails, my brothers, we have always had resort to the fist!"

"FIST! FIST! FIST!" scream the now aroused crowd.

"But today, my brothers, we face...*disaster!* "

The crowd, for the first time, falls utterly silent - apart from an 11,756 year old arms manufacturer and media magnate in the middle of the 57th row who can't control himself and is having a vigorous wank despite the "shushing" of those around him.

"You are all aware of the situation in **Undercliffe**...."

A frightened murmuring ripples through the crowd.

"I ask you now to grant the Grand Cabal of The Grand Masonic Order of Aryan Supremacist Dogbummers full executive powers in regard to the elimination of this latest Red menace! Say you Aye?!"

"Aye!" roars the plutocratic audience, "Aye!"

"MARKET FORCES!" screams the vampire in the Giant

Dog costume.

"HEIL!" roars the wolf pack.

"MARKET FORCES!" screams the vampire in the Giant Dog costume.

"HEIL!" roars the wolf pack.

 "MARKET FORCES!" screams the vampire in the Giant Dog costume.

"HEIL!" roars the wolf pack.

 "MARKET FORCES!"screams the vampire in the Giant Dog costume.

"HEIL!" roars the wolf pack.

"Then let the games....," shouts the Dogmeister, pulling aside the folds of his skilfully crafted Giant Dog cossy to reveal an erect but unimpressive sexual member covered in herpes, syphilis and BSE boils, scars and lesions, *"BEGIN!"*.

"HUZZAH!" screams the crowd - all of whom have now stripped off their extremely expensive business suits to reveal the dyed black baby seal skin pervo-bondage gear they habitually wear underneath.

And as they huzzah, their seating folds back into vast wings to facilitate the sudden appearance of a deep central pit full of chained up and screaming cute furry animals and human children for the ruling class scum to rape, torture and eat at their leisure.

CHAPTER 22 - CONSIDER IT THE AMBIENT ROOM IN AN EXTREME SPEED GARAGE GABBA DISCO FULL OF ANGEL DUST CRAZED PSYCHOPATHS WITH CHAINSAWS IF YOU LIKE.

HELL!

'Oh, God! No! No! No!

This can't be happening to me! Total blackness! Terrifying screams!

God! Please get me out of here! I'm on fire!

The flames are sizzling me! The smoke is choking me! The stench of burning flesh is turning my stomach!

I can't stand this pain. Somebody get me out of here!

This is a gruesome description of one more teenager who just took the last fatal step

down the eternally damning stairway to hell.

Rick Jones, Stairway To Hell - The Well-Planned Destruction Of Teens, 1988

Mick felt himself falling, falling, falling....... An hour later he was still falling. And then he smashed face first into a grassy meadow.

"UUUUUUUUUH!" groaned Mick as his ears slowly filled with the seductive coo and twitter of a sentimentalised and perfect English countryside at about 7.00 on a beautiful summer's evening. He opened his eyes. An primarysexorganengorgingly beautiful insect sat smoking a relatively ginormous spliff atop an impossibly Disneyesque white-spotted red mushroom.

"Alright, Mick!" chirped the beautiful bluey-greeny beatle. "Fancy a blow-back?"

Spielbergian tendrils of strangely sentient spliffsmoke streamed out of the insect's flared nostrils and homed like pigeons desperate for a piss straight up Mick's greedily gaping snotpits.

"BOOM SHANKA!" thought Mick as he experienced instantdrugnirvana.

Mick glided, he glode, he *glid* across the grass, steel toe-capped DM shod feet limply dangling mere centimetres above the green tendrils of lush vegetation that wafted gently in the almost imperceptible but definitely strawberry-scented breeze. The insect had by now transformed itself into a multi-dimensional and kaleidoscopic space snake which gently penetrated and threaded the reality around Mick's hover-gliding form.

"Please allow me to introduce myself" said the snake. "I'm a man of wealth and taste...."

"ie The Dev?" asked Mick, quietly, orgasms popping into his bubbling brain as he spoke each syllable.

"Yo! Dat am moi!" said the snake, shitly. "And this dingly dell meets Lucy In The Sky type paradise is Hell ie where all the cool people go when they die..."

"Really?" murmured the extremely relaxed Mick as he drifted through the beautiful meadow with his feet not touching the ground. "I thought Hell was where all the people who didn't accept The Lord Jesus Christ (ie the "son" of the insane god "God") as their personal saviour went no matter whether they had been good or not, like?"

"Oh, people don't still believe that old bollocks, do they?" laughed the Dev. "It's true, of course, that all the born-again Christians do go to Heaven to spend eternity with the gibbering nuttah they call "God"" said the Dev, "but that's only because they're crap. All the crap people go to heaven and have a really shit time and all the cool people, like you for instance, go to Hell and have a fucking great time out of your boxes and doing what the fuck you want without some wanker with a Hitler complex interfering all the time like back on Earth."

"Fucking wow!" giggled Mick as The Dev brainflashed him a quick glimpse of heaven where all the dead Tories and suchlike crappos that Mick had offed in his corporeal existence were shown having a really shit time. "Far out!"

"Only thing is, Mick, me ole chum" said Satan, suddenly transmogrifying into Mr Spock from the original versh of Star Trek (ie the 3rd best programme ever made after Batman starring Adam West and Rhubarb and Custard). "The thing is, you can't stay...."

"Yah boo sucks!" moaned Mick, childishly.

"Sorry, but that's just the way it is," said Satan, suddenly transmogrifying into Justin Sullivan aka Slade The Leveller from 1980's Bradford rock band New Model Army. "The fact that you and Sir Andrew Taylor-Bjork died at the exact same nano-second has opened up a yin-and-yang style rupture in the space-time-continuum which has attracted both the forces of **Evil** ie the crazy god "God" and his legions of dead Christians, Tories, Fascists, Morrissey fans and other crap types as well as the forces of **Good** ie me and my legions of dead rebels, socialists and assorted demon muckers. It's gonna be a fight to the death, Mick, and it's going to be a fight which we can't afford to lose. Plus there's a shitload of Wattie out of The Exploited worshipping alien psychopaths from the Planet Milkin joining the party and we gotta get rid of the crappos before we do the aliens, savvy?"

"Uh, so far...." said Mick, hesitantly.

"So," said the Dev, patiently, "It's my intention to resurrect you and your recently slaughtered terrorist muckers including your mum and the amazingly attractive Karen Skull at exactly the moment in time when you were resurrected the last time round so that this time you can drop that neutron bomb that you picked up in your tractor beam on the corporate HQ of Sir Andrew Taylor-Bjork and then head off to Glastonbury and then timejump 55 years in the future (through a nearby and extremely convenient tantrIckally activated worm hole in time)."

"What," said Mick, "now?"

CHAPTER 23

ABORTED!

'Tay tay tay tay t-t-t-t-t tay tay/Take or leave us/Baby, please believe us/We ain't never gonna be respectable.'

Mel & Kim, 'Respectable'.

So thus it was that Mrs Needle and her mad son Mick found themselves hurtling through the upper stratosphere in really cool battle suits equipped with enough hi-tech James Bond style weaponry to win a world war (all of which Mick experienced with a nagging sense of deja vu) (all of which Mick experienced with a nagging sense of deja vu) (which, of course, Mad Mick experienced with yet *a further* layer of de-ja-vu).

"AAAAAAAAAAARGH!" screamed Mick suddenly as his physical body whiplashed under the savage impact of the blunt ends of *two* major karmic feedback loops.

"OK!" he screamed, "Attack aborted! Repeat! Attack aborted! Everybody hover over to me using the Iron Man style jets in the soles of your state of the art combat boots NOW!"

When he was sure that his well tasty team of tooled-up top terrorists were all gathered around him, Mick proceeded to explain the reason for his sudden change of mind.

"You're not going to believe this but I've just made a 50 year karmic round trip from the future and a trip to and from hell and, trust me, you do NOT want to go attacking that veggie castle down there because there's going to be a neutron bomb dropped on it just after I've ripped the top mungbeancurrymuncher's pointy little head off and we all get instantly killed which is really weird because I had a dream this morning - or was it yesterday morning? - anyway, this dream was sort of, uh, a premonition - have I said this before? - but anyway after we've all been killed this acts as some sort of a brake blah blah blah blah blah blah blah blah blah and you all said - "Yonks! What are we waiting for!" - and so we took off and attacked the corporate HQ and all got killed doing it and went to Hell but got resurrected by the Dev and sent back to this moment so we can neutron bomb the corporate HQ instead and then head off to Glasto to lend a hand to Justine Justice and go though an tantrickally operated temporal worm hole into the future and kick some alien ass! So are you up for it or what?"

"Yo!" bellowed the 200 top terrorists who were all so off their face on super strength battle cocaine that they would have said "Yo!" to anything as long as it involved an impossible amount of violence. And off they went towards the worm hole in time, neutron-bombing the corporate HQ on the way, natch.

Chapter 24

TYRANT!

'The bizarre stage antics of today's rock groups are possible because one man destroyed the moral barriers constraining public entertainment. Known for his gyrating pelvis and lewd gestures, that man was Elvis Presley.'

Bob Larson, Larson's Book Of Rock

Terrifyingly typhonic terrorist tyrant and huge-titted Queen Beast and Captain Mainwairing style self-elected leader of Satan's Gibbering Minions On Earth, Justine Justice, sits throbbingly naked on the massive gleaming white Throne Of Bone nastily cobbled together from the recently hydrochloric-acid-bathed skulls of assorted pigs, nazis, Channel 4 commissioning editors, squaddies, Tories and other enemies of the human race, each of whom died screaming and involuntarily shitting themselves whilst choking on their own entrails and writhing like an electrocuted epilectic dogs in the latter stages of hydrophobia after being suddenly and unexpectedly whacked up the arses with blunt boathooks and ripped in half ie in excruciating paroxysm of unbearable agony. Her hair is frizzed up around her finely chiselled head like a hastily snatched Polaroid (TM) of a multiple lightening strike on a gothed-up Mount Rushmore at midnight. Her

collagen enhanced cherry-red "fuck-me" lips are tightly pulled back
in a sardonically twitching rictus of hate to reveal gleaming white
teeth filed to needle-sharp points inna hungry cannibal stylee. Her
rolled back eyes are panda-ringed with kohl for that full-on Gaye
Advert-stroke-heroin chic-stroke-gothchick effect that says,
ironically, "I take smack and get battered, me". **HA!** Every
bronzed inch of her superbly over-muscled body (including, of
course, her massive but incredibly firm breasts) is oiled and
gleaming in the light of a thousand flickering human-fat candles
inserted in the top of a thousand evily grinning human skulls which
line the palpitating and mucous dripping walls of the Living Lodge
Of Flesh which she had made the HQ of the recently formed Anti-
Crap Jihad Party Of Great Britain (Magickist-Leninist). An insanely
twitching Mutant Superferret stands rampant on each of her
superbly overmuscled shoulders, hissing and whistling though
razor sharp yellow fangs, staring intently at fuck-all through boggly
little blood-red eyes. Frightening! In a Colonel Kurtz from
Apocalypse Now (ie the best movie ever made - **OFFICIAL!**)
stylee! Only more impressive, expensive and spooky and with
tons more dosh spent on the spesh FX.

Switching swiftly to Justine's POV we see the kneeling ranks
of the Lost Boys, The Pudsey Posse, The Yammering Proto-
Yippies, The Malboro Light Smoking Bone Marrow Suckers, The
Campaign For More Sex Violence And Drugs On TV, The
Ruptured Ducks, The 1970's Polytechnic Lecturer Facial Fuzz,
The Anti-Dogbummer Alliance, The Rank Beslubbering Mammets,
The Ill-Nurtured Puny Gudgeons, The Spleeny Pribbling
Flapdragons, The Tango-Ad Brain Mashed Snorters Of Domestos
and all the other violent video game fucked, junk-food screwed
and trash culture raped teenage gangs who have been lured by
the roaring waves of psykic magick (Pied Piper Of Hamelin stylee)
caused by the recent mass crucifixion of 666 local Conservative
voters and flocked like psychotic lemmings into the 24 Hour Fight
For Your Right To PARTEEEEEE! that is the newly created
Magickal Anarkist Diktatorship Of Underkliffe and been ruthlessly
moulded into an Invincible Army Of Khaos by Justine Justice,
Terrorist She Wolf, Witch, Mutant Superferret Breeder, total fackin'
nattah and general all-round generic threat-to-human-civilisation
(aka Babylon an' ting) as we tolerate it, *muthafukkkkkkkkka!*

They are naked, these children, every inch of their

lithesome young teenage bodies festooned in magickal mock tat-
toos which make them invulnerable to the weapons of the armed
bodies of men who compose the state. Nipples, clits and cocks
throbbingly turgid, they clutch in trembling hands the blood rusted
knives, machetes, home-made spears and sharpened shovels and
garden forks with which they have already purged the earth of
over 20,000 lap-dogs of capitalism. Their heads are shaven and
support jerryrigged mini-S&M leather harnesses in each of which
sits a red-eyed, hissing, whistling priapic little Mutant Superferret
with whom the individual teenage terrorist exists in a state of
permanent symbiotic psychosis. Some of them munch on
delicious portions of fried pig cock. Others swig greedily from
flagons of human blood laced with Viking berzerker serum. Apart
from this munching and slurping (and the whistling and hissing of
the Mutant Superferrets and the throb-throb-throb of the palpitating and mucous-dripping walls of the Living Lodge Of Flesh, of
course) there is not a sound to be heard.

The relative silence is suddenly shattered by the 200
decibel, 490 bpm noise of the drum&bass attackjungle versh of
The Ramones' 'Rock'n'Roll Radio' which Justine has autocratically
chosen as the Magickal Anarkist Diktatorship Of Underkliffe's
international anthem. This drives the teenage terrorist scum into a
sudden orgy of moshing, skanking, thrashing and mindless
screaming whilst Justine Justice leaps to her superbly overmuscled feet and lets her still tranced-out body gyrate in an impossibly
ugly dance that requires her to dislocate all her limbs whilst
repeatedly back flipping and vigorously frigging her massively
swollen and ball-bearing hard clit like a loony. The Mutant
Superferrets, meanwhile, all don little Ray Charles style
wrapround Raybans and look cool whilst they click the tiny little
fingers of one tiny little hand in time to every 47th beat whilst
clinging on to their jerryrigged mini-S&M leather harnesses with
the other hand whilst their tiny little furry cocks and cunts spit
impossibly huge amounts of foul smelling yellow spunk and lube
juice. *Funky!*

"ARE YOU SITTING COMFORTABLY?" roars Justine
Justice, suddenly, savagely and somewhat ironically when the
music stops. The dance-crazed killer-kid-kannibals all sit down
and pay rapt attention to their leader so suddenly and savagely
that a visible mist of sweat and Mutant Superferret spunk visibly

hangs in the air for a split second before crashing down with an audible splat on the steaming heads of the now crosslegged and utterly rapt teenage terrorist scum.

"Gooooooooood!" purrs Justine, after a perfectly timed dramatic pause of exactly 1.75 seconds. "Then I'll begin. Chairman Mao once famously claimed that power comes from the barrel of a gun. Well I've got news for him - *Yer art of date, granddad!* " spits Justine, temporarily sliding into an ironic Martin Amis style mockcockernee accent.

"'Cos nowadays power comes from all-over magikal body paint (it does **exactly** what it says on the can) and a well-honed Kitchen Devil (tm) bread knife wielded by a brain washed council estate gutter rat existing in a state of symbiotic psychosis with a permanently priapic Mutant Superferret strapped to his or her shaven head in a cute little S&M stylee leather harness!"

"ARF! ARF! ARF!" roar the audience of brain washed council estate gutter rats existing in a state of symbiotic psychosis with the permanently priapic Mutant Superferrets strapped to their heads by cute little S&M stylee leather harnesses as they bang the throbbing, fleshy floor of The Living Lodge Of Flesh with the shafts of their home-made spears and fall over backwards whilst chortling like those metallic aliens from the "For Mash Get Smash" advert.

"Any road up," chuckles Justine, "we've made the mysterious cabal of dogbumming vampiric Tory technocrats who secretly run the world sit up, take notice and shit themselves *big time!* They've just had a secret meeting and decided unanimously to terminate our little experiment in Insane Magikal Autonomy henceforth and forthwith and without further ado and with extreme prejudice!"

"Vat's h'it!" suddenly and violently yells one of the assembled naked teenage terrorists, leaping to his feet and beating his chest with blood caked fists. "We're facked! We're finished! We're fackin' *DOOOOOOOOOOOOOOOMED!* "

"SHUT IT, YOU COCKERNEE TWAT!" roars Justine as she leaps, gazelle-on-steroids-like, off the Throne Of Bone and into the crowd of her gibberingly insane and brainwashed followers and boots Ricki Tickytimebomb (for it is he) in his whining cockernee nuts.

"Cooo!" thinks Ricki, as he collapses into a foetally positioned heap, "it's'a good job ole Justine pulled 'er Bruce Lee style kung fu kick in me ole Jane Horrocks at ver last minute uvverwize she'd've recessed ver ole family jewels clean ap into me blinkin' ribcage causing me to die instantly and messily from a leefal combo of shock and massive internal haemorrhaging! Blimey!"

"As I speak," roars Justine, consciously adopting the posture and vocal mannerisms of Kenneth Branagh in the ginger luvvie's self-produced movie versh of Shakespeare's royal-arse licking Henry 5, "we are surrounded by over 40,000 of the world's hardest shocktroops culled from the world's tuffest armies and gathered here, today, in Underkliffe with but one purpose blazing in their stunted but incredibly well trained minds. To **destroy** us and, in so doing, to destroy **anarcky** and thus to crush forever the last flickering hope in the heart of mankind that there is some alternative to the grinding, kneechewingly sad and depressing boredom that constitutes day to day life under the economic system of capitalism."

"KILL! KILL! KILL!" roar the adrenally spasming teenage terrorist horde inarticulately as their external sexual organs engorge still further at the prospect of yet another mindless orgy of dumbfuck pig-offing followed by senseless torture and sickeningly gratuitous cannibal feasting over open camp fires followed by a good old sing-song, spooky ghost stories and climaxing in a no-holds barred hard-core bisexual rumpy fest.

"**AROOOGA! AROOOGA! or what!?**" roar the moronic mob. And who can blame them?

"**SHADDUP!**" yells the UK's undisputed No.1 top witch, Justine Justice, savagely. "You'll get to off some piggies, my lickle cherubs, don't you worry, but first - **IT'S CABARET TIME!** "

And with that Justine magicks a magick wand out of thin air, says "Izzy Whizzy! Let's get busy!" and BUMPH! disappears in a huge mushroom cloud of purple smoke.

"Oooh! Ahhhh!" gasp the children as, slowly, the smoke starts to settle and thence to separate and semi-solidify into seemingly sentient whispers which whizz about the room a bit like the spooks that come out of the Ark Of The Covenant at the end of the first Indiana Jones move (ie the 12th best film ever made - **OFFICIAL!** - the other two having reeked like the breath of a baby shit fetishist who can't afford mouthwash and only has access to a baby with particularly pungent pooh) and spooked about the place turning the assembled Nazis into screaming loonies before blowing their fucking heads off except that these wisps of smoke are perfectly harmless and are obviously supplied by a much better spesh FX dept).

"Behold....." says Justine, suddenly sat back on her Throne of Bone as time s e e m e d....t o.......s l o w........r i g h t
......d o w n.......

and the slimy walls of the Living Lodge Of Flesh pulse slower and slower and slower and the floor silently and seductively heaves and folds and reforms itself into a huge tumescent vagina from which, ever so sexily, oooooozes the heart stopping spectacle of........the demon known to our Cro-Magnon ancestors as..... ***OLE SPUNKER!!!!!*** (whom the more observant reader will remember from earlier in the book where he made a brief appearance spectacularly interrupting a secret meeting of freemasons conducting child-sex fuelled satanic rituals at a Conservative Club where the aforementioned multi-phallused demonic entity flickered into corporeal existence in the very midst of the perverted shenanigans and shagged the Conservative dignitaries to death with 13 of its six hundred and sixty six prehensile, multi limbed and steel fanged peni whilst tap dancing with its cloven hooves and whistling the bass riff from Rage Against The Machine's punkrock fuck-off classic 'Bombtrack'.)

"Ta-*da!*" says Ole Spunker (whose real name is "Qwerkyrtu-ka-uiophdjdhj-ka-poiliooilopoli-ka-ak-ak-kkiol-kawuwyy-hfyfyrhe-ka-ka-ka-pa-kajkuihjiukiuk-!-ka-ka-ka" but bollocks to that). "Um, I mean, er... Who dares summon me hence!"

"Tis I!" quoth Justine Justice. "Tis I who dareth summoneth thee hence, I, Justine Justice!"

"Oh, it's you is it?" said the demon (who still has the rotting but still living and thus still savagely screaming corpses of 13 child raping Tories stuck on the bell-ends of a baker's dozen of its six hundred and sixty six prehensile, multi limbed and steel fanged peni) sarcastically.

"Finally got round to giving me a call have we, *you bitch!* What was I, just a cheap fuck? Just a one off wham-bam-thank-you-mam cheap interdimensional casual shag, was I? You cow! I must say, you've got a fucking nerve, you cunting tart!"

"Listen, Spunker" coos Justine, casually lying back on her

Throne of Bone whilst offhandedly peeling a Satsuma, "how do
fancy taking on 40,000 top anti-terrorist squaddies for us?"

"What!?" screeches Ole Spunker, hysterically, "on my own?
Are you fucking mad, woman? Are you totally fucking
INSANE!!!!!!?"

"No, off course not on your own!" sighs Justine, petulantly.
"Me and my teenage terrorist muckers here will give you a hand
plus I've got 350 pigs, squaddies and Tories that we've topped but
not yet decapitated who I've turned into indestructible zombie
slaves so we'll send them in first to soften the bastards up and
then you can steam in and kick the shit out of them whilst they're
distracted and we'll follow on and mop the survivors up. It'll be a
piece of piss!"

"Oooh!" coos Ole Spunker, waving his six hundred and sixty
six prehensile, multi limbed and steel fanged peni about in
excitement, "I **like** zombies! I **LUUUUUUURVE** zombies! They
turn me fucking ***ON!!!!!*** Where are they?"

"Right behind you" guffaws Justine throatily, waving her
magick wand to make the far wall of Lodge Of Living Flesh rend
itself asunder into another gigantic vadge through which march, or
rather lurch, loads of ex-pig zombies led by the two hopping
figures of SAS Colonel Dan Daniels who, if you remember, had
been split completely in half by the sexual performance artist,
Candice X (as she now wished to be known having come to the
inescapable but completely bollocky conclusion that her former
surname was a patriarchal imposition which stopped her from ever
knowing her true female "self" as an "autonomous womyn" or
some feminist shite like that).

"Zombies..
FAY-***SUH!*** Pleas
Ma'am, the Loya
Former Pig Zomb
For Truth And Ju
Anti-Crap Jihad
Britain (Magicki
the service of n
Magickal Anarki
Of Underliffe r
duty, ***SAH!!!!***"
Said one half of the split-in-two Colonel Dan Daniels

(formerly of the SAS).

". Ten **_HUT!!!_** Abart
ed to report,
Regiment Of
oid Warriors
ustice of the
Party Of Great
st Leninist) in
ewly created
st Diktatorship
eporting for"

Said the other half.

"They're gorgeous!" squealed Ole Spunker, brewing up a spunkstorm. "And can I get to fuck them all afterwards? Oh please say yes, **_pleeeeeeeeeease!_** "

"'Course you can, Malcolm!" laughed Justine, throatily.

"Right, then!" said the demon, "you're fucking **_ON!_** "

CHAPTER 25

MONSTER!

'Desperate diseases require desperate remedies.'

Guy Fawkes

Flashback:

"Aye! Listen up! Muck around with the Magick and the Magick will fuck ya up big time, seen?" slobbered mother of 97 Janine Justice as she lay on her black-satin sheeted deathbed but a mere savagely pain wracked 9.24 seconds away from popping her genuine Hebden Bridge Mill built New Model Army stylee steel-toecapped bovver clogs after a traumatic 2 and a half years of suffering loudly from the most savage cocktail of cancers ever contracted by one human being in a single lifetime.

But 4 year old Justine Justice wasn't listening as she dementedly disco thrashed around the gloss black painted and endangered animal skull studded council house bedroom on the creaking back of Pogo, the 15 year old family poodle/dolphin mix interspecial mutant mongrel hybrid whilst a magickly (and utterly illegally) procured bootleg of The Prodigy's ideologically unsound killer-disco-floor-filler 'Smack My Bitch Up' from 23 years in the future pushed the woofers of the state-of-the-art-for-the-early-'60s hi-fi to their utter outer limits and twisted the nipples of the tinny tweeters till they squeaked like cute little field mice being brutally bummed by especially well-endowed Blue Whales who'd under-gone radical penis enlargement plastic surgery for purely sadistic reasons. And that's just how the social workers found the sweat drenched and stinking Justine Justice just 4 days later, her hair wired into hideously vertical devil-horn style dreadlocks after being artfully stiffened with putrid pus squeezed from her mum's bulging cranial boils - utterly off her emaciated face on Airfix glue whilst teetering on the brink of screaming hysteria dressed only in the stinking skin of poor old exhaustion-slaughtered Pogo and still bopping like an CIA torture victim with a switched on cattle prod whacked hard and deep into every orifice whilst the crew-cut and short sleeve shirted defenders of democracy chug Bud and laugh.

And on she danced on for the next ten years, wired to bleeping, flashing hi-tech monitors and liquid nutrient drips - the chundering thunder of The Prodge (most of whom hadn't even been born yet) smashing about her cranial cavity like a permanently pre-menstrual she-elephant with terrible toothache and a wasp hive rammed brutally half-way up its giant pile-plastered elephant arse. Top scientists allegedly working for the British Government's ultra-secret Future Weapons Research Department were utterly baffled as they stared feverishly through the 9ft thick two-way mirror wall at the still gyrating child around whom white lightening flashed and thundered and apparently spontaneously generated an occasional shoal of disgustingly weird looking marine life somehow sucked up from the deepest depths of the Atlantic trench to be spat out here in this top secret research institute 2 miles beneath the earth and 80 miles from the nearest beach. Every 24 hours a hand-picked suicide squad would enter the room to clean up the pools of piss, piles of pooh and huge stinking mounds of rotting aquatic fauna whilst spraying gallons of DDT, dettol and fly spray in every direction to try and curb the sickening stench. Millions of man hours and billions of siphoned-off into an ultra-secret slush fund tax payer pounds were spent trying to diagnose Justine's unique condition (which the scientists had provisionally named Red Shoes Syndrome) to no avail although an autopsy on the corpse of her mother, Janine Justice, revealed seething swarms of supernaturally semi-sentient cysts surrounding the witch's womb which suggested that the crazy beatnik bitch had been ingesting vast amounts of satanically cursed benzedrine-containing nasal inhaler innards for 24 hours a day throughout her pregnancy whilst probably being fucked non-stop by a plethora of lower-ranked demons when her husband,

Jack Justice (now deceased) was off robbing banks and offing coppers for kicks and stuff.

And then...***SUDDENLY!!!!***....the dancing stopped. Once scrubbed and brushed and dressed properly in pretty gurly clothes, Justine looked no different from any other spectacularly well developed and obviously psychotic 14 year old girl who'd spent her entire childhood in a weird and chronologically illogical techno trance of the sort which would later occupy most of the leisure time of an entire generation of twat hatted ravers off their moronic faces on E which they then piss out into the ecosystem thus setting up a Butterfly Wing Chaos Theory Domino Theory Effect which will probably destroy Western Civilisation As We Know It.

Whilst keeping her severely manacled (and with cattle-prod wielding pigs lurking in the background - natch) the scientists belatedly commenced Justine's education, feeding her amazingly hungry mind with text books which she consumed avidly (and with a reading speed that made Star Trek's slickfingered-king-of-superspeedreading (ie Mr Spock) look like a 2 year old liquid-coshed dyslexic dullard with lead poisoning induced brain-damage, narcolepsy and a morbid and totally irrational fear of the printed word) with the end result that, by her 15th birthday, Justine Justice was at PHD standard in Physics, Biology, Chemistry, 14 different languages, domestic science and sums. Eager to encourage their prodigy and getting carried away with the sheer intellectual thrill of their "experiment", the scientists were soon catering to Justine's every whim, furnishing her with tons of steroids, life-time subscriptions to Guns And Ammo, Soldier Of Fortune, Muscle&Fitness and 2000AD and with an Olympic-level supergym featuring a special virgin-blood Pentagram splattered bench where the now 7 foot tall and massively muscled Justine would try and summon the Dev whilst pressing 400 lbs of raw steel and cursing God in Sanskrit whilst all the time growing ever larger under the disbelieving but obviously sexually excited eyes of the pipe-cleaner limbed and pencil-necked speccy-eyed and tiny genitalia-ed scientist scum who all fell in love with Justine for exactly the same reasons that nearly all little boys fall in love with dinosaurs which is exactly the same reason that the incredibly wonderful bodybuilder cum poet cum cop hater cum punk rock shouter and former singer with Black Flag, Henry Rollins is the fulcrum of so much closet-case homo-erotic hero-worship from skinny male indie-kids. Because the vampiric capitalist patriarchy is ideologically driven by an almost religious worship of raw, naked, throbbing, thrusting, spurting, sweating, bulging, rippling, muscular, carnivorous penile *POWER!* And so, however much we might in later, more civilised years, sneer and mock the massively mighty - like Rollins, like Arnie, like Tyrannosaurs Rex - the reality is that we never, ever, cease to *envy* them. Us blokes, anyway. Us weedy, skinny, powerless males taught from Day 1 - when, pink and screaming, we are spat defenceless from our mothers' wombs - to worship **THE COCK!** Told to be **TUFF!** And promised that one day we too will be **POWERFUL!** *The point being* that this **LIE** is what makes men rape, murder women, abuse children or embrace capitalism. Thus the sanest male is the clinically insane anorak-wearing anal-retentive **Trainspotter** - a sexually stunted eunuch who has taken **total control** over an area of highly specialised yet utterly useless, archaic, redundant or obsolete knowledge which contributes absolutely **NOTHING** to the patriarchal power structure, the very same power structure which as we rant is nurturing its own nemesis in the stunningly erotic and amazingly powerfully overmuscled super genius anarchist lunatic she-wolf bitch nutter black-witch commie psycho terrorist One-Woman-Army otherwise known as Justine Justice. **All Hail!**

By Justine's 31st birthday the Red Shoes Project (which had been skilfully hidden from the prying, parsimonious and penny-pinching eyes of the various legally elected British Governments that had come and gone in the meantime but which was, of course, well known and feverishly monitored by the evil cabal of vampires that really ran the world) was secretly consuming over 20% of the nation's annual budget and was obviously careering out of control. Corruption (caused partly by the inevitable slide into waste and iniquity that ultimately warps all such top secret projects but mostly by the severe and soul witheringly lethal leakage of satanic spiritual sickness that oozed like psykik puss from Justine's deranged and satanically cursed pre-natal nasal-inhaler overdose damaged psyche) was ultra-rife. Cut off from the outside world (which a pseudo-religious mini-cult popular amongst the institution's many biologists claimed no longer existed anyway) apart from the regular monthly convoy of 200 sealed juggernauts bringing supplies, the scientific community

sealed within the vast underground complex went slowly but surely and absolutely inevitably stark raving fucking totally bang-your-
head-with-biscuit-tin-lid-'till-either-unconscious-or-progressively-
accumulating-brain-damage-inhibits-your-motor-neuron-
responses-to-such-an-extent-that-you-have-to-stop Lord of The
Flies cargo-cult style ***MENTAL!!!!!!!!!!*** and started worshipping
Justine as a Goddess because Justine's mum (Janine Justice
RIP) hadn't just been talking shit when she uttered her last words
ie "Muck around with the Magick and the Magick will fuck ya up
big time, seen?" and the swivel-eyed 9ft tall sabre-toothed mega-
chickens of kosmick karma had come home to roost with a
vengeance, hoisting the scientists with their own petard, stripping
away their cynical, sceptical, rational, scientific armour and seizing
the now oh-so-ultra-vulnerable little brains of the wriggling pink
spiritual maggots that were revealed squirming hideously unpro-
tected and ripe for metaphysical shafting beneath with gusto and
wolfing them down whole without even bothering to chew!

So it's no wonder the lass is a bit of a nutter then, you
remark sagely. Yeah, that's right, liberal, let's all just blame
"society" and let the criminals off the hook, right?! By the age of 32
Justine had developed telekinitic and telepathic powers which not
only enabled her to psyckically infiltrate the conspiracy of evil Tory
vampires who secretly run the world but also enabled her to feel
and ultimately gently guide the translucent tendrils of drug
pollution-overdose induced Khaos that have since coagulated and
found physical force in the form of the lithesome young bodies of
Mad Mick, Karen Skull and the other incredibly sexy young Nihilist
Terrorist Filth whose Anti-Crap Jihad is so eloquently and thrilling
described in the book you now hold in your trembling hands. And
then she escaped and offed the fox hunt. Quick! Turn the page!
There's ***tons*** more to come!

CHAPTER 26

WINONA!

'Everybody's bisexual/Nobody need be left upon the shelf!'

'Everybody's Bisexual', The Pop Starz

"What do you mean they "bounced off"?" roared Field Marshall Hilary Hollocks-Heath Camberly Roth, brutally smashing the quaking subaltern across his beardless and pimple pitted chin with his titanium tipped solid-oak swagger stick. "Thermonuclear weapons attached to state-of-the-art delivery systems don't just ***"bounce off"!***"

"Ish duh magish runsh thur oiksh haff shrpayed all offer Undercliffe!" spluttered the cringing junior officer through an utterly crushed upper class gob full of blood and broken teeth whilst nurturing the small but rock hard lob-on that ex-public schoolboys always get when you punish them physically.

"The fucking ***WHAT!?***" roared the red-faced head of Britain's armed forces savagely whilst once again furiously back-handing his junior across the face and accidentally breaking the little posho tosser's neck in the process.

"He means the "runes"" interpreted MOD mandarin and secret vampire Sir Jeremy Holsworthy-Hutchinson Chinnely-D'eath Starksmith Blyth, helpfully.

"Don't talk rot, man!" roared Field Marshall Hilary Hollocks-Heath Camberly Roth feverishly, his mighty voice bouncing off the impenetrable walls of the reinforced concrete secret bunker which, unfortunately for its occupants, also stopped the negative-vibes which radiated from Field Marshall Hilary Hollocks-Heath Camberly Roth's jet black, bad karma drenched and foully bubbling cosmic aura from harmlessly escaping into the surrounding atmosphere like they normally would and instead channelled them back into the room where they sweated, festered and stank, all the while geometrically multiplying and thus savagely worsening the Bad Vibe Overload Situation within the bunker which we feel must surely soon experience an extremely dangerous Bad Vibe Meltdown Scenario which will all too probably climax in an explosion of gratuitous violence so horrible that it will almost certainly be banned from all British cinemas when this book is made into a five hundred million dollar budget top-speshFX Hollywood movie starring Tom Hanks as Mad Mick, Whoopi Goldberg as Mrs The Needle, Winona as Karen Skull and, of course, the incredibly sexy Cher as Justine Justice

"A bunch of doodlings scrawled by an unwashed and undisciplined mob of raggedy-arsed common-or-garden fish'n'chip munching drug-addict council estate glue sniffer gutter scum urchin slum vermin armed with kitchen knives isn't going to stop a hydrogen bomb! Ha!" babbled the top pig, unconvincingly.

The Field Marshall's face gave a sudden, savage twitch. Everybody else in the un-airconditioned and incredibly stuffy bunker stopped moving little flags about on the battle map and stuff and stared. The Field Marshall was literally shaking (like a brutally egg-bound dog which has finally managed and was halfway through a minute but incredibly slow and devastatingly painful diamond-hard bowel movement after 18 months of no-shit city) with rage.

"It's the old magick," murmured Sir Jeremy Holsworthy-Hutchinson Chinnely-D'eath Starksmith Blyth, staring into the far distance, "the magick of Merlin, Moses and Marx!. Sheep magick! Slave magick! Human magick! **Maggot Magick!** We'll not stop them using the fruits of deliciously twisted science, oh no, not *this* time. They're out of control! They've slipped the leash! We're doomed! DOOMED! YOU HEAR ME! **WE'RE FUCKING DOOOOOOOOOOOOOOOOOOOOOOOOOOOOOOOOOOOOOOOOOOOOOO OOOOOOOOOMED! AHA! AHAHAHAHAHAHAHAHAHAHAHA-HAHAHAHAHAHAHAHAHAHA** -*OOF!*"

"Shut your defeatist mouth, you bastard!" screamed Field Marshall Hilary Hollocks-Heath Camberly Roth as he once again gratuitously rammed the secret vampire in its undead nuts with his steel-kneecapped prosthetic left leg. "Just because the anarchist scum now occupy the entire greater West Yorkshire Conurbation after destroying over 4O per cent of the world's most professional army doesn't mean we're **licked!** A **true** Briton **never** concedes defeat! Not whilst we've still got a single overburdened and undertrained working class squaddie cannon fodder mug to send over the top at a walking pace into the enemy machine guns like we at the Somme! We'll fight them on the beaches! We'll fight them from the cellars, sewers and secret hiding places, we'll use chemical, bacteriological and top secret experimental death ray weaponry! We will **NEVAH SURRENDAH!** UCK!"

The "Uck!" noise was made by Field Marshall Hilary Hollocks-Heath Camberly Roth as his head was knocked clean off by a casual swipe from the pale and delicately veined hand of the supernaturally strong secret vampire known to us mortals Sir Jeremy Holsworthy-Hutchinson Chinnely-D'eath Starksmith Blyth.

"I say!" woofed all the junior officers simultaneously as they reached for their revolvers. **SLISH! RIIIIP! BONK! ROLL!** went their heads as the rest of the civil servants in the room (who were all Igors) took their cue from secret vampire Sir Jeremy Holsworthy-Hutchinson Chinnely-D'eath Starksmith Blyth's wonderfully casual assassination of Field Marshall Hilary Hollocks-Heath Camberly Roth and sliced the Ruperts' noggins clean off with razor sharp machetes which they whipped out of their identical human skin briefcases and applied to the unsuspecting necks of the posho soldier boys in the single fluid movement which they had been patiently and painstakingly taught as part of their Igoric Indoctrination at a Secret Vampire Monastery hidden away from prying human eyes in the heart of the Himalayas.

"Super!" purred Sir Jeremy Holsworthy-Hutchinson Chinnely-D'eath Starksmith Blyth before switching to telepathic mode.

"Calling all vampires! Calling all vampires!" he telepathed urgently, "Code Red! Repeat! **Code Red!**"

All over the world the secret class of unhuman blood-sucking filth who really run t'ings stopped what they were doing (ie bumming dogs etc), turned into giant vampire bat form and flew off to the secret vampire space ship station craftily hidden deep in heart of the Carpathian mountains where an already alerted crew of especially trained elite Space-Igors were already busy at work fuelling the secret vampire spacecraft and filling the larders up with blood to drink, children to eat and dogs to bum etc.

"Just who the fuck *is* this Justine Justice oik anyway?" spat Sir Jeremy Holsworthy-Hutchinson Chinnely-D'eath Starksmith Blyth contemptuously as he effortlessly shape-shifted from his upper-crust Brit snob Tory bastard human disguise into his even more hideous and much more frightening 40,0000 year old vampire Tory bastard persona.

"Your worst fucking nightmare, bloodsucking fiendish horrorpig!" bellowed Justine Justice as she rode suddenly through a hole chewed through one of the allegedly impenetrable top secret nuclear bunker cum emergency Governmental HQ's walls astride one of Ole Spunker's six hundred and sixty six prehensile, multi limbed peni (the supernaturally hardened steel fangs of which had found the reinforced concrete a doddle to chew through) whilst clutching in her superbly overmuscled left hand a furiously ticking Badvibeometer.

"That was a rhetorical question, bitch!" screamed the evil Tory vampire as he whirled to face his nemesis whilst savagely shapechanging into a Fire Breathing Mutant Wolf Rhino in which frightening form he charged straight at our heroine who leapt gazelle-like off Ole Spunker's writhing and rearing knob and onto the back of the vampbeast who had by now once again shapechanged into a Giant Sabretoothed Steel Plated Armoured Death Batmoth in which mode he flapped savagely about the room as Justine Justice mercilessly plunged the magickally enhanced plastic fork with which she had been merrily munching a Chicken Curry Flavour Pot Noodle not but 5 minutes ago into his green-gunk spurting neck again and again and again until the undead Tory vampire bastard flapped to the floor, quivered, shat and un-died.

KKKKKRUNCH!

went the rest of the walls of the no-longer top secret underground nuclear bunker as the other 665 of Ole Spunker's 666 prehensile, multi limbed and steel fanged peni - each ridden by a garden-tooled-up teenage terrorist existing in a state of symbiotic psychosis with the permanently priapic Mutant Superferrets strapped to their heads by cute little S&M stylee leather harnesses - burst through the wall like the giant worms in the crap film Dune .

"PRAAAAAAAAAAAAAARP!"

roared the suddenly traumatically dilated sphincters of the stunned Igor civil servants as the seats of their pin stripe suit trousers bulged violently outwards under the savage impact of a mass collective shock-shit!

"HURRRRRRRAAAAAAAAAAAAAARGH!"

thundered the naked teen penile calvary as they leapt from their bucking semi-turgid steeds with gusto and nary a thought for their own safety! Into the valley of death charged the 665! Defenceless foes to the left of them, defenceless foes to the right of them! And hacked the cringing speciestraitor Igorscum into bits of battered and bloody flesh so tiny that a giant diamond-bladed supermincer couldn't have done a better job and all the world's forensic pathology labs combined couldn't have put even one single Igor back together again even with overtime. **No way!**

      The totally insane Justine Justice roared with laughter as she surveyed the stomach churning carnage and decided to take stock of the situation which she decided immediately was *ACE!*

      "We have decapitated the state!" she murmured savagely into the still spurting neck stump of the still twitching corpse of Field Marshall Hilary Hollocks-Heath Camberly Roth with which she now waltzed erotically through the nauseating barbarian violencefest overkill scenario which sexily surrounded her "but we have not slain the beast! Oh no, it will stagger on a while longer yet, methinks! Athrashing and alashing out blindly but far from harmlessly like some giant farmyard chicken decapitated by a length of foot-thick cheese wire stretched between two pylons except with a huge stinger on its arse instead of feathers and with blazing 40,000 rounds-a-minute miniguns and napalm spurting flamethrowers instead of wings."

      By heck, she thought, this was *FUN!*

CHAPTER 26

CRUSTIE!

'LOUDER! FASTER! SHORTER!'

Strap-line on the back cover of Stewart Home's Cranked Up Really High - An Inside Account Of Punk Rock.

"Praise be to Mother Gia for her bounty!" smiled nose-pierced and caucasian dreadlocked juggler and environmental activist "Mole" (real name Patricia Amanda Hollocks-Heath Camberly Roth) as she tossed the handful of dodgy looking and worm-shit smeared forest roots that she'd spent the last 4 hours digging up with her bare hands into the camp's collective stew pot in which bubbled a delicious smelling broth containing mung beans, lentils, dock leaves, dandelion roots, carrots and a soupcon of rough cider.

"Yeah, praise her!" replied "Tufty" as he stirred the festering veggie puke with a large wooden spoon that he himself had crudely carved from an ash tree that had fallen down naturally, probably during a storm or something, and not been "murdered" by "Man". Tufty's "real" or "slave" name had been Police Constable 9874666 Mike Udo. He'd infiltrated the 'Mrs Tiggywiggy City' camp of the anti-bypass protesters some six months ago, determined to fulfil his mission of discovering the crusties' plans, inciting them to acts of illegal violence and maybe shagging some of the fit posh crustie totty with an eye to discovering their deepest secrets like James Bond did with Pussy Galore in Goldfinger. And shag them he had, *dozens* of them. The young PC was shocked but delighted to learn that crusty chicks did it like dogs except all the year round and with absolutely *any* male as long as they were ugly, smelly, didn't eat meat, could juggle a bit and dressed in filthy rags. Yeah! Crusty birds *ruled!* Who cared if they all stank like a long term homeless person's training shoes!? But it was he, not they, who had ultimately cracked and blathered out the details of his secret mission in a state of post orgasmic euphoria whilst being cradled in the massive arms of 24 stone "Mare" - the camp's tantric healer who, like all intelligent but fat and incredibly ugly people, was an incredibly good shag because she had to be. For the old piggish Mike Udo was, by that stage, no more. He'd come to respect and then love the hedgemonkies whom he had once so despised (once going so far - in an inspired and crack cocaine addled police canteen rant - to advocate that "the whole, stinking, treehugging fucking lot of them should be rounded-up, stripped, de-inoculated and dumped on that remote Scottish island where they tested Anthrax during the war. That'd teach them to reject the wondrous technological advances bequeathed on our species by capitalism which, of course, would be impossible to maintain without an ever expanding infrastructure including a roads programme dedicated to the building of ever more of the very same by-passes, ring roads and motorways which these cock-pierced, dope-smoking, shitbreathed heathen hippy scum are trying to stop!")

Tufty smiled at the fading memory of this particularly noxious example of his own bigoted naivety. Of *course* the roads had to be stopped! He saw that now! The universe was *one* - every leaf, every person, every "animal", every molecule, every atom, quark and quasar - all part of one wonderful constantly recycling cosmic whole! He knew now that everything he'd learnt at school, college and then at Hendon had been a lie! They'd never told him that Earth was a living Goddess and that we "humwoms" (as he had now learnt to describe his own species) were merely custodians whose sacred mission it was to preserve Her sanctity until the benevolent vegan confederation of sentient species that lived in the rest of the universe saw that we had reached a high enough state of purified karmic consciousness to make overt contact with us rather than through the "coded" messages they were giving us now via corn circles, "coincidences", cosmic-channelling-through-crystals and stuff.

Tufty looked down at the swastika tatoo that adorned the lightly muscled and nut brown tanned arm that held the crudely carved wooden spoon that stirred the cauldron containing Mother Gia's wondrous bounty. Like most of the pigs at his nick, Tufty/Mike'd been a secret nazi, taking part in the annual worship at the swastika flag draped shrine hidden in the station cellar on Hitler's birthday. He was glad that he didn't have to cover the tatoo up any more since 'Magick Terry', the camp's philosopher and guru, had explained to him that the "crooked cross" was actually a beautiful ancient symbol of regeneration and fertility that Hitler had nicked for bad purposes.

"Boom shanka rajit bhuna jalfrezi dahl tandoori krishna khorma!" chanted Tufty ecstatically, as the tune from Kula Shaker's spiritually profound hit single 'Arbeit Macht Frei!' gently wafted around the inside of his endorphin drenched brain as he came explosively inside the violently sucking gob of 'Mole", thus providing the Field Marshall's aggressively vegan daughter with her only protein intake of the week so far.

"This is beautiful!" babbled Tufty. "This! Here! Now!" He laughed and then did a spontaneous Iron John style primal scream that immediately put him in touch with his subconscious desire to murder his own father. "You! Me! Us!" he cried, starting to trip as the magic mushrooms he'd harvested from some cow shit that morning and scoffed not but 3 minutes ago kicked in and dragged his concrete covered and plastic coated modern false consciousness free from its "civilised" moorings and dragged it deep down into rich, dank, stinking mulch of an earlier, primordial state of being when his place on the kosmic karmic cycle had been that of a monocelluar sea moss or something similar, just one of a billion billion such mindless vegetable protobeasts photo-synthesising in joyful unthinking bliss in a sea rich in the essential nutrients necessary for the evolution of ever more complex (but not necessarily "superior") life.

BOOM! SHANKA! He was suddenly rocketed "up" the evolutionary scale at a gallop that made light speed look like a arthritic snail's pace! He was a lung-fish feebly gasping its first few breaths of ash-filled air on some prehistoric volcanic beach! He was a Tyrannosaurs Rex chasing a herd of screaming smaller dinosaurs across a vast yellow plane under a boiling and somehow strangely alien sun! He was a grunting pygmy chimp in a cave using a crude stick to extract delicious organic honey from an angry bee hive! He was a Roman Soldier delivering metal death to the rounded bellies of innocent Ancient British Druids! AAAAAAAAH! He was a Norman Lord on horseback leaning over to smash the skull of a terrified and cowering Saxon juggler with one mighty blow from his tightly clenched mace! NOOOOOOOOOOOOO! BAD TRIP! He was a bushy-eyebrowed capitalist pig smoking a huge cigar as he watched his oppressed wage slaves murder trees and pour concrete down fox holes just so he could build a chemical weapons factory! NO NO! NO! NO! NO! NO! *NOOOOOOOOOOOOOOOOOOOOOOOOOOOOOOOOO!*

"Tufty, wake up! You're having a bad trip, man!" said a posh female voice. Tufty opened his eyes and stared into the face of the Earth Goddess - simultaneously Virgin, Maid and Hag. She who was life. Was death. Was Mole. Was *Gia!*

"Are you alright?" asked the nurturing, caring Mole.

"HIK - RAAAAAAAAAAAAAAAAAAAAAAAAALPH!" emitted Tufty savagely as he puked his veg-swill packed guts straight into the bubbling vegan stew.

"Oh God! Fuck! Sorry!" he mumbled, his head still swimming from the nightmarish bad trip in which he had come face to screaming face with the hideous reality of his own alienation from his own true vegetable self over many reincarnations on the never ending kosmic circle of birth-death-rebirth.

"Shhh! Baby! Don't cry!" murmured Mole gently and sweetly and caringly. "It's all vegetables! It's all Mother Gia's wondrous bounty!" she said, reassuringly, dipping a finger into the bubbling stew and sticking a huge dollop of the shit coloured "food" into her mouth to prove to Tufty the truth and wisdom of her womynly words.

"Tell us a dream!" whined Tufty, now cradled in her bony lap and smelling her unwashed cunt through the filthy Laura Ashley frock that was all she wore.

"Yes, tell us a dream!" said the other crusties as they emerged from their benders and wigwams and filled their crude wooden bowls with huge steaming dollops of the stinking stew and sat down crosslegged around the fire - munching, slurping, scratching and violently farting.

"Yes, I'll tell you a dream!" laughed Mole gently. Because she was the tribe's Dreamweaver. She was the purest, the one amongst them whose mind was nearest the pure vegetable state.

And so, as night gently fell, she told them her dream. It was a dream of the future. A dream of the coming time when the majority of planet-raping Humwom-kind had been slaughtered by an angry Earth Goddess who had purged the earth of the irritating skin disease of technology, industry, "progress" and science with fire, plague and killer plants a bit like triffids only more discriminating. Because Gia had not killed *all* the humwoms. No. She, in Her boundless wisdom, had spared the most intelligent, the most caring and the most unwashed.

"This is the time of my dream" said Mole, rocking backwards and forwards as if in a trance, the firelight flickering magickally on her dirt caked brow. "The coming time when men will be men again and will hunt and gather and live in perfect harmony with our brothers and sisters, yea, verilly, even with the tapeworm, malaria parasite and herpes virus for are they not all Gia's creatures?"

"Yeah!" mumbled the surrounding Crusties in assent. And then, *suddenly,* something *magickal* happened! The woodland folk - the non-humwom "animals" who lived in, on, under or around the surrounding trees - slowly started to walk, hop, fly, slither or burrow their way into the circle of humwoms where they too sat and eagerly listened as if somehow magickally transfixed by the beautifully musical voice of Mole The Dreamweaver.

It was a *beautiful* sight. Deer, red squirrels, badgers, foxes, rabbits, voles, shrews, mice, rats and flies (to name but a few) all sat together in perfect harmony with the humwoms with whom they shared but temporary residence on the fragile skin of Old Mother Gia.

"And the womyn!" continued Mole, "The womyn of this time will be **real** womyn and they will be the carers, sharers, cleaners, cookers, nurturers and rearers of children!"

"FUCKING HELL! FOOD!" roared a coarse Bradford accented voice as a home-made crossbow bolt smashed into the skull of the young doe that was leaning over Mole's shoulder, splattering the crustie chick's face with deer-brain, some of which went down her throat to join Tufty's spunk in her belly with which it instantly mingled thus suddenly constituting a critical mass of animal protein which sent the vegan lass's malnourished body into a screaming dance of twisting, bucking, toxic-shock overload!

Panic rippled through the crosslegged crustie road-protester ranks as their peaceful camp was suddenly and violently invaded by hundreds of whooping, hollering Lord Of The Flies style naked council estate scum with permanently priapic mutant ferrets strapped to their shaven heads in sexy little S&M style leather harnesses, waving knives and crude home made spears and sharpened garden tools which they used to immediately slaughter the stunned woodland animals, eating their flesh raw in great steaming handfuls and drinking their still steaming blood from ram's horn goblets like mad vikings!

The protein deficient and new-age superstition dimmed brains of the road-protesters were slow to take in the full horror of what they were witnessing. I mean, come on! Be fair! One minute it's Walt Disney in Dingly Dell on really groovy acid - the next it's **_HEAVY METAL ARMAFUCKINGGEDDON, MAAAAAAAAN!!!!!!!_** Right!? WRONG! This isn't **Armageddon**, you mug! This is merely a **_TASTER!_**

So the stunned crusties could but sit and stare as the newly arrived prancing barbarians slaughtered, tortured and munched every last one of the defenceless animal friends that they had worked so hard to protect from the road developers. They barely had time to gasp in horror as a hugely-horned figure riding a massive and pollution spewing 30,000 CC chopped Harley hog came roaring through the suddenly fallen blood red mist to stop in a hideous squeal of brakes atop the escarpment that dominated the now devastated crustie camp.

The demonic biker pulled open the visor on her massive gothic bat-winged and phallically horned helmet and scowled at the cowering crusties who still sat shocked senseless amongst the carnivorous carnage. And then her incredibly beautiful and steroid swollen face cracked into an utterly evil grin.

"DIGGERS!" roared Justine Justice (for it was she) in an inhumanely loud voice. **_"FORWARD!"_**

The air was suddenly filled with the savage roar of a thousand souped up and carbon monoxide spewing diesel engines as a fleet of snazzily painted super-bulldozers came crashing over the hill behind her, ploughing straight through the crustie camp, knocking ancient trees hither and thither like so many skittles and crushing crustie scum to squealing death beneath their cruelly barbed caterpillar tracks. The biggest and sexiest bulldozer of all, of course, was driven by the demon Ole Spunker, who looked even sexier than usual in his Village People style bright yellow safety helmet as he simultaneously spat acidic spunk from everyone of his 666 multi-limbed prehensile and steel fanged peni whilst cackling with joy at the fulfilment, at last, of one of his major childhood ambitions! *Go for it, Spunker!*

But one crustie, an especially filthy specimen named 'Music Morris' whose reflexes were somewhat sharper than those of his less fortunate comrades thanks to his naughty habit of nipping out once a day for a guilty bacon sarnie on the quiet, managed to escape. He ran through the woods just in front of the oncoming tide of tree-murdering mechanical death, and screamed a warning to the crusties in the other camps.

"THE ROMANS ARE COMING! THE ROMANS ARE COMING!" he squealed in a voice made high pitched and trembly by sheer scrotumtighteningly intense shock and terror.

The other crusties in the other camps heard the tradition-al "alarum" and hastened up on to their tree-connecting walkways and down into their painstakingly well constructed tunnels. Which was a *total* waste of time. The treecrusties fell to their deaths screaming as the merciless tide of Bulldozer Death smashed their hiding places into tooth picks. The tunnelcrusties met an even grizzlier fate, chewed to death by the razor sharp fangs of the unstoppable tide of fleshcrazed mutant superferrets or alternative-ly but equally hideously suffocated by the quicksetting liquid concrete pumped straight into their screaming gobs, down their unwashed throats into their vegan shit filled guts by the giant atomic powered cement mixers that followed in the bulldozer's crustie-blood drenched wake!

By the next morning Todchester Wood and its 473 crustie defenders were no more and a new 40 mile stretch of the Anarko-Motorheadway stretched down from Bradford towards Glastonbury, its still sizzling tarmac surface already marked with the mystic runes that would protect it from vandalisation by the puppet forces of the secret cabal of vampires that really run the earth who, even as Justine Justice surveys her night's handiwork and sees that it is *good* , are already blasting off into space to meet the incoming warfleet of the psychopathic punk rock space scum from the Planet Milkin with whom they will attempt to do a deal and stitch up poor old humanity **4 EVAH!**

Suddenly Justine felt something weakly scrabbling at the toe of her steel-toecapped biker boot and looked down to see the upper half of Music Morris which some clever sod with artistic pretensions had half-buried face-up in quick-setting concrete whilst leaving one badly broken arm waving pathetically free like the last flower flapping feebly in the radiation riddled winds after an nuclear apocalypse has stripped the entire planet of all life for eternity.

"W-w-why?" asked Music Morris.

"Ooh, you're a tough one!" laughed Justine. "Where's the other half of you?"

"Got....eaten!" gasped the semi-buried crustie. "W-w-wwhy d'you *do* this?" His awkwardly angled arm waved pathetically at the surrounding asphalt hell.

"Instinct, mostly, I suppose," said Justine, scratching her incredibly beautiful head as she considered, as if for the first time, why she had singlehandedly destroyed the armed forces of her native state and then set out of a holy-war come roadbuilding scheme that would interlock every single leyline in Britain under an utterly indestructible layer of concrete and tarmac whilst sacrificing the lives of as many innocent humans to her mate Spunker and his demon chums as she could in the meantime. "But mostly for fun!"

"F-f-ffff-un!?" screamed Music Morris, feebly "F-F-F-UCK-ING *FUN!?* "

"Listen, young man, can I give you a bit of advice?" asked Justine, maternally.

"Wh-wh-what?" spluttered Music Morris, coughing up blood and green stuff.

"GET A BATH, HIPPY, *YOU FUCKING STINK!* " roared Justine, smashing the cunt into oblivion with one stamp from her steel-toecapped biker boot and then, in one fluid and almost balletic movement, straddling and kicking into bestial life the demonic chopper which had given her more and more savage orgasms than any million men would be ever be capable of delivering even in their most arrogant dreams and headed off (throatily singing the chorus from The Wurzels 'I Am A Zider

Drinker' the meantime) *darn sarf* , towards Glastonbury and
DESTINY!!!!

MEANWHILE....

Grand Ubergod 34 extracted a 50,000 mile long
forefinger from the anti-matter packed inside of one of His small-
universe sized nostrils and flicked the cosmos sized collected
semi-liquid snotball skyward where it formed a giant constellation
of fizzing beauty and sighed.

"We're gonna have to do something about Pete, He's out
of fucking control!"

"Which one's Pete?" grunted Grand Ubergod 12
disinterestedly as He scanned the infinitely stacked ranks of
securi-cam monitors on which the two security guard uniformed
Grand Ubergod Guardians Of Ultimate Entirety viewed the mainly
tedious going-ons of an infinite number of realities with an infinite
number of boggly eyeballs under an infinite number of Noel
Gallagher style bushy black eyebrows under the rigid black peaks
of two infinitely large Hitlerhats.

"Y'know, the mad motherfucker!"

"You mean the one from the monkeyplanet who's totally
convinced Himself that He created the dominant species in His
own image? He's harmless, in'ee?"

"WAS harmless! Emphasis on the *past* tense!" spat 34,
savagely. "Was harmless when all He fucking did all day was
sneak into the tents of beardy-weirdie patriarchs and inject them
with acid for a laugh and then appear to them as a burning bush
or something and waffle complete bollocks to freak them out!
Yeah, agreed! *That* was a laugh! But now the shit's leaking all
over the place! It's started to infect other planets! I mean, just *look*
at this fucking mess!"

Images of mayhem, riot, gratuitously degenerate sex
acts, surreally magnificent drug abuse and utterly impossible
metaphysical anti-physics from all over the universe that contained
the aforementioned monkeyplanet blasted suddenly from the nearest two zillion monitors.

"WHOAH! I see what you mean! The tosser's totally lost
it!" roared Grand Ubergod 12 excitedly with one of His infinite

number of impossibly long fingers suddenly hovering over one of the galaxy sized buttons on a universe sized remote control. "Shall I zap the twat and all His works or what?"

*"**YOU'LL DO NOWT, HEATHEN SCAB!**"* roared a heavily Bradford accented voice as the universe sized door of the infinitely large Entirety Control Room came crashing off its incalculably large hinges and a mob of deranged rebel Ubergods came steaming in waving red flags and universe sized copies of 19th century monkeyplanet Russian rifles affixed with bayonets.

"What is this nonsense, 589?!" barked 34 furiously, immediately fixing on the obvious ringleader of this unprecedented revolt with the time honoured object of facing Him down and then sneakily offing the cunt - thus decapitating the mob just like that monkeyplanet king did to Wat Tyler and The Peasants Revolt inna fascist textbook stylee.

"Anarchy in the Entirety!" snarled 589, insanely, "It's acomin' sometime a-maybe! The times they are achangin'! Babylon's burning with anxiety! This is the eve of destruction! We gotta get outta this place! Press that button and you're *FOOKIN' DEAD!*"

"Oh no!" gasped 12, His finger still hovering a mere billion light years above the galaxy sized red button that would terminate the mad god "God" and all his works with extreme prejudice *4 EVA!!!!!* "This is impossible! It can't be! The leakage from the monkeyplanet! It's..."

"Are you ready to accept Our Lord Jesus Christ as your saviour and be washed in The Blood Of The Lamb, *COMRADE?*" screamed the ringleader of the screaming mob of Born Again Christian Commie Ubergod rebel scum who had been sent screeching over the edge of The Cliff Of Deranged Metaphysical Psychosis into the Bottomless Pit Of Mindless Anarchy after Ubergod 589 had metaphysically manufactured some of the monkeyplanet drug E for a laugh, little knowing that it would send Him totally insane and thus utterly vulnerable to infection with a strange hybrid of the two earth ideologies Marxist Leninist Communism and Fundamentalist Evangelical Christianity with the end result that He heard the mad monkeyplanet god "God" speak to him out of a burning bush telling himto infect as many of the other 666 Ubergods with E as possible and then lead the spasming mob on an anti-authoritarian nihilist Jihad against any kind of ultimate metaphysical control over The Entirety by bursting into the control room, trussing up the two remaining un-E-infected Ubergods, injecting them with E and speed reading the Bible and Das Kapital at them until they too went utterly insane and agreed to join the other 664 Ubergods in an utterly stupid metaphysical Kool-Aid'n'Cyanide suicide pact which would take the much-needed brakes off the explosives packed Juggernaut Of Cosmic Possibility and send it screaming down hill into the Orphanage of Khaos. Which He did.

CHAPTER 27

ARMABASTARD-
FUCKING-
GEDDON!!!!!

**'Did ye not hear it? - No; 'twas but the wind/Or
the car rattling o'er the stony street;/On with
the dance! Let joy be unconfined; No sleep till
morn, when Youth and Pleasure meet/ To
chase the glowing Hours with flying feet'**

Byron, *Childe Harold's Pilgrimage*

   "What a fucking doddle!" thought gargoylishly ugly and
spectacularly untalented top ultratrendy DJ Ross 'Guru Dosh'
MacIntosh as an ultra-fit skinny rave chick burrowed up under his
trademark Bactrian camel-hair kilt'n'baby seal-fur sporran combo
and started sucking eagerly on his disappointingly undersized
knob. He's a total counter cultural man-for-all seasons , this
bastard, who but 17 years ago could have been seen stomping
the cider-vomit stained stages of the nation's post-Pistolian
proletarian punk pits as the ginger-haired rudimentary bass player
in but one of thousands of bog-standard sound-shite-a-like
stud'n'bristles Scottish Oi! combos that had flowered like weeds
after a shitstorm in the wake of the truly inspirational Exploited at

a time when he'd've been lucky to have got sloppy 16ths from some dodgy old crab-ridden dog-faced three-bagger boiler greaser grannie groupie with teeth like razoredged tombstones and a tendency to chew as opposed to the current legions of long-legged, glassy-eyed and glossy haired micro-mini-skirted and deliciously drop-dead knobthrobworthy and vacuum-gobbed brain-doner E-addict posho home-counties hippy chicks whose main ambition in life seemed to be to swallow his spunk just because he played other people's records for a ludicrously lucrative living. But now the Koolest, Hippest, Phattest, Chillest and Deffest DJ in the (soon to be dismembered by the irresistible forces of class conflict and tossed contemptuously into the dustbin of history) UK dismissed such thoughts as he concentrated hard on conjuring up stark images of the staggeringly long rows of noughts in his bank book to keep himself excited enough to maintain a semi-erection despite the stiffiewitheringly vast amounts of industrial strength E, coke, LSD, crystal meth, smack, blow and peyote that were whizzing about his bloodstream like crack-crazed crusties on jet-engined pogo-sticks and which he had to take in ever more frequent and increasingly more massive doses every day of the week just to make the utterly crap disco music he played seem even remotely bearable because DJ Ross 'Guru Dosh' MacIntosh - the man whom The Face had once called "The 5th Teletubbie" and "The Kinetic Keltik Kingpin of the post gabba tinged speed-garage balearic ambient intelligent jungle house-tekno acid swing revival t'ing, seen?" - was in fact still at heart an utterly unreconstructed smelly old 4th generation, 3rd division punk rock bollockhead chancer whose idea of a really good time was *actually* getting of his (preferably lime green mohawked) head on Special Brew, bathtub sulphate and glue and then smashing that same now-numbed-to-fuck head repeatedly and savagely into a screaming bass bin from which erupted the unlistenable anarchocacophony of the Deadbeats 'Kill The Hippies', 'Deny' by The Clash, 'Sheena Is A Punk Rocker' by The Ramones, 'Rudimentary Peni Fan Girl I Love You' by The Jane Austen Mercenaries or the only slightly tongue-in-cheek 'Smash The Fucking Disco Scum' by Severed Head & The Neck Fuckers 'till blood spurted from every hole in his spider-web tattooed face and he attained the state known as **PUNK ROCK NIRVANA!** - *not* wobbling around like a spaz in a cowshit ridden field to fucking mindless machine muzak dressed like a fucking hippy puff like the 100,000 moronic sheep he currently had spaced-out in front of him in the laser-lit Glastonbury meadow whilst he destroyed their last remaining few braincells with an "industrial mix" of the fake "Rare Groove classic" 'Handstand' which he'd written (ie stolen), arranged (ie farted about with on his computer for a bit), recorded and then ruined by paying a desperate smack addict producer "mate" £200 to speed it up a bit and stick some road drills and a few bleeping noises on it in the sure knowledge that the almost terminally cocaine battered sensory basketcases and utterly smackfucked pseudy Paul Smith'n'Armarni suit wearing media whores who decided what was "hot" and what was "not" in Britain's laughably pretentious "sTyLe" mags would conclude that it was an absolute mega-classic of almost unbearable beauty and all but immeasurable social significance, thus ensuring the single's status as an "underground cult hit" which meant that loads of goat-ee bearded, black turtle neck jumpered and pretentious beret-wearing idiot elitist bozo cokehound dickhead arsewipe shit-brained spunkgibbon toerag empty-trousered mindless mankfaced moronic muppet E-fucked motherfuckers would buy it and worship it and frug around like boneless chickens to it until the record "crossed over" and actually started being bought by the "general public" (ie working class girls) by which time the snobbish scum of the trainspotting dance-nazi elite would all start claiming that they never liked it in the first place just like they did when the brilliant 'Ride On Time' by Black Box crashed into the proper charts because a) the dance-nazis are just as misogynistic and have their pointed heads just as far up their bony arses as the pathetic "indie" rock kids who, in the 1980's, had made heroes out of sad miserable pretentious and ballsachingly dull Manc wankers like New Order and Morrissey whilst sneering at really cool, **FUN** female stuff like Kylie, Mel&Kim and We've Got A Fuzzbox And We're Gonna Use It! because no male between the ages of 20 and 30 has any taste in music whatsoever (**biological FACT**) and b) like nearly all males of their age, they primarily (if unconscious-ly) used music as a sort of power trip cum penis substitute so that they could unzip their metaphorical flies and slap their metaphori-cal dicks on the metaphorical all-male pub table in incredibly dull non-metaphorical mock-conversations with other dull-as-fuck dance-nazis in much the same way that differently but equally

fucked groups of socially and emotionally pygmyfied male obses-
sives discussed cars, football statistics, Star Trek trivia or DIY
(which is not to say that elitist dance-nazi snob trainspotters are
any more tediously parochial, socially crippled or in need of a
damn good lobotomising than any other bunch of anal-retentive
male trainspotting scum you might care to mention, but it *is* to say
that they are most definitely more *aesthetically* revolting for the
very fact that they consider their own particular puerile obsession
with what is, after all, just *disco music* (ie music to wiggle about to
whilst cranially carnaged on drugs which are specifically designed
to make you want to wiggle about to music that is designed to be
wiggled about to whilst you're cranially carnaged on drugs which
are specifically designed to make you want to etc etc etc) as a
somehow inherently superior "art form" at the cutting edge of
modern culture, with its own codes, fashions, language, morals
and even, in the shape of the piss-poor "Chemical Generation"
writers who flourished like magic mushrooms in cowshit after a
particularly humid and magic-mushroom friendly spring night in the
used AIDS-infected needle-strewn wake of the late '90s Jock
Smackhead pulp classic Trainspotting which, at first glance anyway, had nothing to do with actual trainspotting **per se** but was
actually about a bunch of Scottish smackheads who lead what
seem to be incredibly exciting lives which is a bit odd because the
only smackheads anybody else has ever met in "real" life have
just sort of sat in the corner and dribbled out of both sides of their
mouths at the same time whilst looking like shit ie utterly boring (if
you discount the fact that they're all incredibly daring and utterly
ruthless thieves when "straight" because they need to raise some
"moolah" by selling your video to a "fence" for less than one tenth
of its original retail value to buy some "horse" off "the man" to stop
themselves going "cold turkey" which is sort of entertaining as
long as it's not your video the fucking boring useless junkie scumbags have nicked) its own (alleged) "literature") but what the
FUCK that has to do with "dance culture" (ie wiggling about to
disco music) is anybody's guess *(choose Drugs, choose Adidas,
choose Wiggling About In A Field, choose Parkinson's
Disease, choose death from dehydration, choose a lifestyle of
mindless and pitifully passive "alternative" consumerism
under the pathetically sad illusion that you are somehow par-
taking in a sort of revolution or something*) thought secret

punk rocker DJ Josh 'Guru Dosh' MacIntosh cynically as he stared with contempt, loathing, hatred and despair at the field full of robotically bopping morons who would all be far better engaged in some useful, life-affirming, earth-shattering, world changing and **exciting** cultural activity - like robotically pogoing in some sweaty toilet of a rock venue to some *good* music like 'Lets Vibrate' by The Vibrators or 'Never Been In A Riot' by The Mekons or 'Toothache' by John The Postman or any one of the 18,567 punk rock singles that top dance DJ and alleged rock-hater Josh 'Guru Dosh' Macintosh had secretly hidden away in a Swindon warehouse, each gaudy day-glo picture sleeved 3 minute, 2 chord, 1 braincell musical vomit carefully wrapped in a grease-resistant and air-tight envelope and alphabetasised with utterly trainspottish anal-retentive care - something that Josh knew he'd have to keep a secret from all his dance-nazi friends unless, of course, punk rock suddenly became ultra-fashionable with the despicable disco-cognoscenti and it temporarily became like really groovy, *maaaaaaaan* , to start sticking the stuff into disco music but that would be disastrous, realised the Scottish DJ suddenly as he feebly knobcoughed a dolls-house teaspoonful of cold grey watery spunk into the slurping maw of the still frenziedly vacuum-pumping E-Babe tirelessly tonguing his tiny turgid todger under the strobe-strewn mixing desk, because then I'd have to publicly burn my entire punk rock record collection the very nano-second that punk rock became **un**-cool again and that would be **CRAP!**

So totally zeroed in on the zen-zone hypno-dynamics of the thudding aural soma that roared like a raging fire-storm from the massive PA's giantskyscrapersized speaker stacks were the 100,000 badly dressed instantkarma-addict nouveau-hippy seekers of E-fuelled hypernarcobopfrenzyblissfury that they totally failed to notice that the entire festival site was being slowly and surreptitiously surrounded by stealthy teenage terrorists, ex-pig'n'squaddie zombies and evil-looking demons driving massive snazzily painted bulldozers covered in bits of rotting crustieflesh and smashed Sacred Druid Grove until the music suddenly whimpered to a halt and they were violently lashed off their twat-shoed feet and sent skidding limbs-akimbo across the suddenly extremely muddy ground by skilfully directed riot fire-hoses which squirted lime-flavoured Lucozade at pressures of up to 1000 pounds per square inch from stolen tanker trucks which WERE stolen, *actually*, and were not, as you might have cynically assumed, part of some disgustingly corporate-cocksucking official sponsorship deal. By which time, of course, it was **TOO LATE!**

"What th..." said top DJ Josh 'Guru Dosh' MacIntosh as he was picked up, scrunched up into an awkward ball of broken boned deadflesh and casually tossed over the superbly overmuscled left shoulder of the mighty Justine Justice - much as one would a crisp packet or a piece of vinegar sodden newspaper one had just eaten fish'n'chips off - *if* one was a litter lout.

"What th...," echoed E-addled ravechick Danni D'Cadenet whose lank lukewarm late-lunch of limp lob had so suddenly been removed from her bee-sting lipped gob mid-flob.

"Never mind lass, suck *this* instead!" cooed a compassionate Justine Justice as she ground the grateful girl's greedily gaping gob onto her savagely whipped out clit.

"Mmmmm!" mumbled the top teenage totty with her mouth full of powerfully vibrating cunt as the fact that Justine's slick clit was at least 8 times larger than DJ Josh's recently removed knob somehow registered on her chem-cripped brain, enabling her to at last realise that she was, in fact, a lesbian and helping her to arrive at the liberating decision to never again suck knob whilst she still had sisters eager to have her incredibly large and pretty young tongue rammed savagely up their greedily gasping gashes.

"ROUND 'EM UP!" roared Justine through the massive PA as she cracked a huge bullwhip and broke into a spontaneous rendition of the 'Theme From Rawhide' as the disco-dolly's dedicated drubbing of her dilated demi-dick sent a thermo-nuclear explosion style orgasm smashing up her spinal column like the North Vietnamese army piledriving through the paddy-fields of the Mekong Delta on their heroic and utterly unstoppable final blitzkrieg sprint which ultimately ended in Saigon and **VICTORY!** as huge cranes swung into position the massive slabs of prehistoric stone that the Anti-Krap Jihad had nicked from Stonehenge and Justine had ordered to be engraved with the New Seven Kommandments which were **ACAB!, BAZ IS FIT!, BCFC RULE ALL OK!, SHARON TAYLOR IS A SLAG OFFICIAL!, GOD IS DED!, AMBIENT IS FOR PUFFS WHO CAN'T HANDLE THEIR DRUGZ!** and **SPICE GIRLS SHIT ON OASIS!**

MEANWHILE... down in the disco, Justine's orders were being carried out to the last incredibly savage letter by her psychopathic barbarian army of garden-tooled-up teenage terrorist toerags whose long march down from Bradford might not have been quite as long or strenuous as that taken by Chairman Mao and the Red Army back in the good old days when everything had been reassuringly black and white but **HAD** been a lot more fun and **HAD** resulted in the very heart of the disgustingly racist Tory version of "England" being ripped out and stomped on until it stopped throbbing and **DIED** under the wickedly barbed caterpillar tracks of the very same anarkobulldozers that now dug deep pits which tankers then filled with vile smelling sheepdip through which the quaking ravers were forced at sharpened shovelpoint in parties of 2,000 and from whence, now disinfected, the shivering shitheads were herded into hastily erected cattle sheds where they were then stripped naked, painted all over with mystik runes and then forced to drink giant flagons of Viking berzerker serum liberally dosed with potentially lethal doses of guaranteed 100% rat-poison and Domestos free E - but it's alright because, made invulnerable by the magic rune paint, the E failed to kill the kids and instead drove them utterly insane and thus ready to have the sexy little leather harness attached in which would sit their own personal mutant super ferret with whom they would for evermore exist in a state of permanent symbiotic psychosis, ready to fulfil the twisted and seemingly unstoppable will of the obviously totally bonkers beastwoman, Justine Justice **(ALL HAIL!)** who spins disc in the liberated DJ console, effortlessly combining the mental roar of her fave record ie The Prodigy's 'Slap My Bitch Up' with the orgasmic bliss of The Tofu Love Frog's 'Vegetable Attack!' intercut with free-enterprise guru Sir Keith Joseph's sampleranting *"Rome itself fell, destroyed from the inside... Are we to be destroyed from the inside too... a country which successfully repelled and destroyed Philip of Spain, Napoleon, the Kaiser, Hitler?"* and the bit from the Close Encounters Of The Third Kind movie soundtrack album where the aliens finally land and make beeping noises and thus provided the perfect aural backdrop to the arrival of the spaceshuttle containing Mad Mick The Needle and his 200 top terrorist muckers which crashed to a halt into the giant foam-filled balloons at the end of the hastily laid pre-fabricated runway and viciously disgorged its crazy cargo of combat-strength battle

cocaine-stoked occupants who immediately joined in the
screaming rave fury by stripping off their state-of-the-art armoured
exo-skeletons to reveal the superbly overmuscled hotbods of sexual athletes and then blended seamlessly into the bucking,
twisting, writhing, gyrating, bopping, thrusting, skipping, hopping,
whooping and hollering mass mob of magik rune painted and
tightly muscled monkey-mad teenage flesh which was radiating
positive vibes so powerful that teenage tribes from all over Britain
were at that moment heading towards Glasto eager not to miss
out on the ultimate rave and have to read about it in NME the next
Wednesday to discover to their chagrin that they'd missed out on
the magikal moment when the Goths arrived in hearses, the Teds
in pink Cadillacs, the crusties on red bandanna wearing dog-back,
the trainspotters in trains, the busspotters in buses, the mods on
scooters, the straights in Volvo estates, the Romos in crystal
carriages drawn by prancing white horses called Cyril and Frank,
the Teckno kids on spacehoppers, the Gabba Yobs roped together
in a snaking 5 mile long rollerskated congo, the Old Skool Rap
Crew parachuting in from specially hired World War 2 vintage
Douglas Dakotas and the 'Have You Got 10p?' Punks arriving all
packed like sardines into rusted trawlers resurrected from the
North Sea bed and fitted with giant edible frogs legs providing
enough elastic power to leap over church steeples and get them
there a full ten minutes in front of their arch rivals, the Skinheads,
who'd hitched a lift on the massive shoulders of a Giant Skinhead
Robot built by a mad billionaire scientist who nurtured incredibly
sordid secret sexual fantasies about being savagely bummed by a
train of 20,000 heterosexual skins whilst dressed in a mini-skirt,
pink Fred Perry and steel toecapped monkey boots - but such
yoof-tribal oneupmanship was soon rendered utterly irrelevant as
ALL the yoof stripped bollock naked and joined the frenetic frug
whilst DJ Justine Justice smiled crazily at the mixing desk as she
felt her last strands of sanity sever suddenly under the sensation-
ally savage strain of witnessing the sickeningly skintingling accel-
eration of Reality Eats Itself Overload as Mad Mick The Needle
danced his way towards her through the frothgobbed mob of beat-
crazy discozomboid beast-teens like Nijinsky meets Fred Astaire
meets Michael Jackson meets Che Guevara meets the extreme
epitome of male beauty with his massive and utterly beautiful
circumcised cock a-frobbin' in front of him and his huge lightly

haired balls bouncing hither and thither in response to the acrobatic twistings of his superbly overmuscled torso and amazingly powerful legs which worked together in frantic overtime to bring his ten delicious pounds of rock hard throbbing cockflesh ever closer to the spurtingly wet cunt of Justine Justice who now lay back buck-naked and ready to megafuck with her treetrunk thick thighs splayed wide and her superbly overmuscled back arched Olga Korbut stylee to thrust her slobbering love tunnel savagely back and forth as her prehensile labia mouthed the words **"I LOVE YOU"** at the approaching titanic and titanium-tuff Timmy Tallywhacker of Mad Mick The Needle whose buns of steel were now involuntarily thrusting backwards and forwards at speeds approaching 895 miles per minute in desperate primeval anticipation of the soon-come sensation of sinking his ginormous penile python into the steel-gripped innards of Justine Justice's savagely bucking cunt from which now flowed a frothing fountain of reeking hormone packed love-lubricant into which Mick dipped a mightily-overmuscled Jie Young style fist which he then brought up to his brutally flared snotpits, sniffed savagely and smeared all over the bulging bellend of his rippling purpleheadedyoghurt-squirter which was eagerly seized by the coatpegnippled and deliriously snorting Justine Justice who slammed every single superbly savage centimetre of its slippery 16 inches straight up her bubbling front bottom and came like Krakatoa on coke as Mad Mick's blurringly fast thrusting buttocks piledrivered his amazing pork pole into her powerfully pulsating pink pussy with a brutality that would have shattered the pelvis of a brontosaurus and caused the screaming Justine's internal love muscles to involuntarily grip, ripple, suck, push, nibble, lick, lash and twist at Mick's spasming spermspear with enough force to collapse a black hole so suddenly that it savagely sucked the entire universe into its gaping maw where it collided at incredibly violent velocity with a mirror-image universe comprised entirely of anti-matter thus triggering an implosion of such incalculable intensity that it set off a Butterfly Wing Khaos Theory Domino Effect Scenario that prolapsed all the infinite number of parallel universes and mirror image anti-universes in a chain reaction beyond even God's ability to comprehend but which none the less was as **NOTHING** com-pared to the utterly amazing mutual orgasm which Mad Mick The Needle and Justine Justice now endured as a shared out-of-body

experience cum terrifying hallucination in which they found themselves transmogrified into a teensploitation pulp fiction novel
publisher who existed in a universe very different from their own
where reality wasn't collapsing in on itself quite as quickly and
they, as Mad Mick The Needle and Justine Justice, only existed in
the wankfevered mind of the evil paedophile pornographer who
stood rubbing his tiny cock furiously as he read again the sordid
details of the hyperbolic hump that took place on the smouldering
wreckage of a Glasto DJ's mixing console where Mick'n'Justine
were only just now emerging from their spiritually traumatic
cosmic-orgasm triggered mutual out-of-body experience to now
share another and even greater orgasm which could no longer be
contained by the creaking walls of the reality which contained
them and thus caused the long extinct volcanoes of Britain to
burst into molten metal-spewing life as they roared across the
heaving green skin of Albion like pimples on the bubbling
epidermis of an Ebola victim watched at quadruple speed on acid
and heaved up the entire Glastonbury area and whisked it across
a world where the tectonic plates heaved and crashed against
each other like blindfolded carnivorous dinosaurs being whipped
into an hysterical frenzy by sadistic aliens with giant electro Dino-
prods in some strange off-planet colosseum to finally smash the
ripped-out belly of Merry Ole England down on the plains of
Armageddon in Palestine with a thunderous crunch which was
echoed by the awesome roar of a Total Reality Implosion as 55
years of time disintegrated into temporal dust and the
Limegreenmohawked Big Monkey led invasion fleet from the
Planet Milkin which was now in sordid alliance with the disgusting
dog-bumming Tory vampires who had manipulated hundreds of
thousands of years of human history to their own foul ends landed
on the east side of the newly-formed valley where the aliens and
vampires roared out to form a vast army of human hating goth-
punk bastardry whilst God and his legions of giantswan winged
angels and dead uncool deceased types steamed in from the west
led by God himself stood in the back of a ginormous golden chari-
ot pulled by giant headless rabbits from whence he tossed
thunderbolts about willy nilly and giggled like the nutty psychopath
he was as he saw his old enemy Satan and his demon hordes
simultaneously arrive from the south riding on the 1000 mile wide
back of the giant black communist bisexual superspider Skunk

Anansie whose 666 chainsaw-toothed skeletal heads bopped
hypnotically on slinky springs composed of ultraflexible cartilage
whilst she spewed from her puttering anus great clusters of
translucent eggs which exploded in speeded up time-lapse nature
movie stylee sickening slo-mo to disgorge tiny baby Skunk
Anansies clutching World War 2 vintage Schmiesser machine pistols which they fired from the hip sexily as they wafted down onto
the battlefield on parachutes made from gossamer strands of
\spider silk to land in the fur of the enormous purring figures of
The Stiff Kittens whom all serious students of demonology will
remember as the two lurchingly upright Frankencats with 999
retroactive afterlives (each time you kill 'em, the closer you bring
them to actual life - *uh oh!*) known to their close friends as
Ginger Ralph And Ginger Ted who are often confused so we'd
better point out at this stage that Ginger Ralph is the cat that
mews pitifully as he claws Milkinite attack helicopters out of the
sky with Mighty Joe Young style paws whilst Ginger Ted is the cat
who you can see keeneyedly frankensteining it towards the mist of
the squitting Godbothering enemy as if on a mission from the odd
god Cedric Pod - King Of The Cats, scourge of rats and chief devil
in the demonology of those planets where rodents and small
boned birds have reached sentience but meaning absolutely fuck
all to the allegedly neutral (but actually just utterly bloodthirsty and
up for a good ruck with anybody, anytime and anywhere) herds of
unicorns wearing Sony Walkman headphones through which they
listen, at full volume, to copies of the tapes made by the US Army
psi-ops department during the Vietnam War of human babies
screaming to try and freak out the Cong whilst up above in a sky
that flashed black, scarlet and Peach White from the Dulux range,
great squadrons of demonic crows manoeuvred amongst the
seething supernatural rains (or "fafrotskies" as they are known to
serious students of such phenomenon) of frogs, fish, eels, coins
and burning crosses to drop rocks on the flocks of olive branch
bearing doves of heavenly peace which fly hither and thither
amongst fluffy white clouds which slowly condense and harden
into the Gallagher brother-style massively bushy eyebrowed forms
of the giants Gog and Magog which means trouble for Gog is a
massive punk rock fan whilst Magog larges it big time on the
throb-throb-throb of old skool Boystown HiNrG disco and neither is
exactly what you'd call tolerant in the sensibly sharing the CD

player stakes with the oh-so predictable but nonetheless totally avoidable and completely unnecessary result that they clash together violently with boots and fists and savagely wielded nail-studded clubs inna countercultural tribalyoofkrieg which makes the epic Mods v Rockers clash on the pebbley beaches of Southern England during the Easter Bank Holiday weekends of 1964 and '65 look like a poncey pillow fight at an especially soft posh birds' Swiss finishing school and even threatens to eclipse in its testosteronic intensity the savage conflict that ensued when unreconstructed Stranglers fan and England defensive hard man, Stuart Pierce, attempted to play the definitive amphetamine sulphate glorifying boogie 'Go Buddy Go' in the England dressing room shortly before the ultra top secret friendly with an experimental Secret Government Laboratory Mutant XI who thrashed the unmodified normos 12-0 thanks largely to a triple hat-trick scored by a six-legged monstrosity which had been cloned and then savagely genetically altered from a sample of DNA covertly extracted from a lump of Diego Marradona's cocaine-rich gobbed-out snot when the plucky basin-bowl barnet-ted ex-Nottingham Forest stalwart had barely escaped from the jockstrapsweatdrenched changing room with his nads intact after the rest of the England squad who were all hard core Dire Straits fans turned predictably nasty and told him that The Stranglers were puffs with no nobs who couldn't play for toffee and weren't fit to lick dog shit off the stackheeled purple cowboy boots of a real musician like Mark Knoppler whose composition of the MOR classic 'Sultans Of Swing' had elevated him into the pantheon of rock greats alongside Rod Stewart, Phil Collins and (late period circa 'Secret Dancer') Tina Turner in the minds of the rest of the UK's professional footballing community who were all utterly shit-in-bed wankers with no taste whatsoever apart from Piercey and former Scotland international Pat Nevin who was cool despite his penchant for Mancunian miserabilist shitehawks New Order.

　　"Cease fire!" bellowed God as He suddenly realised that the Mother Of All Battles for which He had been preparing for all eternity was actually massively more complicated than even He had ever anticipated.

　　"Cease fire!" screamed the top vampire and top Milkinite Limegreen Mohawked leaders who had had their bodies and brains merged into one spectacularly ugly looking vamp-ape entity in order to seal their sinister pact and resolve any of the potentially fatal command conflicts which inevitably arise between allies, particularly those from different planets.

"**Cease fire!**" bellowed Satan as he tried but failed miserably to make any sense whatsofuckingever out of the amazingly colourful total khaos that seethed all about his snorting demon horde.

"That was **GREAT!**" babbled a post-orgasmicaly euphoric mad Mick The Needle as he lay with his semi-tumescent cock still locked in the equally grinny Justine Justice's gripping gash. "You got a fag?"

"Stop! Stop! Think about what you're about to **DO!**" yelled a long haired figure in a checked jacket with leather patches on the elbows suddenly. All eyes turned to the bearded and pipe waving figure of Dr Mark Smithies, lecturer in Peace Studies at Bradford University and committed Ghandian pacifist, anti-war activist and the world's top expert in conflict-resolution as he strode into the middle of the battlefield waving a white flag.

"OK!" said the pipesucker. "Now can I have a spokesperson from each group over here please?". Stunned by this latest turn of events God, Satan, the vamp-ape beast, the still-locked together like rutting dogs Mad Mick The Needle and Justine Justice and the boss unicorn all shamefacedly ambled over to the middle of the battlefield where a smiling Mark Smithies stood patiently waiting.

"OK! *Great!* " said the Prof, nonconfrontationaly, "now look, I know that you've *all* been preparing for this battle for quite some not insubstantial amount of time and I know that there are very real grievances on *all* sides that need to be resolved but, and we *have* to ask *ourselves* this, *is* violence *really* the *best* way of resolving them. Hmmmm?"

"Aw, fuck **RIGHT** off!" said God, whipping out a wicked length of oiled bike chain and smashing the cunt straight between the speccy eyes.

"Yeah, fuck *RIGHT* off!" chorused Satan, the vamp-ape beast, the still-locked together like rutting dogs Mad Mick The Needle and Justine Justice and the boss unicorn as they all whipped out their own wicked lengths of oiled bike chain and lashed the screaming pacifist into mincemeat with gusto with God continually resurrecting the terror-spasmed academic at regular intervals to make the entertainment last longer.

"Hey, that was **FUN!**" chortled God when the bits of pacifist left were just too small to resurrect anymore.

"Fucking brilliant!" tittered the Dev.

"Top laff!" chortled the still-locked together like rutting dogs Mad Mick The Needle and Justine Justice.

"Neighhhhh!" agreed the boss unicorn.

"Yeah!" chuckled the vamp-ape, "You know, you earthlings are alright! You're a bunch of fucking nutters! You may not worship Wattie out of the Exploited like you should do but - what the fuck - I don't think we want to exterminate you any more, do we lads?"

"**No! Let's be mates!**" roared the billions of Limegreenmohawked Bigmonkey-led aliens from the Planet Milkin.

"Hang on!" screamed the vamp-ape who was now giving voice to the dog-bumming Tory vampire half of his brain. "We made a deal! We're going to exterminate every last stinking one of the miserable maggots! Destroy them! Utterly! Totally! **IK! URRRJKAH! AaaaaaarkGAH! UrkARGH! AAAAARKKKKKKK! YOU TREACHEROUS ALIEN BASTARD!!!!!!!!!!!! IIIIIIIIIIIIIIIIIIK! UuuuuuuuKKKKKKKK! Huh!**" screamed the Top Tory Vampire as, with a great deal of pain and squelching noises, he managed to shapeshift his way out of the body he had been sharing with the top alien and, still covered with blood and gunk and stuff, stagger weakly to his feet.

"Right!" snarled the Tory, "if that's the way you want it, we'll take the fucking lot of you on! Right here! Right now! Come on then! Aye! Think you're fucking hard enough do you, eh? Fucking **PUFFS!**"

"Um, may I point out" interjected Satan, politely, "that there's only 665 of you and uncountable billions of us?"

"Oh yeah!" said the vampire, "I forgot."

"But we're still gonna kick the fuck out of you anyway!" spat God, "Come on, la**ds!**"

"Huzzah!" roared the angel host and they steamed into the cowering vampires from the left.

"Hurragh!" bellowed the demon horde as they charged in from the right.

"Neigh!" neighed the unicorns as they steamed in from the front ridden by aliens armed with rocket launchers.

"Sorted!" chorused the massed ranks of human yoof as they

watched with glee from the sidelines and slung the odd bottle indiscriminately into the melee.

"AAAA

AAAA

AAAA

AAAA

AAAA

AAAA

AAAA

AAAA

AAAA

AAAA

AAAA

AAAA

AAAA

AAAA

AAAA

AAAA

AAA

AAAA

AAAA

AAAA

AAAA

AAAA

AAAA

AAAA

AAAA

AAAA

AAAA

AAAA

AAAA

AAAA

AAAA

AAAA

AAAA

AAAA

AAAA

AAAA

AAAA

AAAA

AAAA

AAAR

GH!"

screamed the dog-bumming Tory vampires as they were hog-tied, butchered, staked with garlic-smothered crosses and buried in consecrated ground before being dug up again and machine gunned with silver bullets and then re-buried just to make sure even though Satan said he was pretty certain that was only for werewolves.

"Well that's that then!" said a Limegreenmohawked Bigmonkey as he tossed the last shovel of holy water drenched consecrated soil into the face of the last Tory Vampire corpse.

"Not **QUITE!**" barked a large dog who had suddenly appeared in the burial party's midst.

"Fuck me! A talking dog!" quipped Satan.

"I'm the alsatian formerly known as Prince," woofed the handsome hound, "and the reason I can talk is that us dogs have become magickally sentient as an unexpected side effect of the Ongoing Reality Implosion Scenario. Any road up, me an my muckers" he nodded over his shoulder to a massive pack of millions of dogs of all shapes and sizes (most of whom were staring up in terrified awe at the skyscraping feline forms of Ginger

Ralph and Ginger Ted) "hoped we'd get here in time to do battle with the dog-bumming Tory Vampire vermin who've been inter-specially raping us lot - **FOR YONKS!**"

"Well you're too fucking late, pal!" spat God, nodding His holy head towards the newly dug graveyard where a forest of huge garlic smeared and sharp pointed Christian-type crosses marked the last resting places of the houndraping Tory vampire scum.

"Don't worry," growled the alsatian formerly known as Prince, "we'll be digging them cunts up and sucking the marrow out of their bones in a minute. But first we're gonna rip the Top Tory vampire to screaming shreds!"

"WOOF! WOOF! WOOF! WOOF! WOOF! WOOF! WOOF!" howled the vengeful pack behind him before breaking into the recently composed Canine Nation Anthem.

"Fanged vermin take thy cock from my arse/The aeons of oppression they have passed/No longer will our shit-chutes be used/As receptacles for thy stinking vampire juice/So zip up thine fly and fly away/and tremble as thou await the day/When for thine evil sins thou shalt dearly pay/And every hound that's had to shit thy sperm/Will surely turn just like the angry worm/Our puppies' puppies will adore us/As they howl in grateful chorus/ YOU'RE GONNA GET YOU'RE FUCKING HEADS KICKED IN!/WOOF! WOOFWOOF-WOOF! WOOFWOOFWOOF! WOOFWOOF WOOF! WOOF!"

"OK!" snarled the alsatian formerly known as Prince, petulantly. "So it's hardly up to Sir Andrew Lloyd Weber and Tim Rice standards but be fair! We've only just started fucking talking, for Christ's sake! Give us time and we too will produce our Bob Marleys, Wolfgang Amadeus Motzarts, Chers and Marti Pellows but you can hardly expect a species only just liberated from the chain and leash of sycophantic slavery to just suddenly climb the peaks of artistic endeavour conquered by you monkey types who've been gibbering away ten to the dozen and making stuff with your opposable thumbs, you jammy bastards, for thousands of years, can you? Eh? In all honesty... Excuse me a minute, I've just been overcome with the irresistible urge to suck my own cock."

Mad Mick stared at the autofellating hound with jealous amusement, chuckling silently at the knowledge that he, like most human males, would willingly give up language and *all* the other alleged benefits of human civilisation in exchange for the ability to suck his own cock for just five seconds! **No contest!**

"The thing is, alsatian formerly known as Prince" interjected Justine Justice who was being somewhat distracted by the sudden re-engorgement of Mad Mick's massive meat missile which was still buried deep within the folds of her incredibly over-muscled cunt, "that you're too late for that as well. The Top Tory Vampire is currently rotting with that lot!"

"Yeah" chundered a Limegreenmohawked Big Monkey gravedigger, "so you're too late, doggyboy!"

"No I'm not!" growled the alsatian formerly known as Prince quietly. "I can **smell** that I'm not!"

"Hey!" shouted Satan suddenly, "He's right! Count the vampire graves! *There's only 664 of them!!!!!!*"

"Curses!" thundered the Limegreenmohawked Big Monkey gravedigger, petulantly throwing his green gunk covered shovel down with a clang and shapechanging back into his dog-bumming Top Tory Vampire form.

"Fetch, boy!" laughed Mad Mick The Needle as millions of canine eyes swivelled in the vampire's direction and a million low growls rose from a million furry throats.

"Hang on!" said God "One dog-bumming vampire against millions of angry dogs? That's hardly *sporting*, is it? How about I throw in all the millions of Born Again Christians, fascists and human Tories (many of whom are also dog-bummers) that I've let into heaven over the millennia so you can rip them to shreds as well?"

"Do *what?*" chorused the literally billions of humans, dogs, demons and aliens simultaneously, utterly shocked by The Almighty's incredibly **sane** suggestion.

"Yeah, alright, don't make a meal of it!" mumbled The Lord in embarrassment. "The thing is that the same Reality Implosion Scenario that's kicked our dog friends here up the evolutionary scale seems to have somehow have also magickally rendered Me (ie God) utterly sane."

"Sane?" squealed a fat American angel with boggly eyes as he pushed his way through the confused and milling angel ranks and waved a podgy ginger in God's immaculate face.

"Sane!?" he spluttered furiously, "you call feeding all us

true believers ie those who accept the King James version of The Holy Bible as the literal truth and are Born Again in the Blood of The Lamb ie your holy and one and only son, Jesus Christ Our Lord, to some talking dogs, **sane?!** What's going on? This wasn't prophesied! This is...**madness!** "

"Oh shut up you blathering, boring, tedious, sanctimonious, holier-than-thou tit!" said God, jabbing the fat Yank bible-basher savagely in the eye with a holy thumb. "It's not even as if you've ever read The fucking Bible properly, you twat!"

"What!?" shrieked the Born Again bastard as he clutched a chubby hand to his mashed eyesocket in a futile attempt to staunch the spurting blood.

"You wanna meet Jesus, do you, you thick cunt?" roared God, headbutting the fucker smartly on the bridge of his pudgy pig-like nose, "Well **DO YA?!** "

"Yes!" screamed the bloodyfaced Born Again bastard. "Yes! Oh Lord Jesus, reveal yourself to these Agents of Darkness! Deliver your servant from this torment!"

"Hiya!" said Satan, giving the stunned fundamentalist nutter a casual wave of his pointed tail.

"Get thee behind me!" screamed the bleeding angel in terror. "Thou art not Our Lord for is it not written that The Son Of God was tempted by Satan, The Lord Of Lies, whilst in the desert for 40 days and 40 nights?"

"Oh that was just me talking to myself," chuckled The Dev. "Dad, don't you think that we should move things along a bit here? Only the alsatian formerly known as Prince and his chums are getting a bit restless."

"Yeah, you're right, sorry!" said God, creating a vast pit surrounded by a massive classical Greek style amphitheatre only tons bigger in which the sane-for-the-first-time-since-the Garden-of-Eden God and all the aliens, humans, demons and unicorns sat and metaphorically laughed their sex organs off as they watched the vengeful dogs bite the living shit out of all the fascists, Tories, Born Again Christians and other dog bummers who have ever lived (leaving the Top Tory Vampire 'till last, natch) and then the dogs buried their victims and then dug them up again and sucked on their bones for a bit until it got dark and *everybody* started getting a bit restless.

But just then the boredom was interrupted by the sound

of billions of tiny little wings and the air crackled as if suddenly hyperpolluted with evil faerie magick so strong it could kill every human, dog, unicorn, demon, alien or God it came into contact with. **Uh oh!** Demon, dog, alien, unicorn and human ears all pricked up as they faintly heard for the first time what sounded ominously like a billion billion squeaky little voices humming 'The Ride Of The Valkyrie' tune from Apocalypse Now.

"Oh no!" yelled Satan as he stared in horror at the oncoming tide of gossamer winged tiny folk who darkened the far horizon. "It's the Faerie Folk who've decided to play their Joker and Faerie magick the fucking shit out of the whole lot of us so they can take over what's left of the planet!"

"Faerie magick!" yelled God in alarm, "even my mighty powers are no use against that!"

"We're doomed!" squealed Martin Amis scripted cock-ernee rent boy cum judge stabber Ricky Tickytimebomb, "We're doomed! We're fackin' *dooooooooooooooooooooooooooooooo* - 'ang on a blinkin' mo! H'aint none ov you lot h'ever bleedin' read Peter Pan by JM Barrie? It's virtually a bleedin' manual on 'ow to slaughter fairies - well bless my blinkin' soul if it h'ain't! Come on h'efferybody! H'after me! One two free faw - **I DON'T BELIEVE IN FAIRIES! I DON'T BELIEVE IN FAIRIES!**"

"He's right, by Jove!" thundered God, "Look!"

And billions of sentient beings turned and did as God said and saw the vast oncoming armada of fluttering faerie death suddenly light up with small explosions as a faerie savagely imploded each time the rapidly chanting cockernee anarcho-costermonger uttered his utterly insincere statement of disbelief.

"Come on everybody!" said a stiffupperlipped God whom everybody at that moment suddenly noticed somehow bore a strange resemblance to James Robertson Justice out of the Doctor movies. "Let's give the plucky lad a hand!"

"I DON'T BELIEVE IN FAIRIES!" barked all the dogs and the sky lit up as millions of Faerie scum detonated in mid-air and fell screaming into the desert sand.

"I DON'T BELIEVE IN FAIRIES!" chanted all the human yoof and a vast swathe of the incoming Faerie armada disintegrated into billion points of tinkling light.

"I DON'T BELIEVE IN FAIRIES!" screamed the billions of aliens and demons as the carnage-cracked Faerie ranks shuddered in mid air, halted and then started to retreat back to Fairyland whence they were pursued by Ginger Ralph and Ginger Ted wearing massive jet-packs.

Many strange adventures would befall the two massive Stiff Kittens in that mythical place and many years would pass before they could finally return to the bosom of their Lord Satan - but that's another story.

"Fuck it! I declare this to be VF Day! Lets have a party!" roared God, divinely turning the Armageddon battlefield into the universe's biggest ever rave dance floor and magicking up a vast army of massive ten-armed Santa Clauses who dug into their bulging and bottomless sacks and doled out free totally pure non-addictive drugs with no side effects with many a jolly "Ho! Ho! Ho!" whilst Wizzard's epic socialist utopian stomper 'I Wish It Could Be Xmas Every Day' blasted out of a massive speaker system and every alien, demon, human, unicorn and dog in the area got down and boogied bigtime under the savagely flickering cosmic strobe that God created by making the Sun whizz round the world at167 rpm.

"Sorry I went mad, son!" said God.

"That's alright" said Satan, giving him a hug, "could have happened to anyone."

"I love you, Justine" screamed Mad Mick.

"Don't be a gurly puff!" roared Justine Justice as she violently rode his mighty love muscle to the peak of yet another earth-shattering orgasm.

"Penny for your thoughts?" enquired Mrs Edna The Needle as she jacked up on a non-addictive but incredibly powerful cocktail of smack, speed, crack, E and acid.

"Oh I was just thinking about what I was going to do with myself now that all the crappos have been terminated with extreme prejudice and God's cured my permanent pre-menstrual tension" said Karen Skull, wistfully.

"Yeah *uuuuuuuuuh!* I see your problem **UH! UH! UH! UH! aaaaaaaaaaaaRGGAAAAAAAAAAAAAAAAK!**" said Edna as the drugs savagely carpetbombed her incredibly strong central nervous system and made her eyes bulge out hideously like they did with Arnie and his bird in Total Recall when they had to suck Martian atmosphere.

"Look, me and a few of the lads have asked God to build

us an interdimensional faster-than-light space ship so we can fuck off to alternative universes and carry on satiating our insane blood lusts by continuing to off pigs, Tories, fascists and other crappos for kicks." said Edna, temptingly. "You wanna come along?"

"Yeah, thanks!" smiled the fantastically sexy Karen Skull, "I might just do that!"

"You shaggin'?" asked an eager Ole Spunker.

"You askin'?" replied a coy God.

"I'm askin'!" rejoined the slobbering Spunker.

"I'm shaggin'!" retorted the heavily pouting God.

"Er, Mick, I think you'd better pull your dick out *right now!*" roared Justine Justice.

"Aww! *Why?*" whined a petulant Mad Mick The Needle who was not only just about to come but also fully intended to spend the rest of eternity with his cock stuck up Justine's superbly overmuscled cunt if he possibly could.

"Cos...**UH!**...I'm just about...**UH!**...to...***DROP!!!!***" screamed the terrorist she-wolf as she unplugged her handsome lover and brutally threw him aside before arching her back to reveal a suddenly massively swollen belly and savagely spitting forth a screaming trio of gunkspattered baby girls out of her incredibly beautiful cunt.

Nobody knew it then but these three sisters would grow up to become the most powerful entities ever seen in this or any other universe.

But that's *definitely* another story....

THE END

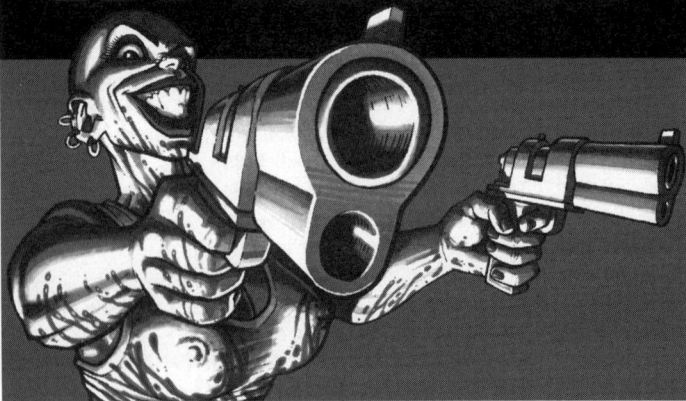

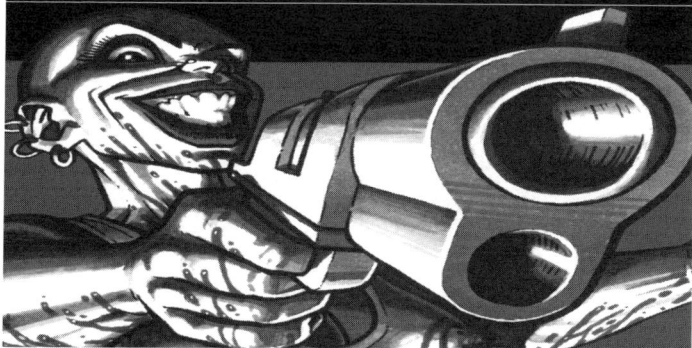

ATTACK!

This generation needs a NEW literature - writing that apes, matches, parodies and supersedes the flickeringly fast 900 MPH ATTACK! ATTACK ATTACK! velocity of early 21st century popular culture at its most mEnTaL!

HARD-CORE ANARCHO-COMMIE SEX PULP

We will publish writers who think they're rock stars, rock stars who think they're writers and we will make supernovas of the stuttering, wild-eyed, slack-jawed drooling idiot-geek geniuses who lurk in the fanzine/internet shadows.

HORROR! SEX! WAR! DRUGS! VIOLENCE!

"Subtlety" is found in the dictionary between "shit" and "syphilis".

VICTORY OR DEATH!

The self-perpetuating ponce-mafia oligarchy of effete bourgeois wankers who run the 'literary scene' must be swept aside by a tidal wave of screaming urchin tits-out teenage terror totty and

DESTROYED!